"*The Strange* is an adventure tale of the best kind: an unusual setting with vivid characters and an unpredictable ending. With every turn of the page, I wondered what would happen next."—Charlaine Harris, *New York Times* bestselling author of *An Easy Death* and the Sookie Stackhouse series.

"Very readable, compelling storytelling, a wonderfully engaging central character, full of atmosphere and beauty and strangeness. Thoroughly excellent space-western. Written in the spirit of Bradbury's Mars and capturing something of Bradbury's brilliance."—Adam Roberts, Arthur C. Clarke Award nominee, BSFA award-winning author of *Jack Glass*

"Ballingrud's brilliant fiction brims with imagination, integrity (I do not use that term lightly), and an authentic world-weary dread that bores directly into your heart."—Paul Tremblay, award-winning author of *The Cabin at the End of the World* and *The Pallbearers Club*

"Nathan Ballingrud's *The Strange* is a thrillingly inventive blend of the science fiction, western, and horror genres, a roaring adventure story of a girl, her gentleman robot, and a planet of ghosts. The perfect novel to take inside your heat tent and curl up with on a cold Martian night." —Owen King, *New York Times* bestselling author of *The Curator*

"*Star Wars* meets *True Grit* in this cinematic tale of a human girl fighting to keep hope alive on a Martian world. Nathan Ballingrud compellingly blends frontier western with rootin-tootin space opera, and the result is epic in scope, thematically rich, and gleefully spooky in places. This is an atmospheric, immersive delight, and so evocative that I kept expecting red sand to trickle out from between the pages."—Josh Winning, author of *The Shadow Glass* and *Burn the Negative*

"*The Strange* breathes vivid life into a Mars that's both fascinating and frightening. The journey of Annabelle Crisp across those red sands—she's a wonderful character, full of energy and determination—was a battle for answers, for autonomy, for humanity itself. I rooted for her every step of the way."—Aliya Whiteley, Arthur C. Clarke Award shortlisted author of *Skyward Inn*

the
Strange

Nathan
Ballingrud

TITAN BOOKS

The Strange
Print edition ISBN: 9781803362694
E-book edition ISBN: 9781803362700

Published by Titan Books
A division of Titan Publishing Group Ltd
144 Southwark Street, London SE1 0UP
www.titanbooks.com

First edition: March 2023
10 9 8 7 6 5 4 3 2 1

A CIP catalogue record for this title is available from
the British Library.

Printed and bound by CPI (UK) Ltd,
Croydon CR0 4YY

To Mia,

the toughest, most resilient person
I have ever known.

I'm proud to be your dad.

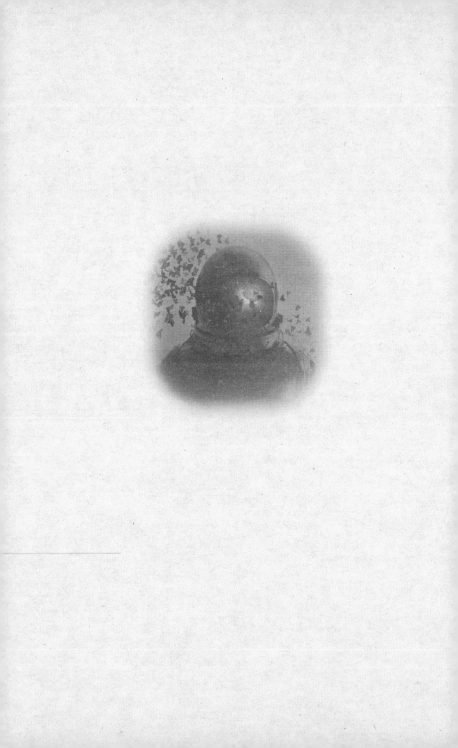

"Doesn't an old thing always know when a new thing comes?"

RAY BRADBURY,
"—AND THE MOON BE STILL AS BRIGHT"

part one

what
happened
to me

1

I was thirteen when the Silence came to Mars, settling over us like a smothering dust. We don't talk about those days much anymore, and most who lived through them are dead. I'm old now—extravagantly old, I like to say—and I'll join them soon enough. Maybe that's why I find myself thinking back on those years more frequently, in the night's long hours: the terror and the loneliness that afflicted us all, and the shameful things we did because we were afraid.

Maybe that's why I've been thinking, too, about old friends and old enemies, about how sometimes they were the same people. And maybe that's why dear old Watson has come to visit me at last, gleaming in the lamplight, full of his own enchanted tales.

All my life I've wanted to write adventure stories, but I've always been more suited to reading than to writing. I never believed my imagination was up to the task. It's only now, close to the end, that I realize I never had to imagine one.

My name is Anabelle Crisp. This is the story of what happened to me, what I did about it, and the consequences thereof.

• • •

IT WAS EARLY evening and we were closing up the Mother Earth Diner. Normally my father liked to keep the place open well into the night. We'd been living with the Silence for nearly a year, and during that time it seemed that more and more people wanted a warm, bright place to be when darkness fell. My family was happy to provide that place. We specialized in good Southern cooking—beans and rice, collard greens, barbecued pork, that sort of thing—and we had our walls covered with pictures of famous Earth cities and landmarks. The Silence had imbued those photographs with an elegiac quality, it was true, but that only heightened their appeal.

That night, we were closing earlier than usual. The Moving Picture Club was presenting a picture show in the town square, which would draw most of the folks away from us. That was fine with me; I was hoping to make it down to the square to see it myself. They were running *The Lost World* again, and though I'd seen it twice before, I was eager to go again. Arthur Conan Doyle was my favorite writer. In my excitement, I was rereading *The Casebook of Sherlock Holmes*, its spine cracked from the love I had shown it.

Joe Reilly was our last customer of the evening. He was despised by many in New Galveston, and it was his habit to come in when he was most likely to remain undisturbed. I would have been happy to bar him entry altogether, but Father wouldn't have it. So I served him with curt silence. He ate quickly, wolfishly, and said, "You closing early tonight, Anabelle?"

"You know we are."

"Well. I guess I ought to let you get to it." He laid down his money and headed out. It was a relief; usually he lingered.

I brought the dishes to the back where Father and Watson, our Engine, were cleaning up. Father had been talking under his breath and went quiet when I came back. He was talking to Mother again. I knew it gave him comfort, but it hurt to hear, nonetheless. He tried to do it only when I wasn't around, but sometimes I guess he couldn't help himself.

Watson was a Kitchen Engine—a bipedal construct, humanoid in form, utilitarian and featureless. I called him Watson after the character in the Sherlock Holmes stories, but he wasn't much more than a dishwashing program that my parents had overlaid with an inexpensive personality template—English Butler—to amuse themselves and their customers. He was no more programmed to be a detective's sidekick than I was raised to be the world's greatest amateur sleuth. It was a lie I chose to believe in.

I was only in the back for a minute, so when I returned to the dining area I was surprised to see a man at the counter. He sat hunched over his clasped hands, studying the entanglement of his fingers like he might puzzle out some mystery there. The hair on his head was long and tangled, blond, dusted with the soft pink shades of the low Martian desert. He wore one of the heavy-weather jackets favored by the nomadic cults, protecting them from the fatal cold of the nights outside the city. A symbol branded onto the leather of his right sleeve identified him as one of the Moths—named after the strange, body-harvesting moth native to Mars, the kind that nests in the dead. He raised his head to look at me and I was struck by his face, which was beautiful in a hard, unforgiving way—the way a desert is beautiful. His eyes were pale green, faintly luminescent; I would have mistaken him for one of the miners if not for the symbol on the jacket. I thought he must have been my father's age at least—somewhere in his forties—until he spoke and I heard the youth in his voice.

"I was beginning to think I was gonna die here before someone decided to serve me."

His rudeness surprised me. I did not know him, which was unusual in New Galveston but not impossible, especially if he belonged to one of the desert cults. Still, my father and I were respected in the community and generally treated accordingly.

"I'm sorry, but we're closed."

"Sign says open."

"I was about to turn it off."

"But you ain't yet, so I guess you must be open. I'll take some black coffee."

Not knowing what else to do, I turned around and put some water on the range to boil. It bothered me, this outsider coming in and delivering orders like that. And it bothered me even more that I obeyed.

For a few minutes there was nothing to do, so I leaned against the counter while he sat there watching me. I slid my book under the counter, not wishing to provide this man an opening to further conversation. I heard Father messing around in the back, cleaning the dishes and putting them up. Talking to Mother. It was private: a quiet expression of grief, unremarkable and without harm; but now that this man heard it, I was embarrassed.

"Who's back there?" the man said.

"My father. This is his place."

"Who's he talking to?"

"Our Engine," I said. The lie was easy by now. "He's a dishwasher."

"Dishwasher, huh? So where's your mama?"

"Earth." I felt the blood in my face.

"So you help him run the place? He lets his little girl out here to deal with all the dissolute human scum that comes through these doors while he hides away doing women's work with Engines in the back?"

"Our customers aren't scum. Generally they are more polite than you are."

"Well, I'm sorry if I offend."

"If you were really sorry, you would collect yourself and walk out that door. As I said, we're closed. They're showing a picture in the square tonight and I would like to see it."

"Little girl, I have come from the desert. I am tired and I am in need of shelter and some pleasant company. But more than any of that I am in need of hot coffee. And under this roof I find I am able to acquire all of it at once. I ain't inclined to leave."

The water started to whistle behind me and I poured it over the coffee grounds. "Well, *I'm* not inclined to be very pleasant," I said.

"Yeah, you made that clear already. What are you so fired up to see, anyhow?"

"They're showing *The Lost World*." Saying the words conjured the image of those beautiful dinosaurs, and I felt an unwelcome childish thrill.

He laughed and shook his head.

I wished I hadn't answered him; now I was ashamed as well as angry. When I poured the coffee into his mug, I allowed a generous portion of grounds to slide in with it.

He said, "Ain't you seen it a hundred times anyway? And won't you see it a hundred times again? There won't be any more pictures coming from home now. What we got is what we got."

I didn't answer him. It wasn't something I hadn't thought of before. But I still held on to the notion that maybe we could make new pictures somehow. Eventually. I held on to the notion that the interruption in our normal life we'd been suffering under for so many months would soon be righted. All it needed was the application of hard work, reason, and mostly patience. The world moved according to a long-standing order, and it would come back as soon as people started acting regular again.

I wouldn't trouble to argue the point, though. He had his cup of coffee, and as far as I could figure it, my obligation to him had reached its conclusion. "Ten cents," I said.

He wrapped his dirty hands around the cup and closed his eyes, breathing in the smell of it. "That don't mean anything," he said.

I felt my patience snap. "It means you owe us ten cents! You can't just force your way in here when we're trying to close and then not pay for what you order!"

He put down his mug gently and said, "Force? Little girl, calm yourself down. I will pay you when I'm ready to pay you. And if you think money means a goddamn thing anymore, you're more childish than I thought. The old things don't matter anymore. Don't you get that?"

I heard the door to the kitchen open behind me, and my father said, "Belle, are you shouting? What's going on out here?"

Father looked tired. Those days, he always did. He wasn't very tall, and he'd been thin even when in good health, but in the months since the Silence started he'd come to look almost skeletal. His hair had thinned away to nothing on top, and what was left was mostly gray. His clothes, wet with water from washing dishes, hung loosely from his body. His face was worn. He was turning into an old man right in front of me. It was hard to look at him anymore without feeling a bewildering tangle of sadness and fear.

"I told this man to pay for his coffee and he won't do it."

He put his hand on my shoulder. "Anabelle, it's just coffee," he said into my ear. To the dusty scavenger across the counter, he said, "My daughter is headstrong. It's what keeps me honest." I bristled; he had no right to apologize for me. Not when I was in the right. He offered the man a smile. If you did not know him, it might have seemed genuine.

"Your sign said *open*," said the man, as if my father had challenged him in some way.

"Of course. We're closing up, but you're welcome to stay and finish."

"Why don't you go ahead and shut it off."

"I don't mind staying open a while longer. To be honest, you're doing me a favor. I have work to do here anyway. And I wouldn't mind the company." Father walked around the counter with his broom, ready to clean the main floor.

"I said shut the sign off."

Father stopped, turned to look at the man. Another surge of anger galloped through my blood. I was always hot-tempered, and it got me into trouble sometimes, but some folks brought it out. Some folks just needed to be hit in the face.

I wanted Father to put him in his place. I wanted him to grab this intruder by his filthy collar and drag him kicking and hollering through the diner and throw him outside. I wanted him to blacken those pretty eyes. But it wasn't his way. He'd always been a mild soul. He liked tranquility and he liked good manners. I used to wonder what it had been that caused such a delicate-natured man to volunteer to be one of the first permanent colonists on Mars, those ten years ago. Brave men did that sort of thing. My father was not brave.

Mother was.

"All right," he said. He flicked his eyes to me and then back to the man. "Just stay calm. I'll shut it off."

"I am calm, old man. I'll stay that way too as long as you do what I say."

Father walked to the sign hanging inside the window, and as he did this I calculated my odds against the intruder. I had boiling water to hand, but it would take me two or three good strides to fetch it, another to turn around and fling it at him. That left him too much time. We'd taken the knives to the back to be washed; the fryer was off, the oil cooling. Watson remained in the back, scrubbing plates, as useless as a potted plant. So I glared fiercely at him and I hoped his imagination was sufficient to interpret the magnitude of ills I visited upon him in my mind.

The vacancy of his expression as he looked back at me suggested it was not.

Father pulled the cord on the neon sign. It sputtered and went out. He flipped a switch and half the interior lights went out, too, leaving only the kitchen illuminated, and a few emergency lights here in the dining area. He stayed quiet as he walked back around the counter, until he stood beside me. "There," he said. "We're closed. Anabelle, go back in the kitchen."

"You just stay where you are, Anabelle," the man said.

"Do as I say. Right now."

I moved to obey, even though every impulse told me to stay.

The man slapped his hand on the countertop. *"Do you not listen? Do you not—"*

My father raised his voice, too, but before I could parse what he was saying, the stranger removed a pistol from his belt, hidden beneath his coat, and with a grace and a practice I would not have attributed to one with such a rough aspect, he flipped it once in the air so that he held it by its barrel, and he brought it down in a vicious strike against my father's temple, dropping him to the counter like a sack of oats. Father slid to the floor; I tried to hold him up, but he was too heavy. The intruder had the gun by its grip again, the transition too fast for me to follow, its open end pointed at my face.

"Now goddamn it, you stay right there!"

I was terrified. I did not move. I watched my father bleeding quietly onto the floor, which was filthy from the treads of our feet and the sand blown in from outside. He was as still as a moon in the open sky.

"Help me with him," the stranger said. He climbed over the countertop and slid down on our side. He hooked his hands under my father's shoulders and looked at me. *"I said help me, girl!"*

I did. I would like to tell you that I fought him, that I grabbed whatever was at hand and attacked him without regard for my own safety. But I was afraid. His quick action had taken the fight straight out of me. Now I was alone with him, and I was afraid. So I took my father's ankles, and when the man instructed me to help carry him into the back, I obeyed.

We called this room the kitchen, even though most of the actual cooking was done on the range up front, where the customers could watch you. This back room was narrow and used mostly for washing dirty dishes and storing ingredients. A large, waist-high icebox fit snugly next to the sink. On the other side of the sink was the back door, with a heavy security bar fit across it. We liked to pretend New Galveston was too small to accommodate the sort of criminal to make such a measure necessary, but Father maintained that bad men could be found everywhere. Though I had always believed him, I was sorry to see it proved so powerfully.

Watson stood by the sink. He looked so intimidating: his large metal body solid and strong, like a big, invulnerable barrel. His arms were made of steel and could crumple a human skull in the grip of their rubber-padded pincers like a grapefruit. The light from his eyes, in that moment, made him look deadly, like something from a dime novel. I wished with my whole heart that he would surprise this man—that he would surprise *me*.

"Oh dear," he said.

The man did not spare him a glance. We laid my father on the floor. As soon as I released his ankles I backed up against the wall, next to a shelf stacked with jars full of preserves, with flour and sugar and oats. Each one a missile I was too scared to use. I felt my breath passing into and out of my lungs. I felt the pulse of blood in my head, so heavy that it made me feel faint.

The stranger stood over my father, examining him the way a veterinarian might a felled horse. He glanced at me. "He ain't dead, just so you know."

I nodded, but I wasn't sure I believed it. I'd seen dead people before—once when two boys were horsing around on a tractor and one fell beneath the disc harrow dragging behind them, and several more later on, when the influenza cut through us all like a holy judgment. All of them looked just as still, just as expunged of possibility, as my father did then.

"Here's what's going to happen." When I didn't look in his direction, he clapped his hands together once, sharply. "Do you hear me, little girl? Pay attention. I am going to open that back door there and make a signal. Then some of my friends are going to come in. They're going to take a look around here and see what might be useful, and then they're going to go ahead and take it. After that, we're all going to leave. All right?" He took a step forward and said, "Are you hearing me?"

"I hear you just fine! You're a thief! That's all you are is a damn thief!"

He had the nerve to look angry. "You better be glad that's all I am. You better hope that's all I stay. You might not think it, but this can get a whole lot worse. So just stand there quietly like a good little girl and let this play out the way it's meant to."

The stranger slid the security bar from the back door and pulled it open, letting in a cool blast of night air. He leaned out and made a low trilling sound, like the Martian cricket that was always infiltrating our greenhouses. After a few moments he stepped away and two others came in.

A man and a woman, both dressed for the cold, each face scoured ageless by the harsh and unblocked winds of the plain. The man was tall and bald, with the same reflective green eyes as the stranger. He ignored my fallen father and me, moving instead to the shelving behind us and scooping preserves into a sack. The woman had black hair chopped short and a stocky frame, her face pockmarked with acne scars. She glanced at me and then at my father. "Dead?" she asked.

"Now Sally. What do you take me for?"

"You probably shouldn't ask."

She joined the other in the scouring of our stores. While they ransacked for food, the stranger went to the table my father used as a desk and overturned the small boxes he kept there, scattering receipts, pens, paper clips, and the hard round cylinders we used for Watson—for recording messages, for music, for backup. He gathered these latter up and slipped them into the pockets of his jacket. It was this loss, even more than that of the food, that would hurt us.

The whole operation took less than five minutes. As they filed out into the night, silently and quickly, taking with them whatever they could of our food and water, the man who started it all made a stop at the icebox and opened it up, removing from the foggy interior a choice bit of frozen Kansas beef.

On his way to the door he stopped by Watson and patted his cheek. "You ought to come looking for me, big fella. It's a different world out there for folks like you." Then he looked back at me. He touched a finger to his head, as though he were raising the brim of an imaginary cap, and said, "Name's Silas Mundt. I don't reckon you'll see me again."

"You better pray I don't," I said.

"Enjoy the picture show, Anabelle. I believe you can still make it if you hurry."

And then he closed the door behind him. I hefted the bar back into place, locking us in, and then rushed to my father, who was indeed still alive, and breathing shallowly. I cleaned the blood from his head with the hem of my dress. Only then did I allow the tears to come, and they came with a force that frightened me.

It would be some time before I allowed them again.

2

This all happened a long time ago: in 1931, almost a full year after the Silence began. Back then, we still measured years the way we did on Earth. That would have made me fourteen. Seven, according to Martian reckoning. But nobody used the Martian way then. That would come later.

What I remember most about being a girl during the first year of the Silence was the terrible presence of the saucer. I could see it from my bedroom window in our little hab, and I would stare at it sometimes in the evening, as the sky was opened up to the stars, drawing out crowds of earthgazers. The saucer rested in a declivity just beyond the border of the town. Its dome rose above the low metal roofs of the habs like a squat silver hill, reflecting the light of the setting sun. Sometimes Mr. Reilly, its pilot, would go inside and fire up the engines—just to keep them in working order, he'd say. When he did that, the lights around its circumference would ignite in a bright blue radiance. The light reflected from the sides of our habs, making New Galveston look like a handful of blue diamonds dropped in the desert.

Mr. Reilly didn't run the engines often, though. The reason he gave was that it used fuel, and fuel had to be conserved if we were ever going to dare the trip home. But the real reason, which I knew even then, was that seeing the saucer all lit up made people a little crazy. They started thinking too hard about climbing in and going home. And nothing fired up an argument in those days like talk of going home.

Serious arguments were things to be avoided, if possible. Sheriff Bakersfield had only a few cells in his jail, and there were no facilities available for long-term confinement. What's more, we didn't know if we'd be able to keep growing enough crops to feed everyone as it was; we didn't want to face the question of whether we should use some of that food for permanent prisoners.

So mostly the saucer stayed quiet and dark. It had acquired the somber aspect of a monument. Sometimes it felt more like a tombstone.

I felt its presence as I ran toward the town square, even though I couldn't see it from my vantage point. It was like a manifest insult.

The picture had already started. The screen looked like a silver pool turned on its side, shedding a flat light in the darkness. Rows of wooden chairs were set out in rank and file before it, with people affixed to them like dark little mushrooms. The mighty heat lamps that surrounded the town and permitted us to survive outside at night had been brought more closely in, creating a wide pocket of afternoon warmth; it was an indulgence, but one the governor allowed from time to time. The movies soothed anxieties.

On the screen I saw the jungles of Earth—something I had never seen in real life, something I would never see. I grabbed the first two grown men I encountered and ordered them to follow me and to arm themselves and to fetch the doctor and to fetch the sheriff and to secure the town and who knows what else. Though it must have surprised them to receive directives from a half-grown girl, they could see the distress in my face, and they moved to action.

In minutes we'd managed to transport my father to our hab, where Dr. Land hovered beside him, crumbs from his dinner still stuck to the long ends of his fine white mustache. Our hab was standard-issue for a family of three: two bedrooms, each with space for little more than a bed, a bureau, and a breath; one living area composed of a small dinner table and chairs, a writing shelf that folded flat against the wall and hitched there, a kitchen, and barely enough space for whatever personal effects might have accompanied us from Earth. All of this crammed like gunpowder into our little aluminum bullet. When the rain fell against our roof it sounded like the German infantry, or so my father told me.

When I joined him at his bedside, forcing my way through the clucking neighbors gathered in the living room, my father had come back to consciousness and was vomiting into a pail Dr. Land had positioned by his head. The stink of it filled our little home. It shocked me: it made what had happened suddenly real, irrevocable. I suppose I expected to enter that room and see Father standing straight and sure, knowing precisely what to do, restoring order. Instead he was sick. I didn't understand why being struck should make him vomit, and that it did so seemed to indicate a peculiar weakness in him. It was as though he was dissolving in front of me.

He beckoned me closer, saying my name in a muted voice. I stood there silently and let him touch my face.

"Are you all right? Did they hurt you?"

"No, but Dad, they—"

"Hush." Once assured of my safety, he seemed to have no interest in learning the particulars of the robbery. "Let me lie, Anabelle. Go on back and lock up. Get someone to go with you."

Dr. Land put a hand on my shoulder. "Oh, there's no need for an escort, I don't think. This whole town is bustling with the news. Those boys are long gone by now."

"They weren't just boys," I said. "There was a woman, too."

The doctor cast a doubtful eye upon me. "Well, in any case, I think you'll be just fine on your own. Go on and do as your daddy tells you."

Father had turned his face to the wall. He did not look at me as he said, "Please, Anabelle. Do as I ask."

As I headed to the front door, I cast a glance into my own room, where Watson waited for me, heavy and solid in the shadows, the orange light from his eyes like little candles in the gloom.

"Shall I accompany you, Miss Crisp?" he said. I thought of the hero I'd named him after and felt ridiculous. John Watson, the character, was an ex-soldier, a capable fighting man, and a sharp intellect. The idea that a Kitchen Engine could protect me was absurd, as he'd already proven.

"No," I said. "You're useless."

He turned away, back toward my room. As his head rotated away from me, the lights of his eyes disappeared from my view. It felt like an omen.

THE DINER WAS only a couple of blocks from our hab. I looked down the road to the town square and saw that the film had been shut off, the screen folded up and put away. People were collecting the rows of chairs and taking them back to the classrooms and the churches. A woman saw me walk by and hollered something at me, but I didn't stay to find out what.

A cluster of men were gathered at the diner, which looked as bright and busy as a workday lunch rush. I pushed my way through the front door, into a discussion already underway about what to do.

Wally Bakersfield, the heavyset, middle-aged sheriff of New Galveston, was in the middle of surrendering. "Pursuit at this hour would be too dangerous," he said. Hearing that almost dropped me to my knees. I had assumed that there would be only one option here, and that all voices would be unanimous in its support. That Sheriff Bakersfield of all people advocated bowing the head to these wretches indicated a weakness at the core of ourselves, one I would not have given credence to even an hour earlier. I was reminded of my father vomiting into a bucket. "Best to wait until morning," he said. "We'll have daylight on our side."

"By that time they'll be miles away!" I shouted. Several of the men, who had not seen me enter, turned to look at me with expressions as various and cloudy as their own cowed hearts. "They'll disappear into the desert! You all know that!"

A big blond farm boy—one of the Dunne boys, a beefy clod named Fenris—put his hand on my shoulder and suggested I go back to check on my father, who was no doubt in need of a daughter's ministrations. He smiled at me the way you smile at boisterous children, or at good-natured dogs in the high reaches of enthusiasm.

I *wanted* to go. I was small in a grove of tall men with loud opinions, and though I was typically not shy with my own, that was with my peers. These were adults accustomed to being taken seriously, accustomed to reacting to hardship with wisdom and careful methodology, accustomed most of all to doing these things free from the buzzing of little girls.

But it felt wrong to leave the diner to this crowd of angry men. There were nine or ten of them at this point, stalking around like ants from a kicked nest, talking in big voices about what they would have done if they'd been here, and the necessity for prudence now that it was past.

One of them came out of the back room and said it was all picked over; there was nothing left. They speculated about my father's future and came to grim conclusions.

"It's just too risky, keeping all this food in one place," someone said. "He was asking for trouble."

"I fear that if it weren't the outlaws, it would have been one of us before much longer."

"Now, Jacob—"

"You know I'm right. It's just going to get worse. You mark me. Once the larders get light, you watch what happens."

"We're a God-fearing people," someone else said. "Not savages. God will see us through."

"God never set foot on *this* rock. It's red for a reason. Red and cold."

"Don't let Preacher Spivey hear you talk like that! He'll drown us in sermon." This was followed by an easy laughter.

I couldn't abide it any longer. These men were jawing like they were sharing a smoke after dinner. "And what of the thieves that came in here and attacked my father and stole from us? Why do you keep going on like you was some kind of philosophers, when you could be out reclaiming what we lost? There was only three of them!" I turned to the sheriff. "One of 'em's called Silas, and he's with the Moths! There was a woman, fat with short dark hair! Two of them's eyes were shining green."

He cut his eyes away from me. He looked troubled, and I thought I knew why.

"Dig Town," someone said.

"Assemble some men who ain't scared of the dark and bring them back here!"

"You curb that ignorant tongue, young lady!"

It was Jeremiah Shank, the most loathsome man on Mars. He was tall and too thin and I was sure he walked in the favor of the Devil, whose approving gaze pinched his face into a permanent scowl. He worked as the colony's cobbler, and he wasn't a very good one. It remains my fervent belief that he made every shoe a fraction too small in an effort to pull the spirit of the colony into accord with his own.

"Will you have us race into darkness to be set upon like lambs? Will you have them fatten their stores with our own flesh? You're a child, with a child's notion of the world. Go back to your daddy, as you were told."

It was especially galling to hear direction from him; everyone knew his own children had run off to Dig Town once his wife had died. He had no standing to say anything to me, as far as I was concerned.

I felt the hand on my shoulder again. Fenris leaned into my ear and said, "Come, Anabelle. You're not doing any good here."

"But I'm supposed to lock up," I said weakly, and I felt the heat of tears gathering behind my eyes. The diner belonged to my father, and to my mother, and to me, too. It had been invaded twice now tonight, each time by offensive, entitled oafs strutting about like it was their own. It felt abhorrent to leave them there, like leaving a mob of unruly boys in a room full of delicate things. It felt like surrendering ownership of something precious.

"I'll walk you back," Fenris said.

"I needed your help earlier tonight. I don't need it now."

He looked properly chastened, though I wondered, unkindly, whether it was real or only for show. I always thought that there was something of the actor in Fenris, that he knew how he was supposed to behave and acted accordingly, though he did not feel it in his heart. Looking into his face, which radiated kindness, I wanted to slap him for the liar I believed him to be.

But I did not. I shouldered past him, hot with shame, and I left the diner in defeat. The light from the windows painted a bright wash over the ruddy sand at my feet, and the clamor of their useless talk followed me like a stink in the air.

The paths connecting the homes and the buildings of our colony were well trod, both by human feet and by the plodding of our Engines. I could have followed the packed dirt to my own front door in my sleep, and according to my mother had once done that very thing, but the thought of going back to the sick-smelling hab, where my father languished in his compromised dignity, held no appeal for me. I turned right, off the road, toward the swelling darkness of the desert night.

Colonists often had difficulty getting used to the colder temperatures of Mars, upon their first arrival. The sun is smaller here, the days shorter and cooler. Twilight is the common mood of our sky. I was only five when I came here, overwhelmed by everything new and wonderful, but I still remember the unpleasant shock of it. You did not want to be caught outside the protection of the municipal heat lamps at night, and I found myself wishing for my coat as I approached New Galveston's edge. I wrapped my arms around myself as a strong gust of wind carved into me, spraying my face with sand that collected in the corners of my eyes and sifted down my shirt. I peered through it, across the flat black plain to the distant rise where I once would have been able to see the low lights of Dig Town, where they mined the mineral called the Strange, which gave the illusion of life to our Engines. But Dig Town was mostly dark these days.

Beyond that was the vast, haunted Peabody Crater: where the Moths dwelt, where the old War Engines still roamed, where spirits were rumored to walk.

I looked for any sign of the thieves: the light of a lantern, the movement of a shadow. There was nothing, of course, other than the long coils of sand that seemed to extend into the night like mystical, winding trails, their far ends connecting to mysteries and riddles, to fantastical cities, or to the long death of the world.

The stars overhead were a shimmering curtain. Somewhere up there was Mother. What she was thinking—if she was thinking anything at all—was just another mystery.

FATHER WAS ASLEEP when I got home. The door to his bedroom was ajar, and by the splinter of light that extended into it I could see his back as he faced the wall. Still wearing his undershirt, he looked small and boyish in the double bed. His work shirt was draped over a nearby chair. The sick-bucket rested on the floor within easy reach, exuding an evil stench.

I retreated to my own room and changed into my nightclothes. As I settled into bed, the orange glow of Watson's eyes rotated again into view. I could hear the grit in his servitors: no matter how much we cleaned and polished the Engines, the sand would never completely come out. They needed deep maintenance, new parts. Parts that would never come.

Well, I thought. *Somebody will think of something. The Engines won't die. They can't.*

"Are you well, Miss Crisp?"

"Yes, Watson."

"Mr. Crisp is ill. He's still suffering from the attack."

"Yes, I know. No one is doing anything about it." I felt despair threaten again.

"Surely it will be put to rights soon enough. The guilty will atone. Justice will prevail. This is civilization, after all."

"Yes, Watson. Let's go to sleep now."

"Good night then, Miss Crisp. Dream well."

Watson always bid me good night that way. It amused me that he issued it as a directive, as though it were a job one could perform well or poorly. I wondered what he understood about the notion of dreams, wondered if he was curious about what they were like. On good nights, when I felt cocooned in the security of my family and the optimism that comes from faith in the world's order, I would allow myself to consider the possibility that he did not have to wonder at all, that perhaps Watson and all other Engines dreamed as we did. I imagined that such dreams would be beautiful, as stark and clean as bones scoured by sand. A series of numbers, an ordering of geometrical theorems. A catalogue of answers to impossible questions, glimmering like steel in sunlight.

But that night I knew the interior of his mind for what it was: programmed algorithms; the illusion of personality. He was as cold and as dark as the space we had crossed to come here.

Again, I heard the grating sound as he rotated his head away from me. The light from his eyes lit the corner of my little room and faded, as he dimmed them in deference to my need for sleep.

3

Mother left for Earth a month before the Silence.

I remember the night it was decided. Mars was different then: vibrant and thrilling, still riding the crest of expansionist excitement. New Galveston was the first official colony established here, but there were other, older settlements: Dig Town, the collection of wattle-and-daub homes and network of tents that had gathered around the great hole they called the Throat, the principal mining site of the Strange; Brawley's Crossing, an unofficial settlement of stowaways and explorers that predated our own town by at least a decade; and a spiderweb of smaller towns and villages full of philanthropists, pioneers, hermits, and reprobates—the driftwood of civilization that had been accumulating over the years since Chauncy Peabody's celebrated landing in 1864.

But New Galveston was the jewel. We represented the first organized effort to build a permanent presence here. We were the ones who benefited from the direct exchange of goods with Earth, we were the town that made all the travel brochures and inspired the dreams of working folks yearning for the opportunities that once lured whole families to the

American West. Laborers came in droves to lay ties for a railroad, which we believed would one day be the glory of Mars. Wealthy adventurers came to wander into the deserts, and famous personalities vacationed here, eager to take in the exotic atmosphere of a wild new place.

The last night of my normal life found me with my parents on the outskirts of town, on our way to the local baseball game. A barnstorming team was visiting from Earth, featuring players from the Cuban and Negro Leagues for the first time, and Father had heard that their pitcher could throw harder and faster than any white man who'd ever taken the mound. He did not believe it, and we all headed for the game in curious disbelief. My father was eager to see our own Martian Homesteaders put a dent in this upstart's fancy reputation, but I was secretly hoping to see a dazzling display of strikeouts.

A train of people made the easy walk to the ballfield, the warmth of the afternoon still riding the breeze, a last lingering comfort before the evening chill settled upon us. The sky was bright, spangled with shades of red, the night still crouched behind the curve of the world. People brought picnic baskets; their Engines walked or rode on treads beside them, including our own Watson, who'd been turned into a pack mule for our sandwiches and our lemonade.

It was Watson that stopped us, rotating his rust-mottled head to observe the Postal Engine racing to catch us.

"I believe we are wanted," he said.

The Postal Engine hurried along, navigating the furrowed track with ease. It came to a ratcheting halt a respectful distance from us. The train of people parted around it, some of them giving us lingering glances. Standard practice was for people to pick up their own mail at the post office; if the Engine came for you, it usually meant an emergency.

"An urgent message for you, Mrs. Crisp," it said in its cheery metallic voice.

Although no great calamity had yet befallen me, I felt a sickness in my gut. The Engine's sprightly tone rang like a funeral bell, inspiring a sudden, peculiar loathing. Its voice appalled me. It was as though its engineers had been so intoxicated with the excitement of Mars that it must have seemed impossible to them that one might ever again receive bad news.

"Let me have it," Mother said, and the Postal Engine extruded a cylinder from one of its ports, which Mother took. It then pivoted on its treads, its function fulfilled, and trundled homeward. My parents exchanged a glance. With a command word—"bluebonnet"—she shut down Watson's awareness and ejected his personality cylinder from a port in his head. In its place she inserted the recording cylinder.

Watson hummed for a moment, and then he spoke to us in Aunt Emily's voice.

"Alice, it's Mother. She's suffered another setback. Dr. Spahn gives her six months, at best. Her memory is fading. Some days she doesn't even know who I am. She calls me by your name. I think you should come, if you want to see her before the end. I'm sorry, I know it's not easy. But I believe it's now or never."

Of course, it was a ridiculous request. The trip home would take two months, and surely there was nothing for Mother to do except to send her condolences and to suffer her loss here, in the comfort of her family's presence.

But passivity was never Mother's way.

Father took her into his arms and held her tightly. Her face was clouded, but it did not seem to me that she was on the verge of ruining my life.

We didn't go to the baseball game. We weren't there to see Satchel Paige shut out the Homesteaders, setting a strikeout record on Mars that has yet to be broken. How strange that this, of all things, still galls. That I should lie here in my cot, staring up at the fluttering canvas of my tent so many years later, and still feel deprived of having seen something wonderful.

After putting Watson's cylinder back in place, we returned to our hab in a troubled silence. Although neither of my parents would speak it out loud, I understood then that she really was going to go.

But I didn't expect her to leave me behind.

When she told me, she might as well have slapped my face. I stood in the doorway to my parents' room, watching her pack for the long journey: her books, her pretty dresses, her toiletries. The ship to Earth was leaving the next day, just after another arrived, each loaded with passengers and cargo. Three saucers made the regular circuit. The one arriving tomorrow would not head back to Earth for another four months.

What we didn't know was that the one arriving the next day—the *Eurydice*—would never leave. And the one that took my mother away—the *Orpheus*—would never return. This was her last night on Mars. Her last night with me.

"I want to come with you," I said.

She did not look at me when she said, "You know you can't."

"You just don't want me to."

I remember standing there, small and angry and hurt. I can see myself as though I were watching someone else. I feel no sympathy for that child, roughly moved by the currents of adult motive, so mysterious and so callous to her needs. I could if it were a different person. I could hold her close and whisper the sweet lies adults tell children. But because it's me, I feel ashamed of her for treating my mother so coldly.

She looked at me then, finally letting me see the grief she felt. "How can you say such an awful thing?"

"I'm small. I won't take up too much space."

She sat on the bed she shared with Father and held her arms out to me. Tears glimmered in her eyes. I went to her, feeling a flare of hope, and she hoisted me onto her lap like a child half my age. I laid my head against her shoulder, feeling the heat of her skin, taking in the clean, wind-scoured scent of her hair. I remember wondering if Earth would change the way she smelled, and it made me afraid. But the fear went away when she held me. I believed she would make the difficult decisions, that she would bear the pain the world portioned out to me, the way parents are meant to do. She would keep me from despair.

But, "You must stay, Anabelle," she said. "Not because the saucer can't accommodate you, and not because I don't want you to come. You must stay because you're a growing girl and you're in school, with friends here and a father who needs you. You have to help him mind the diner and you have to continue your studies. In a few years, you're going to be a grown woman. It's hard work, and you have to be ready. I'll be back soon."

"It's not soon," I said, letting myself cry at last. "It's a long time."

"You have the recording cylinder I made for you. When you miss me too much, you just take out Watson and put that in instead. I left lots of little messages, for you and your father both. It'll be just like I'm right here."

"No, it won't. It's not the same."

I felt her face on the top of my head, her breath warm in my hair.

"I know," she said finally. "I know."

I pressed my face into her shoulder, soaking her blouse with my stupid, useless tears. "Why can't you just stay! She might not even be alive when you get there!"

She smoothed my hair with her hand and pressed her lips against my forehead. "Because she's my mother," she said. "I want to say goodbye to her. I'm afraid it might be my only chance, and it would hurt me forever to miss it. The way you love me is exactly the way I love her."

That made sense to me, of course. But it also defeated me, because the love I felt in that moment was as terrifying and hungry as any starved dog. It left no room for anyone else, not even for my own father. And if it was true that there was no room in my heart for him, then it must also be true that there was no room in hers for me. I understood at last why it was so easy for her to leave me.

"One day," she said, "you'll want to say goodbye to me, too."

4

The morning after the robbery Sheriff Bakersfield assembled a few men on horseback and ranged out along the road toward Dig Town. I climbed onto the roof of our diner and watched them disappear from sight. I waited eagerly to see them return with at least one of the miscreants walking behind the horses with a rope extending from his bound hands to the pommel of the sheriff's saddle. Despite the meek talk of the night before, there was yet no doubt in my mind that justice would be delivered to all who deserved it.

They came home in defeat that afternoon. It was beyond my comprehension. They led their horses back into town, passing by the diner and beneath my dangling feet.

"You couldn't find them?" I called.

Fenris turned his face toward me, though he lacked the fortitude to raise his shamed glance above the level of my shoes. "We just rode up to its border. We didn't go in."

"What? Why not?"

He said nothing more, just followed the others toward the stables.

I wanted to shout at them, call them cowards, ask them why

they'd given up so easily, why they couldn't even muster the courage to go into Dig Town, let alone beyond it; but I knew they'd developed a callus against my opinions. So instead I stared at them and marked them all for failed men.

Across the street, Jeremiah Shank stood outside the door of his business, looking smart and clean in his starched white shirt and buttoned black vest. It occurred to me that I had never seen the man dirty, which only gave me further cause to hate him. He watched the horses go by, and when they had passed, he fixed his gaze on me.

"You're going to have to accustom yourself to disappointment, young Miss Crisp," he called.

"Then I should thank you for providing me an excellent lesson," I said.

He turned and went back into his store.

I decided to linger on the rooftop a little longer. Father was moving around downstairs, against the doctor's wishes. He wanted to restore order to the Mother Earth Diner, and to open the doors again as quickly as possible. The men who'd gathered last night to rationalize their own lack of initiative had caused more upset to the place than the thieves, who at least had been quick and methodical in their enterprise. I wanted to help, but I could sense the darkness falling upon him again, the kind that dragged him into isolation and bitterness, and I did not want to be around it. I feared the attack had compromised his ability to fight it off.

Normally if I was not working at the diner I'd be in school, but Miss Haddersham had said there'd be no classes that day. Though people strutted about with their brave words and their sturdy chests, fear had settled quickly over New Galveston.

That was the effect Dig Town had had upon us since the Silence. It had become a haunted place.

For years there'd been nothing special about Dig Town; it was just where the real work of our colony was done. The Strange— that miracle ore—was hacked from the Martian rock and sent back to Earth, where it was processed into a substance that we could add to our Engines, giving them personalities—the illusion of intelligence. Starting out as nothing more than a few dozen tents surrounding the Throat, Dig Town had grown to become a small town unto itself. It had its own mercantile, its own infirmary, its own church. It was where Mr. Wickham maintained his machine parts shop. This served the purposes of the miners quite well; they had their basic needs fulfilled immediately, and came to New Galveston only when they wanted to.

After the Silence, that separation came to serve our interests, too. It used to be that the Teller Mining Company rotated its employees back to Earth every three months, limiting their exposure to the Strange, allowing them to decontaminate at home. None of them were allowed more than one rotation a year. The miners who came to town in those days had been like any other working men, and their business was welcome.

The Silence changed that, as it changed everything else. Now, the Strange worked its fingers deep into the meat of their heads. The mining work continued, to the dismay of everyone in New Galveston, though there was nowhere to ship the rock to, and no way to process it here. It was changing anyone who worked with the ore. The green luminescence of their eyes was the most obvious example of that, but it changed their behavior, too. They became distant, distracted . . . and oddly confrontational. Occasionally some would still make the trip to New Galveston, and when they did, they spoiled the atmosphere around them. People became troubled and uneasy. The Dig Towners seemed to be a harbinger of some dark eventuality, ghosts of a future time come back to warn us.

The Strange was locked safely in the rock, we thought. But if it was changing them, would it come to change us, too? Going to Dig Town forced thoughts no one wanted to confront.

Easier, it seemed, to let the thieves go to ground there, and forget about them.

This was to say nothing of the desert cults, like the Moths. We knew precious little about them. They lived in the sprawling Peabody Crater, which put them uncomfortably close to New Galveston. The Strange was abundant in the crater, its veins breaching the surface in so many places that sometimes its basin took on a pale green hue, as if it was covered in blowing grasses. These cultists, in their unknown numbers, steered their lives according to whatever mysterious beliefs or hallucinations guided them.

We were indoctrinated with fear of them, both at home and at school. They accrued a horrible mystique. We were told they were religious zealots, or bacchanalians, or cannibals. We were told the Strange caused their brains to rot with too many dreams. Since the Earth had gone silent and the long summer drought loomed over us with its terrible promise, the threat these cults posed to us was an urgent and divisive topic of debate, even more pressing than the question of Joe Reilly and his grounded saucer.

Our life here was so tenuous. We manufactured our electricity from solar- and wind-powered batteries, and these powered the heat lamps that kept us warm at night; a determined saboteur could unleash a lethal cold into the city. We relied on greenhouses for our crops; they'd never survive the night temperatures otherwise. One cascade of crop failures and we would be crippled, possibly finished. The greenhouses themselves were strong, built to withstand the Martian dust storms and the fluctuating temperatures, but there were stories of massive storms, big enough to blot out the sky for days and to scour the land to naked rock. If one of those came upon us, the greenhouses would be gone. And those of us who still lived would starve.

So we feared the cults. We feared how they might take advantage of our vulnerability. We feared what they might do to us, what they might want from us.

The posse had dispersed. From my elevated position I cast my eyes over the town. The shops and the homes all grouped together in this great red waste like silver-backed beetles. Beyond, the pastures where the cattle were kept in fading green acres, the domed fields where the crops of corn and wheat and soy and tobacco were planted and harvested, the water tower and the windmills. A ways off to the north, the landing pad where the saucer was parked, gleaming in the afternoon sunlight. And farther still, the shoulders of Peabody Crater, with its sandy floor and its huge, scattered rocks. I wondered if those rocks were where they lived. If they sheltered in caverns and holes like vermin. I had a vision of them crawling through their underground networks, rotting out Mars from the inside.

I could not figure how we could possibly survive if we did not answer this attack.

A single cloud scudded across the high atmosphere. It was the straggling end of the great herds of cumulus that filled the sky during monsoon season; we would not see more for many months. Seeing even this one was remarkable so late in the season, and I could not help but consider its appearance a sign from whatever spirit organized the world. A friendly wink from God or the Devil.

WHEN I DESCENDED the ladder into the diner's back room again, I heard Father talking to someone up front. Cautiously— not wishing to be called a snoop—I peered around the door. Father was standing by the entrance, which was propped open. He was talking to Sheriff Bakersfield. The sheriff was not a regular at Mother Earth, but he came by often enough for me to have formed a favorable opinion of him. I liked his big belly, his white mustache, his kindly demeanor. He seemed grandfatherly, though I doubt he was more than fifty. But my opinion changed after the robbery. I decided he was too old. I decided that the law should be represented by someone younger and more inclined to action. Like his deputy, Mae Ackerman, who was not with him that day.

Jack was, though. A hulking Law Engine, Jack was designed to intimidate. He had guns folded into his arms, and instead of feet he rolled on massive treads. I didn't like him. I'd never seen him do anything to warrant that dislike, but it was so, just the same. And I immediately wondered why the sheriff had brought Jack here but hadn't seen fit to take him to Dig Town, where he might have done some good.

"Was she there?"

"I didn't see her. But I believe she's holed up there for now, yes."

"Then go get her. Bring her back and get her to tell you where the Moths are. Then round 'em all up."

"We can't do it, Sam, and you know it," said the sheriff.

"That's horseshit, Wally."

"No, it isn't. I can't find anybody wants to go to Dig Town. Mae and Jack, sure, but we won't be enough. And if I wheel Jack in there, well, some might consider it a declaration of war."

"Declare war, then."

I felt a fierce swell of pride for my father. There was life in him yet.

"If we get into it with Dig Town, people die. People we need to till the soil and dig for water. We can't afford any losses right now, Sam. Not with the dry season about to start, and nothing more coming from Earth." He paused. "Not to mention, we might not fare too well in a contest with the miners. We can't afford to indulge in revenge."

Father looked the sheriff in the eye. "You're afraid of them," he said.

"I'd be a fool not to be. That doesn't discount any of what I just told you. I know you see it. Let me station Jack down here a few evenings, just to hang around."

"Jack? No, thank you. A Law Engine doesn't quite fit the decor."

"Mae, then."

"That's not necessary."

"I think it is. They might come back. And I don't mean to disrespect you by saying so, but it might be better if they found somebody prepared to meet them. Mae's a good shot."

"We'll be fine. I appreciate the offer."

"Sam, I'm not sure you will be. It's not just the outsiders I'm thinking about. Those boys in the posse were entertaining some troubling notions."

I could tell Father was angry, though he tried to cover it. He shook the sheriff's hand and thanked him. "I won't be driven from my store," he said. "Not by cultists, and not by good men."

Sheriff Bakersfield nodded reluctantly. "My job is to keep the peace, Sam. To keep this applecart from turning over. I hope you understand." With that, he wished my father a good afternoon, and left with Jack in tow.

Whatever help was being offered, I wished that Father had taken it. It's a peculiarity in some men that they cannot accept help without feeling compromised by it. It's better to die alone, it would seem, than to live in the debt of another human being.

So we were by ourselves, and only I was there to see his face as he surveyed the diner's interior, to see the despair settle in. I'd been right: the darkness was back, a buzzard on his shoulder, wings outstretched.

He noticed me standing in the kitchen doorway.

"What did the sheriff mean about troubling notions?" I said.

He shook his head. "Who knows." He paused. "Let's go home, Belle."

"But . . . there's more work to do."

"Tomorrow. I'm tired. Let's you and me just try to forget all this for a little while. We'll come back in the morning, open up again tomorrow night."

This was unlike him, and I welcomed it. I couldn't remember the last time we'd taken time away from the store, just for ourselves. Just me and him.

"Okay," I said, smiling. "I'll lock up."

• • •

EVENING FOUND US reclining in chairs outside the rear of our hab, out of sight of the neighborhood's foot traffic and presenting us with a clean, unobstructed view of the plain to the west, where the light of the day still lingered. We sat in a companionable silence, watching as the moons became visible in the sky, like faint smudges of chalk.

"This reminds me of back home," he said. "Sitting on the porch with your mother, sipping iced tea, watching the stars come out."

I closed my eyes, listening to him talk. I liked it when he got into these reflective moods, telling stories about Mother, about life back on Earth. Although they skirted the center of a great pain, they were a comfort to me, and I suspect to him, too. They didn't come freighted with misery or regret; they were simply good memories, taken from his pocket like a timepiece, polished and cared for in the waning sunlight.

"I remember one late summer evening, the sky looked a lot like this: a deep twilight blue. Fireflies everywhere, like a tide of stars washing across the fields. Do you remember what fireflies were like?"

I shook my head. I wished that I could. They sounded like something out of a fairy tale.

"The moon was out, and we could see Mars, a little red dot. We'd just started talking about moving here. It was your mother's idea, really. She didn't have to twist my arm, I'm not saying that. It's just . . . she was the one with the passion for adventure. She never felt like she fit in." His voice was getting wistful. "She always felt a little out of place, no matter where she was. I like to think she didn't feel that way with me, but you never know."

"I don't think she felt that way with either one of us, Dad."

He gave me that lonesome smile people give when they don't believe what you're saying, but are grateful to you for saying it.

I knew there was more to the story of what brought them here. I knew they were poor, that he'd had a failing restaurant and owed the bank a lot of money. Life had always been a series of beatings, it seemed, and coming to Mars was a chance to escape them. To start fresh. But it was Mother's adventurous heart that served as his lantern and his compass.

"What are you reading now?" he asked.

"Sherlock Holmes. 'The Red-Headed League.'"

"Is that about a society of evil redheads?"

"No but it would be fun if it was. It's about a bank robbery."

"You already know how it ends, though, right? How many times have you read that book?"

I shifted in my chair. He was starting to sound a little bit like Silas Mundt, and I didn't like to think that they shared a similar reasoning. "It's not about knowing what happens. I just like the stories. They make me feel, I don't know. Safe, I guess."

"Safe, huh."

My cheeks flushed. I'd said the wrong thing. "Comfortable is a better word. Those stories are like a blanket. I feel warm when I read them."

It was too late; I could see the shadow in his face again. "I'm sorry I didn't keep you safe, pea."

"That's not what I meant."

He didn't say anything. The sky to the west was darker now. Stars glittered overhead. Earth was there, the brightest of them. He was staring at it. I could feel him pulling away from me.

"I haven't read to you in a while," I said. "I could read you some of the Sherlock Holmes stories. They might make you feel good, too."

"I'd like that," he said, distantly.

"I'll go get the book," I said, though it was fast becoming too dark to read outside.

I'd taken a few steps toward the hab when he said, "Bring Watson and the cylinder out here, will you?"

My heart sank. He meant Mother's cylinder, the recordings she left. When the darkness found him, he would listen to it repeatedly. The world ceased to exist for him, outside of her voice and the memories he favored. He might as well have been back on Earth, and me stuck here, alone.

Maybe that was one of the reasons I'd never listened to it myself. It didn't make me feel like she was with me; it made me feel like no one was.

Still. Father needed it.

I headed into the warm hab and opened the drawer in the kitchen, pulling out the box of loose items where it was kept. It wasn't there. Father must have brought it with him to the diner; he did that sometimes.

I searched for it a few seconds more, trying to ignore the panic welling in my gut. I remembered Silas, collecting our spare cylinders during the robbery, slipping them like silver bars into his filthy pocket. I guessed he must have taken them for the Engine programs, thinking we might have something he needed—depending on which cylinder you slid into your Engine, it would function as a dowser, a helpmate, a postal clerk, a dishwasher in a diner. Or even as a vessel for your mother's ghost.

I let the box fall to the floor, its contents spilling everywhere. Then I made my way back outside. I had my hands crossed over my stomach; I felt like I was going to throw up. Father was still sitting in his chair, staring up at Earth, which burned like a cinder in the night sky. The moons had flared to bright life, no longer chalky images but bright, boiling eyes.

"They stole Mother," I said.

He blinked, looked at me. "What?"

"They stole Mother."

He paused, then nodded. "Oh," he said. "Well then, I guess that's that." His eyes turned back to the sky. I looked for some sign that it mattered to him. I looked for something in his face to pull me back from my own terrible precipice. But there was nothing there at all.

5

Father elected to finish cleaning the diner himself the next morning, deciding to send me back to school. I confess to being relieved. I preferred laboring under the iron hand of Miss Haddersham, who hammered information into our stubborn skulls with all the delicacy of John Henry driving steel. Miss Haddersham considered her students a kind of affliction, I believe, a malady of the soul she'd acquired for the sins of a former life. She was short, soft, and round. Her body was made for grandchildren to fold themselves into, but her heart was designed for a harder purpose: driving cattle or running a prison house. God save the child who misapplied an apostrophe in her essay book, or who failed to appreciate the sublimity of Alexander Pope. She paced before the chalkboard in long, hungry strides, and she patrolled the aisles between our desks like a Hun looking for a breach in the Great Wall.

All of this was made endurable by the presence of my friends, Brenda Lewis and Dottie Olsen. "Friends" might be a strong term; we spent time with each other more by default than by choice. Neither popular nor pariahs, we each struggled making friends for our own reasons. I had a personality some found

52

prickly or overwhelming; Brenda was a Black girl (and despite the egalitarian ambition of the colony's founders, it seemed we couldn't leave our prejudices behind); and Dottie was so intensely shy that a lot of folks thought she must be simple. Circumstances made us allies. We sat together to have our lunch at midday, and when the class broke off into group study, we naturally fell in with each other. I found them at our usual place when we were dismissed for lunch—sitting in the shadow of a storage shed a few hundred feet from the schoolhouse.

They received me with uncharacteristic silence, and I was immediately put on guard. I sat down with them and opened my bag lunch. Father, perhaps feeling sorry for me, had packed me a sticky bun as a treat. I ignored the thin sandwich and took it out first, pulling off a hunk and shoving it into my mouth.

"Where'd you get that?" Dottie said.

"From my lunch bag," I said, waving the bag and bugging my eyes at her.

Dottie lowered her eyes in embarrassment, and right away I felt bad about it.

"Don't act like that," Brenda said. And then, to Dottie: "She got it from the diner. Where else?"

"I didn't mean it," I said. I looked at Dottie. "Want a piece?"

She nodded her head, so I gave her one. Naturally I had to give Brenda one, too, and suddenly half my bounty was gone. I felt resentful about it—they weren't the ones who'd been robbed, after all. But I tried not to let it show.

"I thought you didn't have nothing left at the diner," Dottie said.

"That ain't true. We still got plenty." That was an exaggeration, of course. We didn't have plenty anymore. But we were far from cleaned out. And anyway, I didn't want to risk my sudden celebrity by admitting the truth.

"Is it true one of them was a woman?" Dottie asked.

"Yes, it is."

"I know who it is," Brenda said.

I stared at her. "No, you don't. How could you?"

"She's a carter, like my dad. Takes things from one settlement to another. Her name's Sally Milkwood. She goes to different places than he does, though."

"What, like Brawley's Crossing?"

"Other ones. Farther-out ones."

"There ain't no farther-out ones."

"That's not what my folks say. My folks say there's *Indians*."

She said that last word in a dangerous hush. I found the notion absurd, and vaguely thrilling. Aware that I was in danger of losing the stage to Brenda, I changed the subject to Silas Mundt and the cultists.

"One of them was from a desert cult," I said. "Maybe one of the cannibal cults."

It worked. They watched me hungrily. "How can you tell?" Dottie asked. "Did one of them try to eat you?"

"I think they ate before they got there. Silas had blood on his mouth, though. Probably a little snack. A baby, I suppose."

"Ugh!" They were delighted.

"He had a moth symbol burned onto his jacket." I leaned in a little bit. "One of the ones that live in dead people."

Dottie recoiled. "That's gross."

Brenda seemed unimpressed. "It's not gross. It's a grave moth. They cultivate flora in the bodies. They turn people into little gardens."

I frowned. I hadn't heard that. It sounded morbidly beautiful. "How do you know?"

Brenda shrugged. "I listen to my parents talk when they think I'm asleep. Dad knows a lot about bugs. I think those cultists worship them or something."

"Why would people worship moths?"

"Because the Moth cultists grow ghosts, and moths are attracted to ghosts."

More nonsense. I felt like she was trying to upstage me. "You made that up."

"I did not! I told you, my parents talk about this stuff. I pay attention."

Although it hadn't been an attack, it felt like one. My face felt hot. I wanted to tell her that I would listen if I had parents who talked, but I didn't. My mother was gone and my father only talked to her ghost.

Before I could open my mouth, Dottie fired her biggest gun. "Well, my parents don't believe you were really robbed anyway. They said you're making it up."

". . . what?"

"My mama said you made it all up so you can hide more food."

I was so stunned I couldn't even feel angry. I just looked at her, and then at Brenda, who wouldn't meet my eyes. If this was what my friends thought, how many others thought the same? How many thought we were hoarding food for ourselves? How many thought *we* were the liars and the thieves? Was this what the sheriff meant when he was talking about troubling notions?

I stood up suddenly, ready to fight, alarming them both. Ashamed—by their fear, by their suspicions—I turned and fled.

I left my books and my bag in the classroom, left my lunch and my half-eaten sticky bun. Something was on fire in my head, something I could not recognize and that drove me into the street, away from the school and from the town square, away from the diner and even my own hab, away from Father. Away from all of it.

THERE WAS ONLY one place to go in New Galveston when you wanted to get away from everything. When even the deep desert didn't seem far enough, and nothing would do but another world.

Joe Reilly's saucer, the *Eurydice*, rested on the launchpad half a mile outside the town limit. On windless days the pink sand and dust covered it like a caul, giving it the appearance of a relic from an older age: something cobwebbed and forgotten. A haunted house full of the ghosts of an entire world.

But windless days were rare here, and normally it was scoured clean. The circumference of the saucer was marred by scorch marks from repeated reentries into the atmosphere, and by the tiny dents and pockmarks left by random small meteors found in the dark hollows of space. Despite these scars, the ship looked fit and capable. Ready to vault back into the sky, which was its natural habitat, and take us all home.

In a small wooden shack erected a hundred yards or so from the launch pad lived Joe Reilly. I wondered sometimes what it must be like to be him. Unlike most of us, he hadn't come here as a settler. He'd never had any wish to remain on Mars at all. He was just a pilot running a route. He'd arrived here a little over a year ago as part of his regular rotation, expecting to remain for his typical four-month layover. Then the next saucer from Earth would arrive and he would fly home, his own ship laden with passengers, letters, Martian-grown produce, and unrefined tonnage of the Strange, the cultural offerings of Earthers acclimating to a new world.

Then the Silence happened.

Joe Reilly wasn't the only forced resident. There were the governor and his family, only meant to stay here for a six-year term, half of which had already elapsed; the visitors and tourists from home, including a Hollywood starlet said to be recovering from overwork; a barnstorming baseball team called the Havana Vaqueros, comprised of Cuban and Negro League players; not to mention dozens of visiting family members, prospectors, geologists, and botanists.

All of them, now, permanent Martians.

I stopped at the edge of the launchpad, the tips of my dusty shoes just an inch or two shy of trespassing, and stared up at the underside of the saucer.

From beneath, it reminded me of one of the strange fungus farms Widow Kessler was rumored to cultivate in her basement. While flat and round on top, the underside was a bewilderment of fuselage and piping, great black cones that belched fire and smoke, lights and hatchways and steel plates. It looked like a beautiful puzzle, and it amazed and infuriated me that the minds that had assembled and guided such a magnificent machine could not solve the simple riddle of the Silence.

What happened to Earth? Where did everybody go?

"What are you doing here, kid?"

His voice startled me and I jumped back a step, as though I'd been caught in a crime.

Joe Reilly stood in the doorway to his shack. He was dirty and unshaven, dressed in filthy trousers and an undershirt, his suspenders hanging unused at his sides like yanked circuitry. The room behind him was in shadow; I had the impression that he'd spent his morning in bed, hiding from the world while the rest of us went about the hard work of living in it. It was altogether an appalling image and it bolstered my low opinion of him.

Still, he was a figure of such importance and controversy that he had an aura of mythology about him, and I felt my courage falter.

"Looking at the *Eurydice*," I said.

"What for? Nothing's changed about it."

"I guess I just wanted to get a close-up view of what a wasted life looks like."

Something in his face changed. He seemed always surprised by the hatred arrayed against him, and I felt a small, brief sympathy. He put his elbow up against the doorjamb and leaned into it, staring at the ground between his boots. Then he looked back at me and said, "You know, you really are a hateful girl. Do you have any friends at all?"

That stung. In fact, it was true: I didn't have any real friends. Brenda and Dottie had made that clear. I didn't have the kind of friends you could go to in times like this, when everyone around you seemed to be malfunctioning in some indefinable way. When all you wanted to do was light the world on fire.

"Watson is my friend," I said, regretting it immediately.

He gave me a mean little smile. "Your only friend is an Engine," he said.

"That still leaves me with one more than you got."

He broke eye contact. I knew I'd beaten him, but it didn't make me feel good. He said, "You should try being nice to people, you know? It might change your whole life." He turned around and was about to go back inside when I said, "I want to see inside the saucer."

I couldn't believe I'd managed to say it. I didn't even know I wanted to go in until that moment. He turned back to me. It was clear from his face that he couldn't believe it either. After a moment, he said, "Why?"

"I don't know. I just do."

He stepped into the sunlight, the wind catching his sleep-crushed hair and rippling over his clothes. He looked around, as though I might be the advance force of a secret assault team. But we were alone out there, the town low and wind-scuffed behind me, the desert long and barren behind him.

"Aren't you supposed to be in school?"

I shrugged.

He approached me slowly, stopping a few feet away. He put his hands in his pockets, took them out again. I could tell he was nervous. At this distance, I could also tell that he'd been drinking. Prohibition was still in effect back then, and the sight of someone so brazenly in the grip of alcohol unnerved me. It made me wonder if I'd stumbled into a dark situation. His eyes were bloodshot and his face looked old and worn-out, though I knew he had not yet passed his thirties.

"What do you want to go in there for, Anabelle?"

I'd been braced for hostility or contempt, or at the very least a curt dismissal, but his voice was soft. Almost wistful. He was genuinely curious, and—although I could not be sure of it at the time—he asked with kindness.

"I just want to see." I was quiet, too. The fight had gone out of us both, it seemed.

"It's not a good idea."

And just like that I felt the anger move inside me again, like an old snake shifting beneath a rock. But I kept my reason. I didn't want to be the girl who was too mean to have any friends. "I'm tired of everybody telling me my ideas are no good."

He actually smiled at that one. "Yeah, well. I guess I know how that feels." He looked up at the underside of his ship. I tried to read something from his expression, some indication of his real thoughts. But there was no secret message for me there. His face was just a face, and whatever he thought was locked behind it.

"I don't think it's a good idea because I don't think any good can come out of it. I think you're here to hurt yourself, Anabelle, the way people sometimes do when they're sad. If you go in there, you're going to start thinking about what it'll feel like when the engines are lit, how the walls and the floor will vibrate and how you'll feel it tremble in your gut. And since that won't happen, you're going to come out angrier and sadder than you were when you started."

"You don't know how I'd feel about it," I said, sensing those phantom tremors already. "You don't know anything about me."

"Yes, I do. Yes, I surely do. There's not a person here who doesn't wish for that very same thing."

"Except you."

He turned away from me and headed back to his beaten little shack. "Go to school," he said. "Or I'll report you for truancy."

"And I'll report you for being drunk!"

He waved a hand dismissively and went inside, shutting the door quietly behind himself.

I stood abandoned for a few moments, unaccountably stung by his dismissal of me, and even more by the things he had said. There was no reason to care what this man thought, but he had spoken my secret fear aloud, and it rattled me to hear it.

I sat on the sand, leaning against one of the *Eurydice's* struts. The sun perched at its apex, and Mars was nearly as warm as it ever got. I stayed under the shadow of the saucer, trying to decide where to go. The thought of crawling back under the malignant glare of Miss Haddersham—not to mention into the orbit of my traitorous friends—was too ridiculous to contemplate. Home was no good; Father was in his dark place, and there was no room for me there. And because I was skipping school, I would have to stay away from town. Adults were meddlesome people, and I wouldn't be able to walk ten yards before somebody would want to know my business. So I kept my back to New Galveston and I looked out toward the desert, where our doom seemed to gather in vast, invisible forces. Hunger. Drought. The cultists with their sinister designs. The Strange, a manifest derangement growing through the very rock of the world.

The wind nipped at my clothes and my hair, and the sand blew in great, soft curls out in the distance. I found myself wishing for one of those sandstorms of apocalyptic beauty, like I'd seen in the paintings of the early settlers. Something to carve us back down to our essentials.

I don't know how long I sat there, mesmerized by the zephyrs skimming across the sands. At some point I stopped thinking in concrete terms or with any identifiable intent; instead I fell into a kind of waking trance, my mind dispensing with thought in favor of drifting clouds of mood and perception, so that I became for a while a vessel for longing, for sadness, for resolve, and even for a peaceful resignation. It was a rare thing to be able to indulge in this kind of separation from the moment, and later I wondered if that was what it was like to be a child on Earth, sitting beneath a summer sun while the wind rippled grass instead of sand, having no more immediate concern than what was playing on the radio later that evening, or what your mother might make you for dinner.

"Well, get up, then."

Joe Reilly was standing over me, still in a state of moral disrepair, but with his hair slicked back and his suspenders up over his shoulders where they belonged. I noticed that the sun had shifted its position in the sky, and the day had progressed well beyond noon.

"I wasn't hurting nothing," I said, climbing sullenly to my feet. My leg muscles had seized up and I took a moment to rub some life back into them.

"You really want to see inside the ship?"

I wasn't sure if he was playing some kind of trick on me. I wanted to say something clever, to let him know that I was too sophisticated to be fooled by him, but my mind was empty and my want was great. "Yes," is what I said, and there wasn't even a hint of sophistication in it. Just wide-open hope.

"All right then," he said. "Let's make it quick."

A HATCH OPENED in the smooth plain of metal above me, descending jerkily to the ground with a sound of shearing metal.

"Is it supposed to sound like that?"

He regarded it unhappily as it completed its slide, speaking only when it had finished. "No. It needs to be serviced. It was due for maintenance when it got back to Earth."

"Can you fix it here?"

"I can do some. But I'm just a pilot. This thing needs experts."

"What about Mr. Wickham? He fixes Engines. I bet he'd help."

Mr. Wickham lived in Dig Town, but he was one of the few who made regular trips to New Galveston.

"I said experts. Harry doesn't know his ass from a hole in the ground. Now come on, climb up."

The on-ramp was wide and smooth, allowing for handcarts to pass to and fro. A handrail stretched along one side for the passengers. The interior was lit; since it would be foolish to keep running the lights while not in use, I presumed they were activated by the on-ramp. I could see the ceiling from my vantage point: the joint of two metal plates, with naked rivets running along a welded seam.

I was five years old when my parents brought me here, so of course I'd been in a saucer before—this one, or one just like it. We'd spent endless weeks crossing the distance between planets, but my memory of the interior was impressionistic. I remembered it being very comfortable, the way I imagined the inside of a rich person's house. I remembered a big room with toys and games, where I spent time with other kids. We were all too young to be anything but bored.

Joe walked up the ramp, and I followed him. We made our way down a short, unadorned passageway of metal plate. He passed by an open door on his left, and I stopped to look. Like the hall we were in, the one the door opened onto was naked steel.

It ascended steeply to another door, standing open at its far end. I saw a glittering bank of lights within, and a wall with receptacles for cylinders just like the ones we used to power our Engines. The corner of a scuffed window showed the Martian sky.

"Come along, Anabelle."

"Is that where you fly the ship?"

"Come along."

The hallway curved to the right and we entered the passenger side of the vessel. Here the walls were paneled with wood, the floors were carpeted, and the rooms, when in flight, were illuminated by electric lamps. We passed through a series of them, arranged like a small labyrinth, though I found that I knew instinctively which room would adjoin with another, more often than not. There was a small theater, with tables and chairs arranged around a narrow stage; a library, which Mother had frequently haunted; and a playroom, which seemed so much smaller to me now. The floor was clean and orderly, the toys and the board games and the art supplies all secured in their places. It had never been this clean during flight. I walked into the corner and experienced a thrill of delight when I found my initials scraped into the molding along the floor, along with those of every other child who burned frustrated hours in this room. So this was the ship I'd traveled on after all. I relished the symmetry of it.

Another long hallway curved along the circumference of the ship and led me to the observation deck, a wide room with comfortable chairs and tables and a service counter that adjoined a small kitchen, where my parents had occasionally donated their time. A huge window dominated the room. We'd watched Earth recede behind us as we left—something I recall vividly, as Mother had made such an issue of it, demanding I sit with her on her lap—and later we watched the astonishing gulf of deep space, as still as a painting, during the long months of travel. Finally, we witnessed Mars appear there, too, the glaring red eye that would be our home. We watched it come with hope and fear, but mostly with exhausted relief.

Now, of course, all it showed me was sand and rock. Miles upon miles of sand and rock. A dark serration ridged the horizon, marking the boundary of the vast Peabody Crater. This was where huge deposits of the Strange breached the surface, eroded by the wind and blowing freely over the sand. Where ghosts were rumored to wander. I wondered if you could see them from here.

Caves were said to wend through the boulders littering the middle of the crater, remnants of an ancient meteorite, and it was widely believed that the cultists made their homes there. I imagined them burrowing into the ground, into their dark holes, bearing my mother with them like Persephone into hell.

Persephone, though, had a savior.

"I told you," he said.

"Why won't you take us home?"

"You know the reasons. Let's not go through it all again. Christ, I have to say this every month at town hall. I'm tired of it."

He was right. I did know them. Everyone did. The ship could not take everyone. No one knew what we would be going back to. There was only enough fuel for a one-way flight; if the Earth was ruined, then it was a death sentence for everyone on board. The ship might be useful in other ways: it could be scrapped for parts and used to keep the failing Engines running; the fuel and the oil could be repurposed for the Engines, too, and it was beyond debate that the Engines were vital to our survival.

It was the fear of firing the only bullet in your gun, and missing.

But this was a minority opinion. It was nothing in the face of the bereavement we all felt for our home, and for the people still there—even for those of us who never planned on returning. It was a wonder to me that Joe Reilly had been able to keep his life during that first year after the Silence started. I am convinced that if anyone else had the faintest notion of how to fly the saucer, or even if they believed that they might learn how to do it, then Reilly would have found himself the recipient of a misdirected bullet, or the victim of a freak house fire. At the very least he would have spent his days wasting away in one of the sheriff's jail cells, a traitor to his own people.

But no one else knew how to fly it. It was absurd. Even as a child I was astounded that there were not fail-safes in place. What if the pilot had taken ill, or what if he'd suffered an accident? Who would have flown the ship then? I suppose the thinking at the time was that the next ship would always be along shortly, stocked with an extra pilot once we'd radioed the situation.

That was my first lesson in how tenuous our grasp on civilization really was. It made me wonder if the Silence, too, was all down to some catastrophic bungling, some calamity born of simple, garden-variety incompetence.

We'd been blinded by optimism. We represented the first flush of our expansion into the stars. After Mars, what would come next? The moons of Jupiter? Saturn? Would we follow the Germans' example and launch a generation ship to fly past it all, out into the bright stellar fields? All of this seemed not only possible, but inevitable. No one thought it would end the way it did. No one counted on God's indifference.

THE STRANGE

I knew all the reasons Joe Reilly gave for not going home.
I knew the reasons the governor gave.
But I also knew the real reason.
Fear.

6

The Mother Earth Diner opened again that night. Hardly anyone showed up. On the one hand, that was a relief; I didn't want to face all the questions, and Dottie's accusation caused me to wonder how many others in New Galveston harbored the same suspicion. On the other hand, though, it hurt me to see so few turn out to support us. I'd always held the basic assumption that a strong sense of community formed the bedrock of our life on Mars. Especially after the Silence. For all we knew, we were the last human beings alive. Though I could not have expressed it this way at the time, I had the sense that people were retreating from the idea of a shared identity, into their own private redoubts.

Mr. Shank's words haunted my thoughts.

You're going to have to accustom yourself to disappointment, young Miss Crisp.

I interpreted the emptiness of the Mother Earth as a moral victory for Mr. Shank. It was as though the whole town were siding with him over me.

We did get some regulars, though, along with a few others. Widow Kessler was there, seated in a corner booth. She lived in Dig Town, a fair hike for an older woman, especially after dark; but she travelled back and forth by horse and she had a heating jacket, so the trip was manageable. Agatha Kessler had been wife to Zachary Kessler, a partner in the Teller Mining Company. Together they'd been among the first official citizens of New Galveston, though they lived in Dig Town, overseeing its operation and development. Zachary had died in a collapsed mining shaft a few years ago, and Agatha stayed on as manager of the mine, though her position was largely ceremonial. She was called Widow now, apparently by her own wish. Zachary's body had never been recovered, and some folks whispered that she kept it in her cellar with her fungus farms, and crept below ground to talk to it every night. She shared the reflective green tint in the eyes common to everyone from Dig Town, but despite the unkind rumors, we saw her often enough that they didn't seem sinister at all, merely an interesting quirk.

She liked to abide in that booth with her hot tea and her lemon wedges and watch the high pink sky deepen to a bloody bruise as the Martian evening settled in. She watched the lights wink on in the habs around us, and she remarked to me once that she enjoyed the flickering neon of our own business sign, stuttering pink and blue in the failing light. New Galveston shed a very small glow in the huge countryside, and the night that unfurled over our heads was deeper than anything anyone experienced on Earth. If anything would keep our diner running, I thought, it was the sense of common human warmth we fostered. No one represented the poignancy of this better than Widow Kessler, who rarely spoke, but seemed to need us nonetheless.

Another staple was Arthur Lewis, Brenda's father. He was a tall, angular Black man, popular because of his easy way with people and because he worked as a carter, running goods between New Galveston, Dig Town, and Brawley's Crossing. I guess that exposed him to all kinds of information and gossip, some of which he shared around town, and some of which he kept only for his wife when he thought Brenda was safely asleep.

Mr. Lewis, like many of the less affluent who'd made the trip to Mars, hadn't been assigned a hab of his own, so he'd moved his family into the burgeoning community of small, hand-built homes expanding from the southern side of town, where the ground was unsuitable for farming or grazing. The neighborhood was called the Taproots by those of us who continued to live in the silver habs, and the name had been sanctioned by the governor as a sign of New Galveston's strengthening grip on the planet. It was like our own miniature Dig Town.

That night, Mr. Lewis spoke to me when I slid his plate in front of him.

"How are you holding up, Anabelle?"

"I'm fine," I said. I wondered if Brenda had told him about my fleeing school, and if he was going to tell my father.

"It can be a scary thing to have a gun pointed at you."

"I wasn't scared," I said.

"No?"

"It's everyone else in this town that's scared." I was thinking about how Brenda had told me the name of the woman who'd accompanied Silas. Sally Milkwood. I wanted to drop that name on the table in front of him and see how he reacted. But I held my tongue.

He pushed the collards around with a fork and said, "Well, you might be right about that. But it could be that they're not scared of what you think."

"Whatever you say, Mr. Lewis," I said, and left him to it. I was in no mood for the prevarications of the adult world. No one could think up an excuse for their own failure faster than an adult. I resolved never to fall into that trap.

And then there were the Dig Town miners. There were three of them that night. They occupied a table by one of the windows, their conversation coarse and loud. The miners had become a rare sight at the diner since the rotations home had stopped. Coming so soon on the heels of the robbery, with its rumored connections to Dig Town, their presence felt ominous.

There were maybe half a dozen more. Business was sluggish. Father toiled quietly behind the line with Watson at his side, offering stilted conversation if prompted by a customer, but mainly keeping to himself. He seemed to have the smell of doom upon him, and maybe that's what had kept people away that night. They were avoiding the Mother Earth the way people avoided the terminally ill.

I told him about skipping half the school day as he pushed some onions around on the griddle, intending to beat Mr. Lewis, or any other busybody, to the punch. "Brenda and Dottie were saying things I didn't like. Brenda said the woman who came in is called Sally Milkwood. She said she's a carter like her father but that she goes farther out. I didn't think there *was* anything farther out. Is there?"

He didn't say anything.

"If we know her name, how come the sheriff doesn't just go get her?"

"It's complicated, pea."

"No, it ain't. He's the sheriff, she committed a crime. It couldn't be more simple!"

He just kept pushing those onions around on the griddle.

"There was something else. Dottie said her folks called us liars. That we weren't even robbed, we just said it to hide food. Why would they say that?"

He still didn't say anything.

"Anyway, that's why I left."

"Left where?"

"School. That's when I left school."

"You what?" He looked at me, plainly confused.

"Aren't you listening to me?"

He put the spatula down. The smoke from the cooking onions billowed over him. "Tell me again."

"Never mind." I walked back out into the dining area. I was waiting for him to call me back, but he didn't. Instead I heard the scrape of the spatula on the range again, and then a loud, crackling boil as he dropped something into the fryer.

I'd been debating whether or not to tell him about my real transgression. If he asked me where I'd gone, I think I would have told him. I couldn't explain why I'd wanted to go into Joe Reilly's ship, or what I'd taken from the experience. I'd spent the remainder of the school hours in the observation deck, just watching the sand blowing across the desert. It was the same dull stretch of land I'd been staring across since I was five years old, the same massive crater, but it looked different when seen through that window. I was able to see it the way my parents must have seen it, the way I had been too young to see it when we landed: as a place of grandeur, as a place of mystery. My mother told me that Mars used to be the subject of extravagant literary fantasies, that people with overheated imaginations would speculate on alien cultures and lost civilizations. I knew

I wanted to read those books, and maybe that's when I first entertained the notion of writing one myself. Looking through that window, I could almost see that Mars. I still wanted to see that Mars; not the ugly, mean-spirited one I had to live in.

"Girl!"

One of the miners at the booth was holding up his mug. He was sitting with two of his colleagues, their eyes flashing that unsettling green that came from being steeped in the Strange. Red dust was permanently ground into the creases of their faces and in the wrinkles of their clothing. No matter how much they brushed themselves off before coming in, they always left a mess. The seats of some of the booths were permanently discolored by their presence.

I went to him with the coffeepot and refilled his mug.

"How long before this runs out?"

I looked at the pot, which was three-quarters full. "There's plenty," I said.

"No, girl. I mean all of it. How much longer till we can't drink coffee no more?"

It seemed a ridiculous question. "We grow coffee beans in the greenhouse. We ain't gonna run out."

He slugged back half the cup right there and put it down with a gesture to refill it. "It's not like Earth coffee, though. Not grown from Earth soil by little brown people under a hot sun. I reckon that stuff is gonna be pretty valuable. I'm sure you and your dad won't run out, though. I'll bet those 'thieves' took them a nice supply, right? Might be they were smart." His eyes flicked from me to the door of our storeroom, just for a second. Then they settled back on me again. "Go on, fill it up, girl."

I did, feeling suddenly scared.

He's with them, I thought. *They've come back for more, and they're rubbing our faces in it.*

I wanted to splash the pot into his face, break the glass over his head. My hands trembled as I poured, and I spilled some onto the table.

He slid his finger through it, then slipped it into his mouth. He watched me and smiled. "Careful, girl. Don't waste it."

"Is there anything else?" I hated myself for saying it. I felt like just by asking that question I was offering him the diner, my father, myself. It was as though he had come into our place and spat on the floor, and I was offering him the countertop as well.

He was done with me, though. He turned back to his friends. "No. Go on."

"We have a rifle," I said. My adrenaline was cresting and my whole body trembled. Heat gathered in my cheeks and behind my eyes.

That got his attention. He looked at me again and said, "Now why would you want to tell me something like that?"

"Just so you know," I said. I heard the tremor in my voice and bit it down.

"Okay," he said. "So now I know. Now go on and leave me in peace before I tell your daddy to whip your little behind."

One of his friends finally spoke up. "Come on now, Charlie. Ease up."

"Don't tell me to ease up."

"I hope you come back," I said. It was like hearing someone else speak with my own voice. I couldn't control it. "You filth. I hope you come back so I can shoot a bullet right through those ugly teeth."

He made a wild grab for me, his teeth bared and his face

crumpled in rage. I turned and ran. I don't remember if I made any noise. I suppose I must have. I do remember that the place erupted in shouts, that there was a flurry of wrestling bodies. I turned around at the counter, where my father stood agape in his dirty apron, his spatula held in one hand like a weird offering, and saw three men wrestling Charlie to the ground. Two of them were the men he'd been sitting with; the other was Arthur Lewis.

The remaining few people in the Mother Earth sat where they were, stunned into silence. Only Widow Kessler continued to eat as if nothing was going on, the chime of her silverware a deranged counterpoint of normalcy to the sound of the scuffle.

Finally the miner was allowed to his feet, his colleagues holding his arms and steering him to the door. Arthur stood aside, his chest heaving from the exertion.

"You need to tan that girl's hide!" the miner called.

"You shut your damn mouth," Arthur said.

One of the other miners spoke up. "Now hold on there, chief. That girl gave Charlie lip."

"She did! She insulted me to my face. She threatened to shoot me, goddamn it! That girl is crazy."

Arthur said, "Boys, you take him out of here."

That's when I said it. They might have just walked on out of there, and none of the rest of it would have happened. The whole story would have ended with this dismal coda. But Silas hadn't paid. He'd taken. And now these men wanted to take, too. I couldn't allow it. Not again. "He still owes for his dinner! You all do!"

I felt my father's hand on my shoulder. "Anabelle," he said. There was anger in his voice.

I turned to him in dismay. "But—"

"Be quiet."

He walked around me and approached the miners, putting himself between us.

Charlie's friends released him, and he made a show of adjusting his jacket, straightening his affronted dignity. Dust bloomed from him like a cloud of noxious gas. "You come to Dig Town if you want to collect," he said, staring at my father. "I'll show you what a tanning is like. Maybe you can bring the lesson home."

"You want to talk about a lesson?" my father said. I only now noticed the iron skillet hanging from his right hand, low to his side, like something he was ashamed to be carrying and was only now ready to admit to. "Here's a lesson."

He swung the skillet in a graceless arc and Charlie lifted his arm to deflect the blow. The skillet snapped the bone in his forearm like a great stick. This altered the course of the swing and Father was pulled off-balance; the skillet slipped from his fingers and flew across the floor. It landed with a mighty clamor at the feet of one of our customers, who lifted her shoes out of its path at the last minute with a startled shriek.

There was a moment when the whole of creation seemed to hang quiet: Charlie staring open-mouthed at his forearm, which now bore a slight but ghastly new angle; Father off-kilter, one leg jutting out behind him and his arms splayed for balance, the muscles in his face shaping it into an expression of anger or fear; the others arrayed around us all, in attitudes of comical disinterest or exaggerated dismay, like a rendering of a crowd at a boxing match.

And then the moment tipped into chaos.

Charlie screamed. It was a long, wild sound: pure, unselfconscious pain. He fell back a step and one of his friends grabbed his shoulders. The other went after Father, whose fingertips were now pressed against the floor as he tried to stay upright. Father's lips were pulled back from his teeth and I could not recognize the person he was in that moment. He completed his stumble by landing on his face.

I didn't think. I swung the pot of coffee full into the face of the man going after Father, breaking the glass against his nose and unleashing the steaming contents over him in a hot flood. He did not make a sound. He just dropped to his knees, one hand held in a shuddering claw in front of his smoking face. He made a grab for me with the other, snaring my skirt with his fingers.

By this time Father had retrieved the skillet and he swung it onto the man's head, as strong and sure as any ballplayer, and the man fall hard to the floor, releasing his hold on me. I watched him, waiting for him to move again. He did not.

I became conscious of voices around me, like intrusions into a dream. What few customers we had remained in their seats, too resilient or too terrified to move. Arthur made an effort to restrain the third miner but was shoved roughly to the ground; that one grabbed Charlie, still cradling his broken arm, and hauled him out the front door into the night. Somebody let out a sob. I don't know who.

Father stayed where he was, standing over the prone miner. He stared down at him with the skillet still in his hand, ready to resume its dreadful function.

"Dad?" I said.

He did not look at me. When he spoke, it was to Watson, still parked by the griddle, where burning onions and peppers stank up the air.

"Get her out of here," he said.

7

Watson ushered me out. I was too stunned to protest: as I stepped over the miner, I nearly slipped in the blood that had begun to collect underneath him. As we departed, I left a trail of it on the linoleum from one shoe.

I followed Watson down the center of the road, the wind whipping through my hair, the night gathered in high, starry drifts above us. Phobos boiled with light. A lamp burned in the window of Jeremiah Shank's shop. I wondered if he would be glad to hear the news of a second disaster.

We walked past and headed down the narrow alley to our hab. I stopped when we got to the door.

"We have to go back."

"Miss Crisp, your father was quite explicit in his instructions."

"What if he's in trouble?"

"I think not. Mr. Lewis is with him. The young men have fled, and the sheriff will have been summoned. The danger is past."

I stood at the door to our hab, uncertain. Watson extended an arm and pressed the panel at its side. The heavy door swung open, and the automatic overhead light spilled its white glow onto the rust-colored ground. Mother always hated the harshness of it; she would immediately turn it off in favor of the softer light from the lamps inside. But since she'd been gone, we'd grown used to it. Now it seemed as warm as any lantern. The world inside was small and confined, and exactly as we had ordered it. My bed was in there, my shelf of books. I suddenly felt so tired that the thought of going back to the diner made me want to cry.

"Let's go inside, Miss Crisp. You must be cold."

But something within me rebelled at the thought of going in there without my father. It had been hard enough without Mother. The possibility that this time I might be sleeping by myself was appalling to me. I felt as though stepping inside now would be an acknowledgment of the corrosion that was consuming my life.

"No," I said. "I'm not going in there."

Watson, the noble creature, did not protest, though I'm sure it confounded his every crackling fuse. He only said, "Where shall we go then, Miss Crisp?"

"I don't know." I shut the door and turned away from it. We made our way back down the alley and turned left at its mouth, away from both the diner and the town itself.

I found myself heading back toward the launchpad. Leaving New Galveston behind me was like shedding a heavy coat. The unlighted dome of the *Eurydice* hulked against the night sky, a darkness upon the deep. Mr. Reilly's little shack shed a warm light nearby; together they were the last way station before the desert, which curled and whispered in great, silent plains.

Watson kept pace behind me. He had never been to the launchpad before, and I wondered why he didn't question me about it now. Instead he simply ambled along, his head tilted back, his lamplit eyes staring up at the ship.

I knocked on the shack's door, and after a moment Mr. Reilly opened it up. I was pleased to note that he'd composed himself since that morning: his shirt was clean and tucked in, he'd passed a comb through his hair, and his face looked freshly washed. He shook his head, but he did not look surprised to see me.

"I knew it was a mistake," he said.

"Can I sleep in the saucer tonight?"

He stared at me with an expression I couldn't read. It wasn't the sort I was used to seeing on an adult's face: not pitying, condescending, or impatient. He looked like he was weighing a sad and difficult problem. Instead of answering me, he said, "I was just about to head over for some grub."

"You can't go. The diner's closed."

"Still?"

"It's for a different reason. There was a fight. My dad got in a fight."

"What?" He looked past me at Watson, perhaps just then wondering why the Kitchen Engine had accompanied me. "What happened? Are you all right?"

I felt the tears pushing against my eyes. I beat them back furiously, my teeth clenched in a sudden terrible anger. I tried to answer him, but I could only stand there mute, my hands in fists, breathing hard. He put a hand out toward my shoulder, but I pulled myself clear of him.

After a moment's consideration, he accessed some device inside the door and triggered the ship's loading ramp. The light inside flickered on and cast a bright beam through the blue night. "Go inside," he said. "Don't touch anything."

Watson and I ascended the ramp. When we were halfway up, Mr. Reilly said, "Sleep in one of the berths. Don't go anywhere else. You hear me?"

I nodded.

"I'm closing it after you. If you need to get out, just hit the big orange button at the top. You can't miss it."

"Okay."

"Does your dad know you're here, Anabelle?"

I shook my head.

"I'm going to go down there, okay? I have to tell him. I'm in enough hot water in this town as it is. The last thing I need is anybody thinking I kidnapped you."

I just nodded. I didn't know what to say to that. It was hard to think about anybody else's problems at the moment.

"That button, if you need it, is behind a little cage. You just have to lift it."

"I'm not stupid."

He half smiled at me. "Yeah. I know."

When we were up, the ramp rattled and banged, and rose. Within moments, we were sealed inside the spaceship. It felt good: safe, locked in, unassailable. The whole of Mars could bend its will against me, and I would be protected in the *Eurydice*, immune from harm, the tools of my triumphant return home at hand.

"Do you remember being in one of these, Watson?"

"My core cylinder was transported in a box. I wasn't activated until I was assembled in New Galveston. I've never been in a saucer before."

"What do you think?"

He moved slowly down the corridor ahead of me, and I followed him into the wood-paneled passenger section. "It seems clean and functional," he said. I understood this to be high praise—one machine complimenting another. I wondered if he could feel jealousy.

We passed an open door—one that had been closed earlier that day—which led into what looked like an engine room. It was vast and grimy, the air smelling of oil and chemical fuel. Much of it was dismantled: parts I didn't recognize were spread all over the floor, wires hung loose from their moorings, tools sat in puddles of oil and grease as though they'd been left there in the middle of a job instead of cleaned and put away properly. I didn't know anything about the engine room of a saucer, but we cleaned our appliances and our work area in the kitchen when we were finished, and I couldn't believe a properly run engine room was any different. This was yet another sign, I thought, of Joe's slovenliness.

He's just like Father, I thought. *He's given up.*

We stopped in the theater, with its tables arrayed in a fan around the small central stage. I imagined a woman singing there, her voice drifting through the room like smoke, and I imagined the faces of the people watching her. I wondered if Mother had sat in a room like this on her way home, if she'd listened to Earth songs and thought about the places she would visit when she got there, the things she would see that she had missed.

"Do you like it, Watson? Does it make you want to go to other places? Like maybe Earth?"

"I would be interested to see Earth," Watson said, and that was enough to justify the floating hurt inside me, the one distinct from Father and the miners.

"Follow me," I said. I led him back the way we had come, until we arrived at the ascending tributary corridor, at the end of which I had glimpsed the cockpit. The door at its far end was shut now. We stood at the corridor's entrance, staring at the closed door as though it were a portal to another, more dangerous world. "That's where you go to fly the ship," I said.

"We should stay out of there."

"I want to see inside."

"Mr. Reilly said not to touch anything. And he said not to go anywhere but the berth."

"Oh, don't start talking like them, Watson. I'm not going to try to fly it or anything."

"Well, I can't go with you. I won't fit." I could swear that I heard a note of pique in his voice. The corridor was indeed too narrow for him; he was designed for industrial work. This part of the ship was designed for human beings, or for the lithe deep-space Engines, which were as slender and fragile-looking as tinfoil flowers.

I gave him a smug little smile and waggled my fingers at him. "I guess you're going to have to stay behind then," I said, and proceeded toward the door. I walked quickly, as much to outpace my own misgivings as to prove to Watson that I could not be dissuaded. The comforting hum of his presence receded, until I faced the door in silence. I liked being trusted to be in the ship, and I didn't want to provoke Mr. Reilly's anger. But I had to see the cockpit. I had to see the one place on all of Mars where the means to go home resided; where, with a specific series of buttons pressed and dials turned, I could be on my way to Mother.

I pushed against the door, expecting it to be locked. It swung open easily.

The cockpit was small. There were two chairs, padded for comfort. One faced the pocked and scored observation window; through it I saw the outer edge of New Galveston, softly lit in the night. The other was turned to the right, facing a bewildering bank of controls, like some glittering crust gathered along a cave wall over the ages. It seemed impossible to me that one person could contain all the knowledge required to operate such an intimidating array. Looking at it, I felt a sharp twinge of despair. Maybe Mr. Reilly wouldn't fly the ship home because he didn't know how to. Or maybe he couldn't do it by himself. It was a silly thought, since he'd already flown it to get here, but at the time it seemed credible enough.

I sat in the pilot's chair, reclining into its surprising softness, leaning my head back so I could see the night sky and watch the moons make their circuit. Phobos still glared overhead, while Deimos hovered palely to one side. But for the ambient glow of the city, I might be in space at that moment, sliding quietly through the clean emptiness.

I dozed for a while.

Then something at the periphery of my eye roused me to attention. I sat forward. A single light flared somewhere out in the desert, not too far away. From the direction of the crater. Immediately it went out again. I put my face as close to the window as I could manage, straining to pick out a shape or a movement there.

I must have made some small sound, because Watson called out down the corridor. "Are you all right, Miss Crisp? I thought you had fallen asleep."

"I did," I said. I kept staring. Something inside me fluttered and jumped. I could hear my own blood pulsing in my head.

The light came again, and now that I was looking for it, I could see that it came from a lantern, though it was hard to judge its distance. Not far. It held steady for two or three seconds, and winked out again.

"Someone's out there, Watson."

"Surely it's Mr. Reilly."

"No. They're signaling from the desert."

I was about to say something else—but what? That the cultists were invading? That we should leave the ship? That we should fetch the sheriff, who at that very moment might be standing in the Mother Earth Diner, determining my father's fate? But before I could manage anything, I saw Joe Reilly emerge from beneath the saucer, almost directly underneath me, startling me so badly that I shouted and jumped back. He didn't hear me. He walked a few feet beyond the perimeter of the saucer and came to a halt, a lantern suspended from his own left hand, shuttered and dark. He raised it and opened a directional slat, casting its beam away from town, toward the crater. After a few seconds he closed it again and set it at his feet.

"Miss Crisp?"

"Shut up, Watson."

Finally, movement from the desert. Two people approached. They pulled the heated coverings from their faces and I saw them. I put a hand over my mouth. My skin rippled with fear.

It was Silas and the woman—the one Brenda said was Sally Milkwood. He sauntered into view with an easy arrogance and clasped hands with Joe Reilly. Sally stood a few paces back, her arms crossed over her chest, her gaze crawling over the saucer above them, and—I could almost swear it—over my own face, pale and cold as a gravestone.

Too frightened to leave, I retreated farther into the ship's interior. I lay down on one of the children's bunks, in a room painted with cool pastel colors, one wall decorated in a bright mural picturing an idealized Martian farmstead, with New Galveston rising in grand spires behind it. It was a dream city, a place of silver towers and floating cars, far different from the small, hunched little town I knew. I stationed Watson at the door.

"Don't let anyone come in," I said.

"I'll protect you, Miss Crisp."

I believed him.

THE RAMP DESCENDED into the bleached pink light of morning. I sent Watson down first. He surveyed the launchpad and assured me that it was empty. I crept down slowly, my eyes trained on Joe Reilly's shack. The curtains were closed, the door shut fast. It existed in a kind of perfect stillness; even the wind was quiet. The only sounds came from New Galveston as it gathered its energies for the day's business: the sound of old Engines starting their tasks, the nickering of horses, the low hum of human industry. But the shack and the wide expanse beyond it might as well have been a painting, for all the life it showed.

I only wanted to get home to Father. The world was tilting, everything sliding out of place. I had to go home and protect what was left, while I could still recognize it.

We made it only a few yards in the direction of town—Watson's thumping footfalls breaking the flat silence like rocks to gravel—before Joe Reilly's voice rang out behind me.

"Anabelle! Wait!"

"Hurry, Watson."

"Hold on a minute! I have to talk to you!"

I stopped despite myself and turned around. He'd stepped out of his shack and was hustling toward us in his usual dissolute state, hair askew and dirty clothes rumpled. His shirt was undone in a contemptible display of immodesty. It made me hate him even more, if such a thing were possible. There was nothing good or respectful about him. That I feared him now, that I waited for Silas Mundt or Sally Milkwood to emerge from the door behind him, stoked me into a murderous rage.

I screamed at him: an inarticulate, frustrated bullet of hate. It was an impotent sound. One day, I vowed, I would learn how to direct my hatred with power.

He seemed amazed by it, though. He stopped, arms slightly raised, palms out: a gesture of peace. "Whoa, girl, what the hell got into you?"

"Stay back!"

"Okay, okay." He was still far enough away that we had to raise our voices to exchange words, which suited me very well. He put out a hand, as though to steady a spooked horse. "I need to tell you something before you go into town."

"You got nothing to say to me. I saw who you was talking to last night. I saw it all. I'm telling the sheriff who you've taken up with. You better worry about what you're going to tell *him*."

That shut him up. His hand dropped and he stared at me like I'd just shot him in the gut. Like he couldn't believe the calamity of it. I tensed, waiting for whatever he might do. Watson hummed at my side, apprehending these events in whatever unknowable way the Engines had. He was not designed for confrontation of any sort, so I didn't know how he'd react if Mr. Reilly became violent. But his heavy presence gave me confidence nonetheless.

"Anabelle," he said, finally. "Listen to me. Don't do that."

"You're going to jail, Joe Reilly," I said, feeling a dangerous, giddy power. "And then directly afterward I guess you'll be going to hell."

He dropped to his knees. I remember that very vividly—even more than I remember the robbery that started all this. I felt a cold, bloody joy riding high in my heart. I half expected him to topple onto his face. Instead he sat, his arms limp at his sides, and stared at me in dismayed silence. His face was wide open, struck defenseless, ready for the judgment of the world.

I would give it to him.

I HEADED BACK to the Mother Earth Diner. I tried to be circumspect, as I knew class had started and I didn't want to be hassled about not being there. Nevertheless I felt stares drawing toward me. Two people talking by the roadside actually stopped their conversation and watched me pass, their faces flat and unreadable. I hurried by. Mr. Shank stood on the stoop of his shop. He watched me, too, his hands in his pockets and his gaze strangely formal, as though he had arrived to witness an execution. I stared back at him, feeling a growing sense of unease.

Then I saw the diner, and I understood.

The door was wide open, but the sign was unlit, and the lights inside were off. It looked wrong, crowded with shadows in the morning. I stepped inside. Chairs were toppled, a spill of forks gathered in a corner underneath an open drawer. Condiments had been swept from the tables, shattered onto the floor. This was more damage than had occurred during the fight. I saw the dried pool of blood where the miner had fallen, and my stomach lurched. There was a lot of it. Too much.

Watson came in behind me and moved immediately to the back, where his morning duties typically began. He bypassed all signs of chaos, including overturned and emptied sugar caddies, kitchen shelves barren of produce and bread, and a drift of spilled flour where a bag had been torn open. Past the fryer and the griddle, still cold. He pushed his way into the back room.

I stood silently, waiting for an emotion to coalesce. I knew what I was supposed to feel, and I tried to tap into it. But I came up with nothing. I was like the desert itself, responding to the Dowsing Engines with a dry silence.

Watson emerged from the back. "It's all gone," he said.

I just nodded.

All the food and water, all the dried goods, all the accumulated useless flotsam that collects in the corners of any human endeavor.

Even my father.

Gone.

8

When we emerged from the Mother Earth, it might as well have been into a new world. Eyes that had watched me approach now turned away in shame. Even Mr. Shank retreated into his store, his attention suddenly preoccupied with a bit of lint on his vest. I ran for home, heedless of Watson's efforts to keep up. I had to tell Father, in case he didn't know. Whether it was the cultists again—with the aid of that traitor Joe Reilly—or the miners seeking revenge, surely he would understand that measures had to be taken, with or without the sheriff's help. Even if he already knew about the looting, he would be wondering where I was, whether or not I was safe.

The door to our hab was closed. Small, covered ferns hung from suspended planters on either side of it, giving the impression of untroubled domesticity. I opened the door and knew immediately that Father wasn't home.

The space felt empty. There was no smell of coffee or eggs, no bustle from his room as he roused himself to meet me.

I had known, though. Somehow I had known.

Watson at last caught up to me, his feet crunching the sand underneath. "Miss Crisp," he said. "Here I am."

"He's not here."

I felt a peculiar urge to retreat to my room and go to sleep. I didn't know what was happening, and I didn't know how to face it. I sat at the kitchen table and stared at the wall. The artwork of my childhood years, depicting the saucer traveling through a star-littered spaceway, seemed suddenly cruel in its innocence.

"Shall I brew coffee, Miss Crisp?"

"No."

The very mention of the word brought back the events of the previous night at the diner. I heard the dull sound of the skillet connecting with the miner's head. I remembered the rust-colored stain on the floor. An unhappy notion stirred in my brain, and I said, "I have to go see the sheriff."

"Shall I accompany you?"

Even though he was only an Engine, I did not want Watson to bear witness to what I knew I would find there. "No. You go back and start cleaning the diner. I'll be along shortly."

He went off to do as he was told, and I took the moment of isolation to rest my head on my arms. I wanted to cry, but I couldn't. There was a knot of fear and anxiety blocking that release. Eventually I got up and left the hab, knowing that I wouldn't be able to shake it until I went to the sheriff's office and faced what waited for me there.

ALTHOUGH MOST OF New Galveston was composed of metal habs and the earthen structures of the Taproots, the municipal buildings at the center of town were permanent structures made of brick and wood. If the government was permanent, so the reasoning went, then the town was permanent, too.

Here were the town hall, the courthouse, the First Martian Bank, the governor's house, and the sheriff's station. This latter was a modest single-story affair, squat and solid, as though it had been built to withstand a siege. The cells had been dug out underneath. There were ten of them, and at the time that number seemed insultingly large. It was almost as though someone didn't trust us.

I had never been in the sheriff's station, nor had I ever imagined I would need to be. It was for other people. Bad people. Not people like us. It intimidated me now; I felt as though crossing that threshold would formalize the calamity that had befallen my family.

I pushed through the door into a narrow receiving room. The walls were raw wood, and a photograph of a collection of tents on red sand decorated one of them. A thin young man sat behind a desk. When he saw me come in, he leaned back in his chair and sized me up, like he was wondering how hard it would be to take me down if he needed to. I resolved that it would be difficult, if it came to it.

Before he could speak, I said, "I need to see the sheriff."

"You wouldn't be Anabelle Crisp, would you?"

"I would."

"Well, the sheriff needs to see you, too. Go on through that door."

It led into an open area crowded with file cabinets and small desks. Papers and folders were stacked onto every available surface, with small spaces cleared here and there for work. There were two office doors in the back of the room, but it seemed the real work of the station was done out here. On the floor I could see the dark scuff marks of Jack's treads. I wondered where he was.

Sheriff Bakersfield rose from the chair behind one of the desks and gave me a smile somewhere under that big mustache, as though I were a neighbor stopping in for a chat. He gestured to an empty chair. "Heya, Belle. Have a seat."

I did. One of the office doors opened behind him and Deputy Mae Ackerman walked through. She spared me a quick glance before taking a seat at a second desk behind me. I felt small. I felt like the focus of dangerous attentions. "The Mother Earth Diner was robbed again," I said. "They took everything this time."

The sheriff nodded and looked at his desk. He moved some papers around. "Yeah, I know it. We're going to address that."

"I want to go with."

That gave him a pause. "Go with, where?"

"Out to Dig Town, or the crater, whichever is your first stop."

He pulled a hand across his face and glanced over my shoulder, at the deputy. I did not turn around, but suddenly I could feel her eyes boring into the back of my head. "Let me get to that in a minute. First, I need to ask you about last night."

I felt ill. I didn't want to talk about that. I wanted to stay on the offensive, where I was comfortable.

"I want you to tell me what happened."

"Where do you want me to start? A lot happens in a diner. I guess first Watson goes in and turns on the fryer oil so it gets hot by opening time."

"Don't be smart, Anabelle. You know what I'm talking about."

Deputy Ackerman spoke up. "Watson's your Kitchen Engine, right? Where is he now?"

I turned around in my chair. She was directly behind me, writing on a pad of paper. I noticed she had a little star-shaped scar by her left eye; it gave her a sinister aspect. "He's cleaning up at the diner," I said. "The one that was stripped down to the bone last night. Remember that?"

She just stared at me. Sheriff Bakersfield spoke again, and I swung my attention back around to him. "One thing at a time, okay? First. What happened last night? Between your daddy and the miners."

A sliver of fear slid through my guts. "Where is he, anyway?"

"He's downstairs. He's fine."

"In *jail*? He ain't done anything wrong!"

"Well, that's what we're trying to establish, okay? I need your help. So please, answer my questions."

"They attacked him!"

"All three of them? They just—jumped up and attacked him?"

"That's right." I needed him out of that cell. I needed him home. I resolved to say whatever I could to make that happen.

"Why?"

"Probably they were working with the cultists who robbed the place. And with Joe Reilly, too."

This seemed to catch the sheriff by surprise. "Now what does Joe Reilly have to do with any of this?"

"He's working with the cultists. The moth ones. I saw him."

He exchanged another look with the deputy behind me. I turned around and watched her writing in her notebook. "I can tell you all about it," I said.

"And I'm going to want to hear it," said Bakersfield. "But right now we're talking about your daddy."

"I know it, and I'm telling you what happened! They attacked him because they wanted to rob the place like those others that came before! That Silas Mundt I told you about, and that Sally Milkwood, who everybody in this town already seems to know about! They're all working together!"

The sheriff leaned back in his chair, the wood creaking underneath his weight. He studied his intertwined fingers for a few moments, and then looked over my shoulder. "Mae, why don't you get ol' Jack in here."

The deputy rose from her chair behind me and went outside. I sat for a few frightening minutes with the sheriff, wondering what ol' Jack would do to me to get the answers Bakersfield wanted to hear. A bead of sweat trickled down the back of my neck. I'd been burnt and cut in the kitchen over the years, but I'd never had to withstand real pain before. I fought back a wave of tears. I resolved to hold out for as long as I could.

The deputy came back into the office, and Jack rolled in behind her. He was taller and sleeker than Watson, and cleaner, too, since he did not have to spend his existence in a grease-filled kitchen. He looked like an upright bullet, the shine long gone but still prepared to fulfill his deadly purpose. Mae resumed her place behind me, and Jack rolled over to the sheriff's side like any good hound.

The sheriff opened a drawer in his desk and retrieved a cylinder, which he slid into Jack's chassis. "I want you to listen to this, Anabelle."

Mae said, "Wally—"

Bakersfield held up a hand. "It's all right."

I knew I didn't want to hear it. But there was no stopping it. "Go ahead, Jack."

TRANSCRIPT OF THE ARREST OF SAMUEL A. CRISP
BY SHERIFF WALLY BAKERSFIELD, AS RECORDED
BY THE LAW ENGINE DESIGNATED "JACK."

BAKERSFIELD: Sam, my God, what happened here?

CRISP: (unintelligible)

BAKERSFIELD: Mae, round up some statements from those folks there, okay? Just leave us alone a minute. (. . .) Sam? Sam, I need you to talk to me. Come sit over here.

CRISP: Where's Anabelle?

BAKERSFIELD: Was she here for this?

CRISP: Yes. Oh God.

BAKERSFIELD: I'm sure she's fine. Probably just run home. I'll send Mae down to check on her in just a minute or two, okay? Come on over here, sit down and talk to me.

CRISP: I can't, I have to—I have to find—Oh, my God, is he dead? Is that man dead?

BAKERSFIELD: Sam, sit down. I'm afraid I'm going to have to insist. (. . .) When are you going to put some wider seats in here? I can't hardly fit in these things.

CRISP: I don't know.

BAKERSFIELD: Maybe I ought to cut back on those pancakes some, huh?

CRISP: He's dead, isn't he?

BAKERSFIELD: Yeah, he's dead all right. I'm afraid so. I got a couple miners waiting at my office who say you was the one who did it. One of them has an arm broken so bad he might not be able to work again. Is what they're telling me true?

CRISP: (. . .)

BAKERSFIELD: Now these boys, I know how they are. It's not the first time I've had trouble from Dig Town. I know you remember Garrison and Cone from a while back. So, what I'm saying to you, Sam, is that I know what they told me might have a little mustard on it, okay? I don't expect it went down exactly how they say it did.

CRISP: (. . .)

BAKERSFIELD: Do you understand me?

CRISP: I don't know. I think so.

BAKERSFIELD: It ain't algebra, Sam. It's pretty simple.

CRISP: Okay.

BAKERSFIELD: Just tell me what happened.

CRISP: I killed him.

BAKERSFIELD: Sam—

CRISP: Are you looking for something else? He attacked my daughter, so I killed him.

BAKERSFIELD: Now . . . what the boys tell me is, there was an argument. But Charlie says *he* was the one that got into it with Anabelle.

CRISP: (. . .)

BAKERSFIELD: Sam?

CRISP: So what?

BAKERSFIELD: Well, so what is, if Charlie's the one that lipped off, how come it's this other fella lying dead on your floor? Did this guy attack Anabelle?

CRISP: I don't think so. I don't know. It happened so fast.

BAKERSFIELD: Charlie says you hit him with a skillet and that's how his arm got busted.

CRISP: Yeah.

BAKERSFIELD: He says they was on their way out the door when you did it.

CRISP: They were . . . they were making threats. He was making threats.

BAKERSFIELD: "He" being Charlie?

CRISP: Yeah.

BAKERSFIELD: Threats against Anabelle?

CRISP: Against me. Against us both.

BAKERSFIELD: And where was Daniel this whole time? What was he doing?

CRISP: Who?

BAKERSFIELD: The man you killed, Sam. His name was Daniel. He was married. He had a wife. Turns out she's got a name, too. You want to know it?

CRISP: (. . .)

BAKERSFIELD: Her name is Constance.

CRISP: Are you mad at me, Wally?

BAKERSFIELD: I'm just—I'm trying to figure out what happened here, and you're not making it easy on me. What you're telling me doesn't sound too good, I have to be honest with you. Where was Daniel?

CRISP: He—he was standing behind Charlie, I guess.

BAKERSFIELD: Trying to lead him out?

CRISP: (. . .)

BAKERSFIELD: Goddamn it, Sam, answer my question.

CRISP: I don't know.

BAKERSFIELD: Yeah, okay.

CRISP: Am I in trouble?

BAKERSFIELD: Well, maybe a little bit, Sam. I think maybe a little bit. Let's go on down to the office, okay? (. . .) Mae,

why don't you head on out to their hab and gather up
Anabelle? She's probably pretty scared, so go easy. Bring
their Engine, too. Jack, initiate arrest proceedings against
one Samuel Alfred Crisp, proprietor of the Mother Earth
Diner, on a charge of murder. Goddamn it, anyhow.

IT TOOK ME a minute to realize Sheriff Bakersfield was staring
at me. I rubbed the mist from my eyes with the heel of my hand
and scowled at the floor. I hated him at that moment. I felt
ambushed.

"Now listen," he said. "That boy Charlie Jackson has been a
thorn in my side for a long time now, even before they got all
weird up there, and if there's wrongdoing on his part, I will land
on him with both feet and a song in my heart. You understand?
I ain't no friend of his. Mae, am I telling the truth?"

"Yes, you are."

"See? Corroboration. But Anabelle, your dad just confessed
to murder."

I couldn't take in the magnitude of it. Even when Father told
me that Mother wasn't coming home, that no one on Earth was
ever likely to come here again, it hadn't felt this bad. At least
then there was time for disbelief. But here, the ugly truth of it
squatted in front of me like some great toad, fixing me with
unblinking eyes.

"Charlie started talking about robbing the diner," I said. "I
was rude to him and he made a grab for me. He made a scene.
That's when Father came out."

"Did Charlie strike you?"

"He knocked the coffeepot out of my hand."

"Did he hit you, Anabelle?"

The question infuriated me. Couldn't he hear what I was telling him? "He didn't get the chance. Other folks was on him. Why don't you talk to them? Mr. Lewis was one of 'em."

"Don't worry, we did. Mr. Lewis didn't have anything nice to say about Charlie, I can tell you that."

I felt dizzy, and curled up in my chair, cradling my elbows and lowering my head. I heard a rush of wind. The sheriff spoke my name, his voice coming to me across a great expanse. It was all too much. Everyone was telling him how rotten this man Charlie was and yet it was still my father in the cell downstairs, and no one was moving to let him out. The diner was still trashed and no one was talking about Joe Reilly or the cultists. I needed Mother. Mother should be here for this.

"I want to see him," I said, finally.

The sheriff exchanged a glance with Mae. He said, "Well, I guess that's all right."

Mae stood up behind me. "I'll take her down."

"Does he know about the diner?" I said.

"I ain't got around to telling him yet," the sheriff said.

"I guess you left that for me. Let no one accuse anyone else in this town of bravery. Can I at least tell him that this time you'll send a force out after them?"

Sheriff Bakersfield leveled his gaze at me. Whatever he was about to say next, I knew he didn't want to say it. "It wasn't any cultists that hit the diner, Anabelle. It was people from town. It was just regular folks."

Once again, I felt like I had been cut loose from something solid. I felt like I was floating away. "What? Who?"

"Too many to count," he said. "Just about everybody."

9

The cells were clean and well-lit. They hadn't seen much use in New Galveston's short life. Once it became clear that the Silence was a genuine and enduring condition, we suffered through a few months of lively reactions; fights broke out as fear and anger took hold of people. Old grudges flowered and new ones were sown. Panic made maniacs out of a few. But that communal rage had decreased in the past few months, replaced by a doomed melancholy. Mostly, now, these cells were used to house the casualties of the sheriff's ongoing struggle to contain the moonshiners, who were enjoying a surging business in the wake of the Earth's sudden stillness.

Deputy Ackerman led me as far as the bottom of the stairs and waited for me there. I wanted to retain my anger, but I felt a surge of gratitude for that small privacy.

Father was the only resident. He was in the first cell on the left. It was more spacious than I would have expected, with a cot and a bucket in the corner. At first I couldn't understand why he would need a bucket, as he had no possessions to carry around; when it dawned on me, I felt a wild and disproportionate shame.

Father was lying on the cot with his back to the locked cage door. He was talking under his breath, barely a whisper. Whatever small hope I'd come down there with dissolved on hearing it.

"Father?"

His shoulders tensed, and he stopped talking. He turned half around so I could see his profile. "Anabelle?"

I pressed my face into the bars.

"I was just talking to your mother."

"I know." I tried to say something more, but my throat was full. I was afraid if I spoke I'd start bawling like a child. I wouldn't do that in front of the deputy. Nor would I give my father the added burden of soothing me.

He rolled into a sitting position. "Are you okay, pea?"

I nodded. I could feel my lip trembling.

"What are you doing here?"

"I—" I couldn't finish. Something burned in my heart, some cancerous mix of rage and love and hopelessness that threatened to eat through my skin and fill this underground hell with its corrosive light.

"Is Bakersfield giving you any problems?" He approached the bars and peered down the hall to where Mae Ackerman stood. "You leave her alone. You hear me? She had nothing to do with this."

I touched his hand. "It's okay. They're just asking questions."

"You tell them the truth, you hear me? There's nothing to hide."

"But—"

"Don't argue with me. Don't you get in trouble, too. It's going to be all right. I need you to take care of the diner until this gets sorted out."

I shook my head. "They wrecked it. They wrecked the whole place. We lost everything."

"What do you mean? Who did?"

"Everybody," I said. "Our neighbors. Our friends."

I could see the understanding break over him slowly, watch it change his face. He stepped away from the bars and sat heavily on the bed. He looked confused. The last vestige of resilience inside him started to die. I saw it happen, just like that.

"Dad," I said.

He looked like he was far away from me. Far away from this cell. Somewhere lonely.

"You know," he said, "I know it's not her. I know she's not there. It's just, I really need to hear her voice."

"Dad? What do I do?"

He didn't have any answers for me. I wasn't even sure he knew I was there anymore.

I felt Deputy Ackerman's presence behind me, and then her hand on my shoulder. I didn't even have the will to shrug it away. I just waited for Father to say something to me, to tell me where to go and what to do, to tell me how to live in this dreadful new circumstance. She turned me toward the stair and guided me away. I did not resist.

10

I spent the next few days in the hab. Watson tended to cleaning the diner. I saw no purpose to it—there was no food left, and I would not serve these people even if there was. My mind could not accommodate what they had done. How could we have been living among them so long and not known the hatred they bore us? How could they have come in every day and looked me in the eye, laughed at my father's dumb jokes, and smiled at me when I brought them their food, knowing the whole time that they would strip us down to the bloody bone at the first opportunity?

Now Sheriff Bakersfield and Deputy Ackerman just fretted like neutered dogs, too docile to deliver even a hint of justice.

And I was stuck in the middle of it, a child among adults caught in a derangement I could not understand. Only Watson provided any sense of stability, devoted as he was to fulfilling the functions of his role, however hollow they were.

On the afternoon of the third day of my isolation, he returned from his labors in the diner and declared the place fit to open again.

"Is that a joke?" I said. I was sitting on a chair by the small, curved window, watching the sky. Although it was light, Phobos was visible, like a pale ghost. Once it had seemed friendly to me; I'd called it my little potato moon, which always made my parents laugh. Now its irregular shape seemed sinister, its presence a threat and a warning.

Phobos means fear. I learned that in school.

While Watson reassured me that he was not joking, I watched my neighbors moving through the street outside. Though they were more shadow than people in this light, I recognized most of them by their shapes, by their mannerisms. Widow Kessler's careful shuffle; Jeremiah Shank's straight-backed stride, as though he were a lord among serfs; Preacher Spivey's big, round potbelly seeming to lead the rest of him about, like a dog pulling its master. Not one of these people had come to my door in the three days since the diner had been looted and my dad locked up. Though I would have turned them away with prejudice, their distance hurt me regardless.

"We're not opening that diner ever again," I said. "These people can starve for all I care."

"They won't starve," Watson said. "The greenhouses are adequate for the needs of the population."

"Now you're just trying to hurt my feelings, Watson."

"No, Miss Cr—"

"Shut up."

He did. I wanted to feel bad about it, but I couldn't. I was too hurt myself to spare any feelings on an Engine. The truth was that I didn't want to talk to a dishwasher. I wanted to talk to Mother. I needed her to be there, and I couldn't even use the cylinder she'd left me. I'd never thought it a substitute worth a damn until now, when I needed her voice and her canned counsel more than I needed the air that surrounded me. Instead I had this stupid kitchen appliance that couldn't stop talking about feeding our attackers, like nothing at all had happened. Engines weren't people. Especially Watson, I thought. I imagined him stepping over my bloody corpse as he hurried to serve hot eggs to Silas Mundt and Joe Reilly and those grotesque green-eyed miners who crawled out of the Martian ground like devils from a dream.

This wretched town, full of wretched people. Cowards and thieves, every last one of them.

I would not abide it any longer. I started packing. When I was finished, I said, "Watson. Come with me."

SUNLIGHT GLARED OFF the *Eurydice's* metal hull, so that it looked like a fallen star wedged along New Galveston's flank. The ship cast its long shadow over Joe Reilly's shack. I approached it cautiously. Though I knew him to be a coward, I remembered my father's warning: cowards were the ones who would hurt you. This man had had some time to stew over the threat I'd given him, and I could not predict his reaction when he saw me again.

I knocked on his door. It was early afternoon; surely by now he'd have roused himself from his stupor.

He did not answer. I knocked again, shouting his name, and waited there for several minutes. Finally it became clear that either he wasn't in or he wouldn't answer the door to me. I hadn't accounted for such an obvious possibility. I turned to leave, embarrassed and exasperated. The clattering sound of the ramp descending from the saucer's belly stopped me.

I waited to see who would emerge. Was he alone, or was he with the cultists? Was Sally Milkwood with him? Everything I knew of the cultists was what I read in my books and heard from kids at school. I imagined them pouring out in an evil tide, their knives gleaming, ready to flense the meat from my bones to cook over their cannibal fires.

But it was only Joe himself, stepping cautiously down the ramp until he stood at its base, where he remained with a look I could not read. His face was pasty and slack. I realized I couldn't read his look because there was nothing there to read: he was a man defined by his passivity, and now he stood awaiting the next gust of wind to blow him along.

Well, here I am, I thought.

"They're coming for you," I said. Of course it was a lie. They didn't give a damn.

He absorbed the news physically. He took a step back and tripped on the ramp's edge, landing on his backside.

Encouraged by the absence of any retaliation, I approached him. Watson kept pace behind me. "They're most likely going to hang you."

"Well," he said. He stared into the open desert. "I guess that ought to satisfy you, at least."

"If I go up in the *Eurydice,* will I find my mother's cylinder?"

He looked at me, plainly confused. It was the first actual expression I'd seen on him that day. "What?"

"You heard what I asked."

"I did, but I don't understand it."

"The Moths stole the cylinder with my mother on it. Is it on your ship?" I felt the swell of a huge sadness, and I struggled to hold my composure.

"I know you hate me, Anabelle. But that's a low thing to accuse me of."

"Then what are you doing? What's your business with those people?"

He wouldn't look at me. "It don't matter."

I didn't have it in me to argue with him. He wouldn't tell the truth anyway, and I was afraid that if I heard another lie I might start weeping. I would not give him that satisfaction. "So they have it?"

He sighed and shook his head. He stared at the ground between his stretched-out legs. "Have what," he said.

"The cylinder," I said, straining for patience.

"Well, if they took it, then I guess they have it."

"You're gonna take me there."

That got to him. He sat forward, meeting my gaze at last. "The hell I am."

"You take me or you swing. You might be a coward, but I know you ain't a fool. It's an easy choice."

He cast a glance toward town. Maybe he was wondering when the sheriff's posse would arrive for him. Maybe he was wondering if they'd even waste time with a trial. Of course, I had no idea what his relationship with the cultists really was; but he took the threat of hanging as credible enough, so I knew it was rotten. I just hoped it was bad enough that he'd go where I pushed.

"I don't know where they are," he said. "At least not exactly." But I could tell by the tone in his voice that he was about to give in. This was nothing but whining, which I heard enough of on the schoolyard.

"That's all right, because I bet I know who does."

"And who's that?"

"Sally Milkwood."

He gave me a pleading look. "No, Anabelle. Come on."

"Start packing."

"Sally isn't somebody you want to tangle with, kid. Let this go."

"Watson has a cargo compartment on his backside. Feel free to use it."

"We're taking the Engine?"

There it was. He'd given in.

"The crater's full of sand," he said, desperate to throw out whatever hindrances he could think of. "He can't cross it without treads."

"I know it. They'll have those at Mr. Wickham's shop in Dig Town."

"For Christ's sake!"

I stopped, stared at him. His face was red; he looked like he was about to pass out.

"You don't know what you're talking about, Anabelle! The crater is full of the Strange! This isn't something you do just 'cause your ass caught fire. This is life-and-death shit! This is serious!"

"They stole something from me," I said, calmly and quietly. "They stole something I need and something my father needs. I've sat by while everyone around me just shrugged their shoulders and let it happen and made up reasons why we had to allow it. And then, while we was down, they turned on us, and they took even more. You better believe it's serious. There's gonna be a reckoning, and I'm gonna deliver it."

He sighed and paced a tight circle two or three times. When he spoke again, he'd managed to calm himself down, too.

"People get lost in the Strange, Anabelle. You haven't heard the stories I have."

"I hear all kinds of stories. It's all fairy tales. It's all excuses so none of you has to do a damned thing. I don't believe in fairy tales, Joe Reilly."

"People come out different. That's the God's honest truth."

"Watson, go tell Sheriff Bakersfield that Mr. Reilly is here awaiting judgment. Tell him he's waving a gun."

"Very good, Miss Crisp."

"Jesus Christ. Just wait a minute." He rubbed the heels of his hands into his eyes. "Fine, I'll take you. I'll take you."

I checked the sun's position. It was late afternoon. Phobos was a chalky shadow in the sky. "We got a few hours of daylight left," I said. "Enough to get ready. I want to be moving before dusk."

part two

what I did about it

11

We set out as evening fell. It was not the most auspicious time to begin a journey, but Dig Town was not far—an hour's walk, at most. Joe Reilly carried a backpack with our heat tents. We packed whatever other small items we thought might come in handy into Watson's chassis, scooped from the ship's inventory and stored in his small cargo compartment: food and water, a cookstove and pot, tinder for fire.

Anyway, neither of us wanted to wait for daylight. Joe because he was afraid of being hanged, me because I couldn't bear to be near any of them for a minute longer.

I expected a feeling of grandiosity as we took our first steps away from town. Here was a beckoning adventure, the kind I'd read about in the magazines. I wanted that feeling of momentous occasion, of thrilling possibility. But there was nothing like that. It was just a long, boring walk—three miles to Dig Town, and then God knew how many beyond, until we found whatever dark cranny Silas and his cohort used for shelter.

New Galveston receded steadily behind us. I found myself looking back often, until it was nothing but a soft glow on the edge of the horizon, like a lamp somebody had left on in an empty room. The twilight sky was as beautiful as I had ever seen it: the sunlight was a pink and purple flourish on the horizon, and the Martian moons shone. Without the habs and the municipal heat lamps to act as buffers against the coursing wind, there was nothing to protect us from its bone-numbing chill. It came barreling in from the dark plains like some ancient intelligence, primal and ravenous.

Now that the journey had evolved from a scheme born from my anger into reality, I felt the first gust of doubt. I wondered if I'd made a dangerous mistake. Maybe I was just a stupid child after all, and had started a process that would kill me.

Joe Reilly must have seen something of this in my face. He laughed. "Getting tired already, kid?"

"No."

"You're starting to fall behind."

"I'm keeping pace with Watson," I said. This was partially true. Watson's slow legs hampered his progress. But it was also true that I was tired. The day had undermined me.

The ground between New Galveston and Dig Town was hard-packed and well-traveled, so Watson could manage it well enough. But once we went into Peabody Crater, where we'd contend with rock and drifting sand, things would change. I feared for his ability to keep up with us, even with treads. The wind would blow the sand hard at us, and it would clog his gears. I could do simple Engine maintenance, but I didn't know enough to see him through anything serious. I hoped Joe did.

"Are you doing okay, Watson?"

"I am in capital condition, Miss Crisp."

Joe said, "Why does he talk like that, anyway?"

"Like what."

"Like a Limey."

"That's his cylinder."

"Yes, Anabelle, I know that's his cylinder. I'm asking why it's programmed to sound British."

"Because it's *Watson*," I said, as though speaking to an idiot child. "Don't you know Watson?"

"Would I be asking if I did?"

I didn't want to tell him, but I couldn't think of a good reason to hold back beyond pure mulishness. "He's Sherlock Holmes's sidekick."

He thought about it for a moment. "I think I heard of him. He's from those detective stories, right?"

I let silence serve as my answer. I wasn't inclined to educate this man in literary matters.

"So does that make you Sherlock Holmes?"

I flushed. "No."

He laughed but didn't push that line. He just said, "Pretty fancy for a dishwasher."

"Watson ain't fancy."

"No, he sure ain't. Just like everything you see around you, kid. None of this is like the stories you read in your books. It's all dirty and dull and real. I just hope we don't have to die before you figure that out."

DIG TOWN RESIDED at the top of a small plateau, situated beside a steep drop-off into Peabody Crater. Coming to it from New Galveston, the series of shacks that made up the town looked like a crown of spiky hair atop the head of a buried giant. From a distance it had looked like the miners' community stayed dark at night, but upon getting close, I could see that there were in fact a few lamps burning, a few homes that still seemed to harbor heat and light.

Still, its reputation as haunted seemed well-earned. I was grateful for Joe Reilly's company as we ventured into that blighted place, though I would have let you pull my tongue from its root before admitting it.

Sometimes, when the air was still or the wind was southerly, the sound of working machines would drift down to us in New Galveston, giving the impression that Dig Town was a place of constant labor. So as we ascended the mild slope into the settlement, I expected an atmosphere of busy industry, a bustling of men and a grinding of machinery. But when we entered, it seemed dead. What few people I could see lingered on porches or moved sluggishly along the tangle of dirt roads wending their crooked ways through town. No machines voiced their power. No foremen bawled commands. The air was heavy with a chalky green dust, as though the great hole in the earth exhaled the grit of the Strange into the atmosphere. I took a handkerchief from my pocket and wrapped it around my lower face. I must have looked like a bandit, but I desired to keep as much of that grit out of my lungs as I could manage. Joe Reilly observed this action without comment. He did not repeat it for himself.

Of course, we attracted attention: a girl, the pilot who wouldn't fly, and a Kitchen Engine. While no one was sufficiently roused to address themselves to us, we pulled every gaze as though magnetized. I felt their eyes on my skin. Everyone would know of what'd happened at the Mother Earth. They would know who I was, too.

It struck me that I did not see a single woman. I knew Widow Kessler lived here, but were there any others at all? Was this a place of men and for men? I felt vulnerable in a way I was unaccustomed to. Watson's bulk, normally so reassuring, seemed only to invite greater attention. If only he wasn't so loud.

Mr. Wickham's place of business was a large shack a short distance from the mine. The word "Parts" had been applied with simple white paint over the door and had flaked to a ghostly hint of itself over time. The chimney was cold and the windows were dark. I hesitated, but Joe Reilly approached the door and rapped his knuckles on it.

A muffled voice sounded from within. Joe took it as an invitation and allowed himself inside. I followed close behind, while Watson waited at the door.

The interior was dark but for a few slender strands of moonlight slipping in through ill-fitted boards. It was crowded with metal parts: drill bits great and small, wheels, metal wagons, dead cylinders, Engine parts of every vintage. A cold hearth dominated the back wall. The place smelled of machines: oil and grease, metal and ash. The whole room had the feeling of a heart gone still.

After a moment, I was able to distinguish Mr. Wickham from the scrap. He was seated at a table near the hearth. His huge form, so striking when he was out in the world, seemed to blend naturally with the great pieces of machinery stacked and suspended all around him.

"Well, this ought to be interesting," he said. He did not rise from his chair, nor did he invite us to sit. He looked like a creature from a fantasy, sitting in the shadows with his drooping black mustache and his reflective green eyes. His arms were huge, as though he were fashioned for the particular purpose of flinging men through the air like sticks.

Joe Reilly said, "We need some desert treads, Harry."

Mr. Wickham glanced at the pilot, but only for a moment; his attention stayed fixed on me. "This maybe isn't the best place for you to be walking around in, young lady."

He had always been pleasant to me on the occasions he'd come to New Galveston, so this statement unnerved me more thoroughly than had our reception outside. "I didn't do anything wrong."

"That don't always make a difference."

Joe said, "We'll be on our way as soon as we get those treads."

Mr. Wickham looked behind us, toward the open door. From his vantage point he could see that Watson waited outside. He appraised the Engine for a moment and then looked back at me. He had not addressed Joe once, nor even acknowledged his presence. "What are you up to, Belle?"

I was glad of the question, because it recalled me to my purpose. I decided not to tell him about Sally Milkwood. I didn't know whether he knew her, or whether I could trust him not to warn her if he did. "I'm going into the crater to hunt those bastards that stole my mother. The ones no one else around here has the stomach to face."

He let the accusation float by. "I thought your mama was on Earth."

"I mean her recording cylinder."

"Oh, I see."

Joe spoke up. "Harry, if we could just—"

"Reilly, you shut your goddamned mouth. You don't get to talk where I can hear you. Do you understand me?"

Joe put his hands in his pockets and half turned away. He

nodded and looked at the floor. He was a beaten dog, here the same as anywhere else.

Mr. Wickham put his hands on his knees and pushed himself standing. I heard his joints pop. He extended a hand to the wall to steady himself when it looked like his legs might not be up to the task. I'd never seen him struggle before, and I wondered if he was ill. It'd been some time since he'd come down to New Galveston. He brushed past us and headed to the door, where he cast an eye over Watson's chassis, at the legs made for short, easy treks, at the rubber-soled feet designed for navigating slippery floors. He did not seem impressed by what he saw.

"You're taking a dishwasher."

"They raided our diner. If I leave him, they'll strip him down, too."

I wondered if he'd offer to watch over Watson while I was gone. He didn't. "Belle, that recording cylinder isn't programmed with your mama's personality. It's a message she left you, that's all. It's not like what Watson here is."

I wanted to be angry with him, but he did not sound patronizing. He sounded as though he was trying to understand my motivations, trying to piece together my reasoning like a jigsaw puzzle. So instead of barking at him, I said, "I know that. I'm not stupid."

"Stupid is the last thing you are. But the world isn't the way you think it is, and I worry for you when you find that out. And you might have chosen better company for the journey."

"Watson is my best friend."

"It's not the Engine I'm talking about, and I think you know that."

"Mr. Reilly knows how to get me there."

Mr. Wickham gave me a level stare. "I doubt that very much, Anabelle. I doubt that man knows much of anything beyond a hundred-foot radius of his own front door. I think you need to be aware that by going out there—with him and some Kitchen Engine, or even by yourself—you are going to a place you might not come back from."

I listened in silence. He was telling me I was probably going to die. I was not accustomed to adults speaking to me so frankly. Wasn't he supposed to care about me, since I was still a child? Wasn't he supposed to try to stop me? It was exhilarating and terrifying at once.

"Mr. Wickham? Where is everybody in Dig Town?"

He tapped Watson on the shoulder and gestured for him to go around the side of his shop. Watson went in the indicated direction as calmly as though he were merely here to receive his long-overdue cleaning.

"They're down in the mine. They pretty much live there now. I'll be joining them soon, I guess." He started to follow Watson around the side of the building. "This'll take me a while. Don't touch anything in the meantime."

"Actually, we have another stop to make anyway," Joe said. "We'll give you the night, come back in the morning."

Mr. Wickham kept on going, as if he hadn't heard.

"I'M CURIOUS WHAT your plan is," Joe said. I followed him out onto the road, under a dense curtain of stars. He seemed to know where he was going. It was a natural question to ask, but it caused a spike of anxiety in me. I didn't really know what I was going to do.

"I'm going to force her to take me out there, same as I forced you to take me here."

"Threatening Sally with the law might not have the effect you think it will."

I let that go by. We'd see soon enough.

"And once you get out there? You think you're going to threaten the Moths with Sheriff Bakersfield?"

I cut a glance at him. "I guess you think I'm going out there to talk."

"Well, what the hell else would you be going there to do?"

I didn't want to say the words aloud, for fear he'd laugh at me. And I feared that laughter might undo my resolve. But the truth was I had no desire to barter or plead. It was my ambition to descend upon their camp like an angel from hell, burning them all down to the soles of their shoes. I had no idea how I'd do it, but I was determined to leave that place a smoking ruin.

Still, I knew we were just a couple of city folk going to a camp of lunatics and thieves. I didn't answer.

Joe didn't press me further. He just shook his head and kept walking.

If there was an organizing principle to the roads in Dig Town, I could not apprehend it. It seemed its layout had been conceived by a child. The steam rising from the mine froze in the Martian night and drifted back down over the city in an icy mist, covering the roads in a light snowfall which would burn away at the touch of sunlight. Our footsteps crunched through it, ruining any chances of passing unnoticed. Occasionally I saw a movement at a window as a curtain was pulled aside and a ghostly face peered out, eyes reflecting the weak light in pale green discs. There were rarely any lights on inside; most who still resided aboveground lived in darkness, as though they were preparing to join the others below.

The Strange was already coursing through their blood, changing them. Making them different.

My skin prickled with fear. I imagined that dead miner's friends huddled in the shadows along the road, peering at me from alleys or from behind curtains, sliding long daggers out of their sheaths. A door opened behind us; I turned and saw the shape of a man standing against the star-washed sky, staring after us. Joe yanked me quickly along, not pausing to look himself.

We quickly approached the edge of Dig Town and stopped at a small home on the outskirts, situated at a slight remove from the leaning wooden structures that preceded it. Though it boasted a wooden front wall and even a porch, the rest of it had been built directly into the sloping earth. It seemed a hybrid between the homes around it and the ones you could find back in the Taproots: cheap, earth-made, integrated with Mars in a way our habs in New Galveston never could be.

The warm glow of firelight filled its single window. Joe rapped on the door, the sharp sound of it echoing up the road.

The door swung open. Sally Milkwood filled the opening, one hand on the door and the other holding a rifle under her arm, the barrel hovering a foot above the floor. A cigarette hung from her mouth, and she removed it lazily as she looked us over. She seemed so much bigger up close: nearly six feet tall, thick as a barrel, her short, chopped hair ragged around her face like the nimbus of an evil sun. The furrow in her brow made a single dark line down her forehead. I thought I'd prepared myself for seeing her up close but felt suddenly cut loose from myself, as though the ground were falling from beneath me.

A young woman and a teen boy sat behind her, to either side of the lit hearth. Those two looked so much alike—dirty-blond hair, round, freckled faces—that I understood they must be siblings. They looked familiar to me.

She did not step aside, nor did she put down the rifle. "Joe," she said.

"Hey, Sally. Sorry to drop in on you unexpected."

She just stared at him, waiting.

"This here is Belle Crisp."

"We've met."

"That's right, I guess you have."

"If you've come for a batch, you're too early. I told you you were going too hard. If you've run out, that's your own damn fault."

"That's not why I'm here."

She looked at me, her eyes spearing me to my place. "No, I guess not."

The boy sitting by the fire sauntered closer. He had a wide, moon-like face. I recognized him once he got close enough. "See if she brought any sticky buns," he said. This was Billy Shank, and that must be his ugly sister Laura. I used to see them in school, until one day they stopped coming in altogether and rumors arose that they were running a still. These were Jeremiah Shank's kids. Joe must come here for his goddamned booze.

"I didn't bring shit for you," I said to Billy.

"Since when did you ever?"

Sally leaned her rifle by the door and turned back inside without shutting the door on us. She took a stool in front of the fire and ground her spent cigarette beneath her boot. The place looked like a nest for rats. The floor was unswept and strewn with the clutter of people who didn't give a damn about their own lives: gnawed chicken bones, sand and dirt, bunched laundry, and scraps of paper. A small opening in the back wall led to another room, where I saw the outlines of their still.

After a moment's hesitation, Joe asked if we might come in. When Sally didn't trouble herself to answer him, he took a seat on the floor next to her and held his hands out to the flames. "Come on, Belle. Come sit down."

I stepped inside and closed the door behind me. I couldn't bring myself to sit beside them at the fire, though, hovering instead by the door, cold and hesitant.

Sally looked at me, the fire lighting up the smooth plane of her cheek. The light leapt in her eye; I thought of the dark powers ascribed to the cultists, and I shivered.

"Sit down," Joe said again, and I did. The floor was hard earth with a rug thrown over it; I found it surprisingly comfortable after the long walk. The muscles in my legs were painful and stiff. This would be my first night spent away from my heated hab. I studied the fire and thought that soon we wouldn't even have this crude comfort.

Laura just watched me from Sally's other side, a rail-thin creature of bone, gristle, and bile. She didn't say a word nor react to me in any way I could detect, except to stare the way a farm animal stares at a passing tractor. I felt as though I had stepped into a trap, surrounded by hostile intent, and my chief regret was that I was to be done in by a gathering of fools.

Sally retrieved a tin plate from the floor and started chewing at a chicken leg. The grease covered her hands and her mouth; she ate unselfconsciously, as if no eye could reach her. I watched her, fascinated. She was a thief, apparently a moonshiner, possibly a murderer—but she exuded a power and a presence I was not accustomed to seeing in a woman. Mother had been strong, and Widow Kessler commanded deference no matter where she went in town, but this was something else altogether. There was a danger coiled in this woman that hypnotized me. I was hungry to see it expressed.

"You might as well tell me what you're here about."

"You're gonna take us into the crater to see Silas Mundt," I said. I was shocked by the sound of my own voice. It sounded small and pitiful in this wretched place.

That put her back on her heels, though. She squinted at Joe, the fire lighting their faces, and then she looked at me. I did my best to glare back at her, but I was sure she could sense the fear in me. She chewed for a while as she thought. "What are you up to, Joe Reilly? Why are you taking the Crisp girl?"

"Why are you talking to him? Talk to me, I'm the one in charge. We're going to get my mother back."

I waited for Sally to shut me up, but she looked at me like I'd spoken French. "What the hell are you talking about?" To Joe, she said, "Silas start kidnapping folks now?"

"She means the cylinder," Joe said. "The one with her mother's recording. Silas and his crew took it when, uh . . . when they robbed the diner."

Sally didn't say anything to that right away. She leaned back on her stool and pushed her feet closer to the fire. She stared into the flames for a little while, and when she started to talk, it took me a moment to understand that she was addressing me. "There's a whole way things work out here, a way you don't have any knowledge of. That ain't your fault, because there's no way you would. I'm sorry your diner got hit, and I'm sorry your dad couldn't handle the injury to his pride. But you can't come out here and expect people to—"

"My father ain't to blame for a damn thing that's happened!"

Sally spat into the fire. She looked right at me. "Sure he is. Silas came into his place and made him feel small, and that made him afraid. And see where that got him. Killed some loudmouth horse's ass when all he had to do was push him out the door. Now look at him."

"That man had it coming!"

"Kid, that fool didn't have any more coming to him than a good beating. Your dad couldn't handle his fear, and that's the simple truth. Now you better look to your own before you follow him to the rope."

I couldn't take another word of it. The anger boiled up inside of me and I screamed at her, at Joe, at those other two jackasses sitting like gape-mouthed imbeciles at her side. It was just a wordless sound, a shout of hate, inarticulate and unchained. I kicked a stray mug at my feet and stormed outside, my hands clutching my elbows. I never felt more like a child in my life, but I was afraid that if I stayed there I might go after her with my teeth.

I expected laughter, but no sound followed me out. It was some kind of mercy, I guess. But no one called me back, either. I kept going, walking fast, knowing I risked running into trouble out here but determined to put distance between me and that den of criminals at the very least. The wind was cold, the night so dark it felt like a living presence.

Tears threatened but didn't come. As I stormed down the narrow road, I thought of my father sleeping on that cot in his cell, with just that stupid thin blanket to keep him warm, and nothing but the silence of an empty building to keep him company. I thought of my mother, millions of miles away from me, on Earth.

Was she sleeping now? Was she cold, too?

Yes, I thought. *She's sleeping in the desert, in the custody of thieves. She's sleeping in that cylinder and you can listen to her and talk to her just like Father does as soon as you get her back.*

The thought was like a rebuke: How could I have lost control of myself so easily? How could I have stormed out of that shack exactly like the spoiled child everyone thought I was? I had to go back, despite the shame I'd feel walking back through that door. I imagined the snickering of the Shank kids, the knowing condescension of Joe and Sally, and it made my skin crawl. I didn't know how I'd regain whatever authority I might have possessed, but I had to try. I had to endure the shame, and I had to somehow get Sally to guide us.

Looking around, I realized that I didn't know where I was. Stupid to get lost in such a small community, but the streets made no damn sense. I backtracked along the road I was sure I'd been on, but nothing looked right. Each road kept branching into smaller tributary paths, or joining larger ones, until I couldn't even tell which direction I was headed. I had the notion that the shack was a kind of trickster, winking out of sight as soon as I rounded a corner, only to appear again behind me.

I turned around in the middle of a frozen street, the misty snow falling around me more heavily as the temperature continued to drop. I was wearing a coat, but the heavy gear and the heat tents were with Joe. Fear crawled up the back of my neck. It seemed absurd that I might freeze to death in the middle of Dig Town, standing in a street surrounded by shuttered buildings, but suddenly the possibility pushed every other thought from my head.

A figure emerged from the snowy veil. Then another behind it. Two men, their eyes shining that pale under-leaf green. They wore rough work clothes, the sleeves bunched over their elbows: nothing to protect them from the night. They should have been paralyzed by cold, but they seemed as comfortable as though it were midday.

One of them had an arm in a sling. My stomach dropped.

He said, "That's the girl from the diner."

"I told you."

I turned away from them and started walking.

"Hey, girl. Hold on a minute."

I picked up my pace. I'd forgotten the chill: a flush of fear coursed through me. I had nowhere to go. Their footsteps crunched through the ice behind me.

"I said stop!"

I ran.

I used Dig Town's chaotic layout to my advantage. They knew the town better than I did, of course, but the narrow lanes were so tightly packed that I was able to turn corners faster than they could follow. A weird sound bounced along the walls after me: a mixture of keening and something guttural, something despairing and broken, like an old language articulated by the wrong tongue. A language of monsters. It chilled me, and I ran harder. I had doubled back on myself enough that the tracks were confused—the first thing that saved me that night.

In a few moments I was huddled against the side of a small wooden house, doing my best to quiet my breathing while I heard the men crunch through the crust of ice, trying to find me. I couldn't tell how close they were, but their eerie sounds seemed to come from everywhere.

And then, the second thing that saved me: a woman, tall and angular, emerging from an alley and beckoning to me.

Widow Kessler.

Without thinking, I dashed over to her, the echoes of my own footsteps skittering through the dense little neighborhood. Nothing I could do about that. She grabbed my arm in a vise and hauled me quickly behind her. Snow gusted around us as the wind kicked up, and it seemed to me that we were running through a drift of falling stars. I cast a glance at her face, stern and gaunt, creviced like old rock, only barely lit by the ambient light of this drowsing, haunted town.

Almost since I had known her, she'd been little more than a figure of sorrow, wearing black in mourning for her dead husband, still answering to a name that defined her by his absence. It seemed pathetic to me sometimes, the way she surrendered her full claim to personhood, accepting her new life as a dead man's shadow. To see her now, a flare of purpose and hard motion, was to see someone altogether new.

She was the first adult I had seen act with something other than derangement in a long time; caught in the fog of my own terror, I followed her gratefully.

12

Though most homes were empty, occasional windows shed little blooms of light; we passed them quickly. I could still hear the footsteps behind us, and now I heard one of the men call out, but they sounded farther away than before. I sensed people stirring around me; a curtain was pulled aside and a face appeared in the window. I kept my gaze to the ground, following the widow's dirt-scuffed shoes. Fear clutched my bones. I could sense it in her, too.

"In here, child."

A door opened, from darkness into darkness, and we stepped through it. She shut it behind us. After a brief rustling, a match flared, and the smell of sulfur filled my nose. The Widow Kessler touched the match to a lantern and light flourished, revealing a small, cozy home hung with draperies and decorated with a mixture of the standard-issue furniture that came along with the habs and personal items of polished Earth-wood, the kind only the rich could afford. I was reminded that she was the nominal manager of the mine, and had once been considered part of the rising Martian aristocracy.

I wondered why she chose to live here, in Dig Town, shunning the comforts she could surely afford in New Galveston. My mother once observed that following her husband's death, Widow Kessler had chosen to move into her own grave, and to live there until she was ready to lie in it permanently.

There was only one room here, but a large curtain was bunched in the corner to section off a place for privacy. A simple cot was propped there, along with a small chest, opened to reveal folded clothes of humble design. Although there was less space here than in the habs in New Galveston, it felt larger and less cluttered. More like a home.

She stood there for a moment, looking at me with stern bewilderment, as if I had intruded into her home unannounced and unwelcome, and she had not dragged me here herself.

"What shall I do with her," she said. She was clearly speaking to herself, or perhaps to the dead husband she chained to herself like a dragged weight; an answer was not expected of me. I thought of my father's lonely conversations with my mother and wondered if this was something that happened to all adults who found themselves suddenly bereft of love. It did not seem such a terrible thing: if all one had was a ghost to talk to, one might as well embrace it.

She turned away from me and went to a small range. "Do you like tea?"

I nodded, but her back was to me. "Yes, ma'am," I said after a moment.

"I'll make you some tea."

There was a small table nearby, with two chairs. I thought, perhaps cruelly, that two chairs were an extravagance for a widow. I took one of them.

"What are you doing in Dig Town?" she said.

"I'm getting treads for Watson."

She poured a measure of water from a large clay jug into a kettle and set it on to the range, which I noticed was already glowing with heat. It took the range in our own hab a good five minutes to get that hot—another reminder that she had not surrendered all the privileges of her station. I recalled the searching questions of the miner that night—how much longer until all this runs out?—and wondered if she'd known all along that something like this might happen. A dangerous luxury, perhaps, to keep these items in Dig Town.

"Do you realize coming here might get you killed?"

"That's because everyone in Dig Town is crazy."

She turned to face me, finally. "Is that what you think?"

"That's what everyone thinks."

She gave me her back again and busied herself with preparing the tea. I became preoccupied with the lantern, and the light it spilled through the curtains. Would those men come here?

"Mr. Wickham said most folks have gone into the mine. Is that true?"

"It is," she said. "Though not everyone just yet. You still need to be wary."

This migration into the dark disturbed me. It was cold enough up here; how much worse in the places sunlight had never touched?

"Why?" I asked.

She poured boiling water into mugs and brought them to the table. She took the other chair, and for a moment we might have looked like a sort of family. "The gardens are calling them down," she said at last. "Sooner or later the whole town will be gone. Best thing you can do is go back home and wait it out. Won't be anyone left here to hold a grudge, eventually."

A whole community moving prematurely into their own graves, just like Widow Kessler.

"What gardens?" I recalled the mushroom farm she was said to have growing in her cellar. It occurred to me that isolation and grief might have deranged her thinking in ways not immediately obvious.

When she didn't answer, I said, "Are you going into the mine, too?"

"Not yet. I have business here, first. All in due time." She watched me while I sipped my tea. It was wonderfully hot, with notes of lemon and ginger. I closed my eyes and felt it fill my chest with heat. I felt suddenly exhausted; my life had been thoroughly dismantled over the past couple of days, and right now all I wanted to do was sleep in this safe, warm place.

Widow Kessler seemed to sense it. "Stay the night, Belle. Don't go outside until morning. And when you do, go straight home."

"I can't go home. I have business, too."

"Here?"

"Yes. And then more out there. With Silas Mundt and whoever runs with him."

She didn't receive the information gladly, but at least she didn't try to argue with me anymore. She only seemed sad, as though she realized whatever fate was closing in on us all could not be avoided, despite her every wish and effort. It made me sad, too, and I wondered if I was just like her, only so much younger, and if all my energies were being wasted.

A voice carried in through the window: the injured miner—Charlie—still hunting for me. I was chilled by it; his persistence indicated a derangement stronger than I'd suspected.

Widow Kessler rose from the table and went into the curtained alcove. She pulled the cot away from the wall; its legs made a dull noise against the packed earth. A small rug was laid beneath where the cot had been. She bent slowly to her knees and rolled it up. A trapdoor was there, with a small recess on one side, so you could lift it open.

"What are you doing?"

"They might come here," she said. "You should hide."

I felt cold. "Does that lead to the mines?" Was she giving me over to them after all?

"It's just my cellar. You'll be safe. Just stay in the main chamber. There are two smaller rooms, and you should stay out of them."

Fear welled up inside me, almost overwhelming me completely. "I don't understand! Why are they chasing me? I didn't do anything! *They* attacked *us!*" I heard my voice crack. I put my hands over my face because I couldn't bear for her see to how stupid and scared I felt. "They robbed our diner! Why did they do that? Why does everyone hate us?"

The widow sat opposite me again. "Because you have things, Anabelle. That man was asking you about coffee that night, do you remember?"

I took my hands from my face. "This is about coffee? That's insane!"

"It's not just coffee. It's food. It's eggs and bread and cigarettes and water. It's orange juice. It's milk that comes from cows raised on Earth-grown grass. It's spare cylinders for the Engines. It's oil. It's gasoline."

"We don't even have all those things! And what we do have, we have to buy! It isn't free for us! It's not fair!"

"No. But we're Martians now, Anabelle. 'Fair' isn't a word we use anymore. The people in Dig Town have been abandoned by New Galveston. The miners are left to breathe in more and more of the mineral, and they're treated like something less than human. Don't let them hear you use the word 'fair.'" She went back to the trapdoor and pulled it open in a silent yawn. Trails of loose dirt spilled into the opening. "It's time."

I stared at the hole in the earth. It seemed to breathe cold air, blowing silence into the room. Going down there seemed impossible. Every cell in my body recoiled from it. I considered going outside, trying once again to find my way back to Joe Reilly and Sally, but that seemed impossible, too.

Widow Kessler stood beside the hole, one half of her face cast in the wild light of the lantern, the other a dark mystery. She was a creature of dignity and threat, heavy with supernatural judgment. "Go on," she said. Her voice had an edge to it.

I approached the cellar with reluctance. As I came to its lip, I saw a ladder built into the wall. I could not see the bottom. I looked at the widow's face, but she was already looking behind me, at the door. I turned, a quick pulse of fear surging through me. But the door was still closed. The lantern sent shadows flickering across it.

I descended the ladder into darkness, and the widow closed it over my head. I heard the sound of the rug and the cot being dragged back into place.

I was entombed.

· · ·

I DON'T KNOW how long I stood there in the cold and dark. I suppose it couldn't have been long at all, but it seemed as though I'd slipped into a place measured in time on a different scale. I thought of the observation window in the *Eurydice*, as I waited for some indication that I still belonged to a world defined by heat and light. I thought of what it must have been like for the passengers—for my own parents—to stare through that window into the abyss between the worlds, where time was measured by the lifetimes of suns.

I felt a terror of that darkness. Martian nights are spangled with stars, draped in the sky like necklaces of light, and our twin moons burned like phosphorus. We only knew real darkness when the sandstorms came, and even then we had our own lights to flower into it.

This darkness was absolute.

I extended my hand in front of me and walked until it pressed into the packed dirt of a wall. I ran my palm across it, dislodging granules of sand. It felt cool. I considered pacing around to get the bearings of the cellar, but I remembered the widow's caution about the other rooms, and that stopped me. How big was this room? And how big were the others? It occurred to me that her cellar might extend far beyond the bottom of the widow's small home, might extend into the bowels of Mars itself, like the Throat. This was Dig Town, after all.

The thought paralyzed me and I crouched in place, my breath coming hard and fast.

Widow Kessler's voice drifted from above. I thought she was talking to herself or to her husband's ghost again, until I heard heavy footsteps, and then more voices. I climbed halfway up the ladder so I could hear.

136

"Thank you, ma'am." A male voice.

"Careful, it's hot."

"Hot is most welcome."

Another man's voice: "You seen the girl, Mrs. Kessler?"

"What girl?"

"The one from the diner in the city. She's running around here."

"So?"

"Thought she might of been drawn to the light in your window."

"No one comes here. You know that." A silence stretched. "You sure you won't take some tea yourself, Charlie?"

"Yeah," said the second man. "I guess I might."

As I strained to listen, something touched my face. My whole body convulsed with fear and disgust, and I nearly fell off the ladder. And then I heard a noise coming from somewhere behind me. Scraping against the dirt. It was a small sound, a tiny sound, but in this black chamber it might as well have been a rat scratching against the interior of my own skull. I gripped the rungs of the ladder more tightly, prepared to launch myself through the trapdoor. To my astonishment, my teeth were grinding in rage. I did not like to be afraid, and my body reacted with fury, as if I was somehow entitled not to be scared, as if the machineries of fate had no business figuring me into their calculations. My clenched muscles started to hurt.

My thoughts fled to my pulp stories. I imagined the wicked princesses of Rider Haggard and wished to be one of them. I would transfigure myself into a devouring flame, a princess of hell, expanding until I took this cellar and the widow and all of Dig Town into my burning belly, and then I would grow further still until all of Mars was a lifeless cinder.

More touches landed on my face, brushing it like tiny fingers. Something landed in my hair, and I heard the vibration of an insect's wings. I shuddered, feeling revulsion, but at least this was something mundane, something of the known world. And then I heard a noise—small, barely there at all. I nearly convinced myself that I'd imagined it until I heard it again. It sounded like a scraping footstep.

A voice whispered, "Agatha?"

I whimpered. It was a man's voice. Gravelly, grave-colored. This was not Haggard; this was Hoffmann or Poe.

It said, "Who's there?"

Still I stayed quiet.

"Is this heaven?"

The question frightened me even more than the circumstance. Anyone who would ask it must be mad. Madness unsettled me more than anything else; Mars seemed to draw it out of people, setting fire to some lonely region of the brain and filling their heads with its acrid smoke. I could almost smell it.

I didn't respond. The cellar was filled with an unearthly silence. I couldn't even hear the people above speaking anymore. Had they heard the voice, too? Were they crouched above me, ears pressed to the floor, eyes wide like green lamps?

After an extended silence I crept down from the ladder and stepped quietly onto the dirt floor. I moved forward a couple of steps, arms extended in front of me so I wouldn't walk into anything—or anyone.

"Hello?" I whispered.

No response. I trailed my fingers along the wall and walked

farther, terrified yet unwilling to stay passive for whatever was down here.

The wall came to an abrupt end, and I felt a subtle drop in the air temperature. I was at the threshold to one of the rooms Widow Kessler had told me to avoid. Cautiously, heart beating, I stepped into the archway.

I had been in absolute darkness long enough that an illumination I would have been blind to in any other context stood out like moonlight. Far from where I stood—too far to be part of the cellar—was a faint green luminescence; the same light shade found in the eyes of the Dig Towners. It backlit what looked like a large pile of black stones strewn over the floor between it and where I stood.

I stepped inside, moving closer to it. I attempted to step softly over the nearest rock, about as big around as a cooking pot; the bottom of my shoe brushed against it, and it collapsed in a puff of dust.

It was a mushroom. I remembered immediately the mushroom farm I'd heard that she grew, and felt a mixture of wonder and relief. I'd always imagined it contained in a series of trays, or pots at least; these seemed to grow wild, covering the floor of the small room like a vast carpet.

They led to a gaping tunnel at the far end of the room, going deeper into the ground.

I stepped closer to it and peered inside. There wasn't enough illumination to make out much detail, but it was clear that the tunnel extended for some distance in a steady decline. A chill rippled across my skin. This was where the man had gone. I imagined the tunnel wending deep into the rock, into some deeper Mars, a colder Mars, where the mad lived.

Frightened, I turned away and hurried across the mushroom-covered floor, headed for the cellar's main room. I tripped over something hard and went sprawling into the fungus, releasing a gamey cloud; each torn fungus spilled that pastel green bioluminescence. I yanked my foot away from whatever I'd stumbled over and turned to see what it was.

A skull stared back at me in the weak green light, its jaw yawning open, the mushrooms growing out of it in a thick, choking tide. The rumors came rushing back to me. Zachary Kessler's broken skeleton lay before me like a ruined city.

13

I must have slept. I remember sensing a vast hollowness beneath me, a darkness that seemed sentient and hungry. I felt as though I lay across the surface of a great staring eye, just a drifting mote—not seen at all. I opened my own eyes to discover Widow Kessler leaning over me, her face compressed with impatience. The trapdoor was open behind her head, a halo of pale sunlight. When she spoke to me, I had the sense that she'd been trying to wake me for some time.

"You have to go," she said.

My whole body ached from shivering all night. It hurt to uncurl my limbs; my fingers felt numb. The memory of the man in the darkness gripped me with a cold hand and I started into a sitting position, casting quick glances into every corner. The cellar was still mostly dark, but there was enough ambient light to let me see the shelves filled with canned goods as well as several stacked crates. I also saw two narrow openings on the far side of the room, small portals into chambers where the light did not reach. My dream, almost faded, stirred briefly into sinister life.

"Someone else was down here," I said.

"No one else is here."

"There was! He came out of the tunnel!"

She gripped my arms. "There was no one down here. There is no tunnel. Do you hear me? Now get upstairs."

I didn't need any further convincing. The cellar had taken on an evil quality, and I wanted to be rid of it. She steered me toward the ladder, and I climbed it with all the haste I could muster. Even with Widow Kessler coming up behind me, my skin prickled as I waited for whatever thing I had encountered to lunge out of the far room and drag me into its bone-strewn lair, the widow cackling madly as it pulled me apart.

Upstairs, the curtains over the windows had been pulled back, the sashes thrown open. Light rode in on a cool morning breeze, gracing the edges of a steaming coffee mug she'd placed on the table, burnishing the wood of her modest furnishings so that they looked like the fancy illustrations in magazine catalogues. It seemed even more welcoming and warm than it had the night before, and I was unprepared for that. I was nearly convinced that last night's experience had been a dream after all. I felt a lump rising in my throat. I didn't want to leave, and I told her so.

"They won't bother you for now," she said. "They're calmer in the morning. But I don't want you here when they come back." She gestured at the table. "Have some coffee. I've wrapped some bread for you. Take it and go back to New Galveston."

I sat at her table and sipped the coffee, still hot. "I told you where I'm going."

"Suit yourself then." She seemed disinterested in further conversation. I wanted to press her on the subject of the thing downstairs, the man who had wandered up from the bowels of

Mars and wondered if he'd reached heaven. But I felt I'd taken advantage of her hospitality enough. And, truthfully, I wasn't sure I wanted to know. I had a more urgent task, so I closed the door on the memory. There were enough horrors in the world without hunting for more.

I FINISHED THE coffee quickly and left with the bread tucked under my arm. Dig Town seemed a different place in the sunlight: reduced, banal. Roads that had seemed sinuous and mazelike now just looked haphazard and disorganized, made not after careful planning but by the wandering tread of the people who lived and worked here, ambulating from place to place according to whim. Wooden huts that in darkness had looked like witches' dens now just sagged with the weight of poverty, looking worse to my eye than even the earthen homes of the Taproots. It was as if the terror and threat of the night before was Dig Town's true animating force, and without it the whole place deflated like a collapsed tent.

I resolved that I would find Watson and continue on with my purpose. And when I returned to New Galveston I would do what I could to hurry both Joe Reilly and Sally Milkwood to the gallows.

Despite the town's demystified state, the paths between the buildings were still confusing, and I took a few wrong turns as I tried to find my way back to Mr. Wickham's shop. I started every time I saw someone peering from a window or walking outside.

I guess that's how I stumbled onto the edge of the Throat.

The enormous hole that sat in the very center of Dig Town dominated the settlement like some kind of terrible dark sun.

It existed in a minor depression in the land, ringed by a tall ridge. The buildings were built around its rim and descended the little slope on the exterior side of the hole, so you saw it only if you climbed the wooden stairs to the catwalk along the ridge and looked down toward the center. Six elevators had been constructed along the edges. They served different purposes; some were huge and built with enormous wooden pillars, which seemed designed to haul machinery and loads of ore; while others were smaller and flimsier, probably meant to lift the miners to and from the depths. More stairs descended toward the hole, where several smaller buildings had been constructed on the interior slope. I imagine that at one time this area was the center of the settlement's activity. But it looked like a ghost town now. I saw no sign of life. The darkness of the Throat resisted the morning sun, seeming to radiate from the center of the world.

I was drawn to it, though it stirred a primordial fear in me. It was the original terror, the knowledge of a predatory hunger lurking beyond the firelight's edge. I climbed to the catwalk over the ridge and stepped slowly down one of the interior staircases, its old wood creaking underneath my weight. No sound came from the Throat, though most of Dig Town's population had moved down there. No laughter, no crying, no speech leaked from that pit. Just a profound silence, as though they had willingly descended into death's province. I imagined some pale king sitting on a terrible throne, the clouded eye of every silent woman and man staring at him in awestruck stupefaction.

Reaching the edge of the mine shaft, I dared a peek into its center. Vertigo tugged at my gut, and I lurched onto my backside, scrabbling away from it. Something awful was down there. Something more than the people of Dig Town, something beyond them. Something alive.

I turned my back to the Throat and made my way back up the stairs to the top of the ridge. I felt just as I had in the cellar: like prey, awaiting the grip of jaws on the back of my neck.

EVENTUALLY I FOUND my way back to Mr. Wickham's shop. Joe Reilly leaned against the tin wall beside the front door, which remained closed to him. He didn't try to disguise his relief when he saw me.

"My God, Belle, where the hell did you get to?"

I stopped a few feet away. I didn't like to admit it, but I was relieved to see him, too. At least he was a familiar antagonist. "Widow Kessler took me in."

His eyes flicked past me, as though she might be found ambling along the road behind. He looked back at me then, all bewildered. "Why did you run off?"

"I just . . . I had to get away from her."

"I know you don't like her, but this place isn't safe for you. I figured you at least had sense enough to recall that."

"My recollection is just fine." I decided not to tell him about the miners who'd pursued me last night. He didn't need the validation. "I half expected you to have run off."

His look soured. "So you can sic the sheriff on me? No, I like my life."

"Is she coming with us?" I asked, not wanting to say her name.

"She's coming."

I was surprised to hear it. "I figured she'd take some convincing."

"She's coming for me. Not for you. I told her what you said you'd do to me."

"Good," I said, though I felt a curious shame about it. I wanted to change the subject. "Mr. Wickham won't let you inside?"

"No," he said sheepishly, as I opened the door and allowed myself in. He didn't follow.

The light was better now than it had been last night, and I found Mr. Wickham easily, fussing over Watson's new treads. It was startling to see my friend so fundamentally changed: his legs and pelvis had been removed altogether, and he'd been fitted onto a triangular base, like a little tank. Mr. Wickham was having Watson roll forward an inch, then backward an inch, each time making some minor adjustment in a panel opened on the side of his chassis. Without turning away from his work, he said, "I'm just about finished, Belle. Another minute or two."

I went to one of the many workbenches, pushed some piled scrap to one side, and hoisted myself atop it. I swung my legs unselfconsciously, feeling briefly like a kid again amidst the smell of oil and electricity, and happy for it.

"How long's Joe been out there?" I said.

He shrugged his big hunched shoulders. "Can't say."

"He's not taking me into the desert by hisself."

"Oh no?"

"We're bringing Sally Milkwood."

Mr. Wickham tinkered for another moment without saying a word. Then he closed the panel and gave Watson a gentle pat, as though he'd been a good and patient dog. He wiped his hands with a soiled handkerchief he pulled from underneath a wrench.

I took his silence as an invitation to continue with my revelations. "She was one of the thieves that broke into our diner. A big, mean woman."

"Hold on now, Belle."

"I guess she stays with the Shank kids when she's in town. They live in filthy conditions. I don't think I'd like to imagine what all they get up t—"

"I said hold on!"

Dismayed, I fell silent. Harry Wickham had never once delivered a harsh word to me, but he looked like a circus strongman, and this burst of anger was alarming.

He must have seen it in my face. He sighed and gathered himself. "I don't want to hear that kind of talk about Sally. I realize she's got some issues, but she's a good woman. She don't deserve to be disparaged in that way."

He might as well have opened his mouth and vomited up a pile of slugs.

"Disparaged? I called her a thief, and that's what she is!"

Mr. Wickham stood. He looked at me like I was the one spouting craziness, not him. "She's rough around the edges. I don't know anyone on this rock who isn't. But she's one of the only people I know who I'd trust my life to. Your chances of surviving just improved twice over. She's not stupid like Joe is. But you lip off to her like that, Belle, she won't hesitate to crack you in the mouth. You need to understand that."

"I invite her to try."

He shook his head and offered me the first smile I'd seen in some time. "You know, you just might be mean enough to make her think twice."

14

Watson retreaded and polished, the three of us walked out of Dig Town unmolested, where Sally Milkwood awaited us. She was dressed for travel, wearing the layers necessary for the open desert, a pair of goggles to keep her eyes free of sand—an item neither Joe nor I had thought to bring—and a pack and a rifle slung over her shoulders. I didn't acknowledge her, nor did she acknowledge me. She did spare a dark glance for Watson, though. I filed that away in my catalogue of grievances. We set out onto the hard expanse leading to Peabody Crater at midmorning, none of us content.

The descent into the crater was easily achieved along a series of steep switchbacks not far beyond Dig Town's boundary. They'd clearly been cut from the rock long before New Galveston's founding, and had to be the primary route by which the Moths—and whatever other cultists might lurk in the crater—accessed the plain.

In school, stories of what mysteries might be found there were a favorite currency. We exchanged outlandish inventions about the place. Some of those stories we heard from adults, but usually we just made things up. For all I know, the adults were making things up, too. We regaled each other with tales of ancient alien cities revealed after the passing of one of the frequent dust storms, its glassless windows gaping like the eye sockets of skulls and its long avenues arrayed in impossible mazes, from which you might still hear the desperate, lost cries of the earliest astronauts from Earth carried on the wind; tales of genies rising from their Martian lamps, green-skinned and several-eyed, eager to grant any wish as long as one was willing to pay a devastating toll; tales of earlier human settlements, established in Roman times or even before, suggesting ancient, vanquished attempts to conquer the red planet far preceding our own, leaving only their dry bones as warning to future generations.

Though I knew all of this to be fantasy, the memory of those stories crowded my thoughts. The desert sands shone in bright pastel pinks and oranges, and the sky was butterscotch yellow. I felt like I was walking into a painting. Nothing about my life seemed real or safe.

Watson rumbled along at my side. I imagined he was enjoying his new method of locomotion. He responded to my occasional observations with his customary deference. "Yes, Miss Crisp." "Oh most certainly, Miss Crisp." "I'm quite sure all will be well, Miss Crisp." I found myself quickly impatient with his innate passivity. This wasn't the first time for it, but perhaps it was the most acute since my mother's leaving. I wanted active conversation, not reaction.

I wouldn't find it with the others.

And so we set out on our long, plodding trek.

Untold years of passing dust storms had filled the crater's basin with sand, irregularly dispersed. Sometimes we would encounter steep drifts that could not be circumvented. We would have no choice but to cross, and it was at these times that Watson outpaced us all, his new treads grinding through the drifts as though he were back home in the diner, rolling over a polished floor.

Joe shuffled through the sand with the same unsure step I had: neither of us was accustomed to feeling the ground shift and slide under our feet. Sally, though, moved with a practiced confidence. She drew ahead and had to stop and wait for us about half a dozen times before she resigned herself to matching our own slow pace. I wondered how many times she'd crossed this desert, with or without Silas and his thugs, and what she'd seen along the way. While I understood the value of having someone experienced to guide our journey, I also recognized that her experience placed her firmly in control. My misgivings of the night before were only amplified.

In the daylight, Sally looked younger than I'd guessed last night—maybe in her mid-thirties. But the life she'd chosen for herself was hard. It had already carved lines in her face and put a few strands of gray in her hair. The flat, mean look, though: that I reckoned she was born with. No wonder the Shank kids had fallen in with her. Like calls to like. Still, she was clearly strong and athletic, and I found myself admiring her grudgingly.

"How long will it take us?" I asked.

Nobody answered. Joe was breathing hard, laboring alongside me. Sally walked a few yards ahead and acted like she hadn't heard me at all.

"I asked a question," I said.

Watson said, "I don't know, Miss Crisp."

"I wasn't asking you."

I felt a pang of guilt for snapping at my friend and patted him lightly on the chassis. He couldn't feel it, of course, but it made me feel better about myself.

Joe paused to catch his breath. He wiped sweat from his forehead. I stopped, too, glad he'd been the first to do it. "Sally?" he said.

Sally walked another ten feet before she stopped. She turned back to look at us impassively. She did not seem to be straining herself at all. "We're headed to the rocks out in the middle. Three days. Maybe more, the way you two are going."

"Why did you decide to come?" I was curious, but I was also stalling for time. Each moment she talked was another I got to slow my breathing. Miss Haddersham taught us that Mars was several degrees cooler than Earth, but I stood there sweating like a farmer regardless. I was used to a different kind of work.

"You two idiots would get yourselves killed on your own. You never cross the desert without an experienced guide. Don't they tell you that in the city?"

I shrugged. "Watson is programmed with local knowledge. He has all the basic survival protocols."

Sally just shook her head and laughed. "Shit," she said.

"You ain't gonna convince me that you come out here from charity, or even from guilt. What's the real reason? You planning on betraying me to your cultist friends?"

"I ain't with them," she said.

"You could have fooled me."

"I guess fooling you wouldn't be no challenge."

"You sure are trying hard not to answer the question."

Sally smiled at me. "You're a firecracker, ain't you?"

"I told you," Joe said.

Though she might have meant it as a compliment, it felt demeaning. *Look at the little girl, all full of brimstone. She sure is cute!* I wondered how hard it would be to shake free of her.

"I'm going because of Joe. And because I think this fool quest of yours is interesting. That's all you need to know."

It wasn't, though. It didn't tell me anything. "What about the Shank kids? Ain't they gonna flounder without you?"

"Hell, Laura Shank runs that still and takes care of her brother. I got nothing to do with it. I don't take care of them, they take care of me. When I'm in town, at least, which I try not to be too often. And now I'm done explaining myself to a child. Are you two ready to start walking again?"

Joe sighed. "Ease up, Sally. This isn't a race."

"The hell it isn't. Get moving."

She turned and started marching again, and we had no choice but to follow. We slid down one dune and climbed another, over and over, hour after hour. At the crest of each new hill I expected to see some variation in the landscape, but there was nothing—just more waves of sand, pink and rust-colored, for as many miles as the eye could hold, the wall of the crater on the far side just a faint discoloration on the horizon. Watson carried on behind us, and already I could hear the grit collecting in his gears. His grand moment of clean circuitry hadn't even lasted a single day. It occurred to me for the first time that this trip might be fatal to him, and that was almost enough to turn me around. What good would it do to get my mother's cylinder back if I didn't have an Engine to run her?

Finally, Sally came to a stop. She peered around for a few moments before declaring that we would camp here for the night. I could detect nothing special about this location that might recommend it over any of the other identical locations we had slogged through the last several hours, each minute of which I felt pain shooting up my calves and pulsing in my shoulders. I knew from his heavy breathing that Joe felt it too. And now it seemed that even Sally Milkwood, though she was born of devil's stock, must have been suffering at least a little discomfort.

Phobos peered over the rolling horizon, about to begin its second circuit across the sky. It was bone white in the late afternoon light. The sky had shaded to a faded rouge, and a low wind—the first movement of air all day long—started to kick up. Night was still at least an hour away, but when it came it would do so quickly and brutally; we would not want to be caught fussing with our camp when the temperature went into free fall.

Joe slid the backpack from his shoulders with a groan, dropping it to the sand. He yanked a few strings and the whole thing unfurled like a set of workman's tools. He pulled two folded heat tents from their places and began to set them up. They were designed to seal the cold weather out and generate enough heat within to keep one person safe and comfortable. I'd seen them for sale before, but this would be my first time spending the night in one. They looked cramped and unpleasant. I didn't think I was claustrophobic, but I guessed I'd soon find out.

Sally had her own, which she also assembled in short order. Watson would be fine in the cold, though I would wrap him in a tarp to protect him from as much of the blowing sand as I could. It all seemed very mundane.

And yet, I was overwhelmed with a feeling that I had crossed a forbidden border, that I had transgressed into a place hostile to me and to my purpose. Even the strangeness of Dig Town and the widow's basement seemed somehow tame compared to this new feeling. At least the people there were known to me once. If they were different, it was because I could compare them with who they used to be.

This, though: this was altogether new. Something seemed to be hidden behind the banal face of the landscape. Something wary and curious.

I turned from my examination of the desert to find Sally staring at me. "You feel it?"

My instinct was to deny anything she thought she saw in me—I wished to remain entirely inscrutable to her. "I don't feel anything but tired."

"And here I thought you were smarter than the rest."

The compliment worked to soften me, and I damned myself for it. "I do feel something," I said. "What is it?"

Instead of answering me, she gestured at Joe, and the two of them walked several feet away from the campsite. They turned their backs to me and Sally started talking. It left me with an ill feeling. Joe Reilly was out here because I had threatened his life; were they planning to leave me out here alone? Were they planning to kill me? It suddenly seemed not only plausible, but their most reasonable course of action.

I looked at Watson standing beside my little tent. I knew he could be of no help.

"Watson, I might have made a mistake."

His head swiveled toward me. "A mistake, miss?"

"Coming out here with them."

"I see. But how else might you recover the stolen cylinder? The sheriff did not seem inclined to help."

"I don't know. But I'm worried about those two. Joe I could handle, but Sally scares me."

He turned his head again, taking them in. The sun had dipped below the horizon, and evening was falling fast. His rich orange eyes glowed like lamps in the twilight. "She is rather coarse," he said.

"Can you hear what they're saying?"

"I cannot. Shall I go ask, Miss Crisp?"

"No." I tried to rub some warmth back into my arms. I didn't want to get into the tent while they were still conferring. "Will you protect me from them?" I hated asking the question, hated the way it made me feel, but I was cold and alone and Watson was the only one here I could trust.

"I am a Kitchen Engine, Model 17643. I am not programmed for conflict."

Of course I knew that. Everything extraneous to that simple duty was artifice. His namesake, from the stories, was an ex-British soldier turned medical man. He was strong, devoted, and capable. Utterly loyal. That used to provide me with great comfort. It was like having a strong uncle to watch over me. Now it just seemed stupid. His whole personality was nothing more than a pretty decoration, like a hood ornament on an automobile. Why did I keep forgetting that?

"Just wake me up if they try to come near my tent, okay?"

"Yes, Miss Crisp."

"Thank you." I felt better despite myself. I resisted the urge to kiss him on the cheek.

The temperature was dropping rapidly. Stars began to frost the sky, and both moons shivered among them. The others were still talking—well, Sally was, while Joe stood there and listened—but I could see their breath clouding, and I knew they wouldn't last much longer. My will broke, and I turned toward my tent. I dropped to my knees, preparing to unzip the end of it, when Watson spoke to me.

"Miss Crisp? What is that, if you please?"

He was looking some distance ahead of us, where sand began to ripple in another series of dunes. I followed his gaze.

Something like a centipede as long as a wagon train undulated over the peaks, turning over itself, looping in great, sweeping circles. It looked for all the world as though it were in a state of joy, as though it were cavorting like a filly in a field. Its body was black. Long, cruel-looking spines ran along its back, coruscating with flickering colors arcing between them like electrical charges. It moved in complete silence, running over the dunes with as much ease as I might tread a wooden floor. And then it seemed to climb directly into the air, where it looped over again and descended back to the shifting ground. There was nothing like this supposed to be living on Mars anymore, nothing larger than the palm of a human hand; and yet there it was, defying gravity, defying extinction itself.

One of the fabled ghosts of Peabody Crater. I was reminded that granules of the Strange blew in the wind with the sand down here.

I watched it mutely, in the grip of a sudden unaccountable happiness. Joe and Sally, having ceased their talk, watched it, too.

We stood transfixed.

"Will it come up here?" I asked. As though I'd broken a spell, I suddenly realized how cold I was. My voice shook, my body trembled.

They both turned to me. They looked like they'd forgotten I was there. "No," Sally said.

There was nothing else to say. I wanted to keep watching, but the chill was becoming unbearable. I knelt down and slid into my heated tube; Joe and Sally retreated to theirs as well. As I zipped myself inside, I glanced up at Watson once more. He had not moved from his position. His eyes glowed brightly as he continued to watch the miraculous creature's glittering configurations in the night. Not for the first time, and not for the last, I wondered what secret thoughts warmed the copper coils inside his head.

15

When we woke up the next morning, everybody wanted to act like nothing happened. Joe and Sally crawled out of their tents and broke them down. Afterward Joe went over to the little stove and started making some coffee. Sally walked down the slope a ways and took a moment to survey the landscape. The dunes were empty now; I couldn't see any tracks where that giant creature had done its cavorting, and I suspected it had never left any to begin with. I waited for one of them to say something, but no one did.

"Well, ain't we gonna talk about it?" I said.

Neither one of them acted like they'd heard me. It was as though I had taken up with a pair of vegetables.

"You saw that worm last night, right, Watson?"

Watson, who had kept vigil beside my tent all night, and who had found no cause to rouse me, confirmed that I had not dreamed it. "I saw the creature, though I don't believe it was a worm."

I knew he was right. In school we learned that the things people saw in the crater were reflections of what was in our minds, or echoes of things that had lived in some ancient time.

But it was one thing to read about it and another to actually see it.

I walked over to the stove and waited for the coffee to get ready. Joe, having exhausted the small list of tasks with which he could busy himself before our trek resumed, sat cross-legged beside me, staring at the little flame beneath the pot. He would not look at me, nor did he look at Sally. He seemed to be in a different place entirely. I wanted to bring him back to where I was: cold, disoriented, uncertain.

"You ever seen anything like that before?" When he kept up his pretense of pretending I wasn't there, I grabbed a handful of sand and threw it at him, in case he needed tactile evidence of my existence.

He blinked and rubbed the grit from his eyes with his thumbs. "Goddamn it, Anabelle!"

"You craving your whiskey?"

Something dark came into his face. "That's not funny."

"Neither's acting like you can't hear me when I'm speaking to you. I asked you a question."

Before Joe had a chance to answer me, Sally came sauntering up, her thumbs hooked in her belt and a mean little smile on her face. "Who the hell you think you're talking to, kid? Your dad let you sass him like that at home? Ain't nobody whupped your ass for you yet?"

This was the second time someone had threatened to beat me for not tucking tail in deference to the idea they had of themselves. I recognized a signal moment unfolding here: Sally wanted to make plain her control. I wasn't about to let her have it.

"Some have tried," I said.

159

She threw her head back and laughed—a series of big, booming *haws* that flew like cannonballs over the open miles. "And what," she said, "you snatched the leather from their hand and delivered a lesson of your own? Who was it tried to chasten you, a little rosy-cheeked cherub from the cradle?"

I felt my face flush. "You stay away from me."

"Girl, I'm gonna knock you on your ass. You been acting like some queen bee ever since I first saw you. You think you're something special because you can push a drunk around? Try *me*, brat. You think you scare me with your threats of the law? The law's gonna hang your daddy for murder. The law sure as hell ain't no friend of yours."

"You don't know what you're talking about," I said.

She smiled at me. "No? Honey, I got all kinds of experience with the law. I know exactly what I'm talking about. Your daddy killed a man. What did you think they were going to do?"

"Come on now, Sally," said Joe.

"You shut up, Joe. You didn't feel like you had a thing to say when she was laying into you, don't start finding your gumption now. You know I'm right, anyhow."

I waited for Joe to argue with her—prayed for him to do it, reduced once again to hoping a grown-up would come to my rescue—but he just turned back to the stove, lifting the pot off the flame and pouring coffee into his mug. Steam billowed from inside it, clouding in the cold air. I wondered suddenly if my father would ever drink another cup of coffee.

I was paralyzed by my fears, by the impossibility of the situation. Both my parents needed me to save them. Both were slipping out of my grasp, leaving me stranded in this haunted place on my own, surrounded by criminals and by a madness that blew out of the very ground.

I must have looked like quite the fool, standing there while these terrors ran loose across my face, because Sally laughed. "First step out of the playpen is rough, ain't it, honey?"

"I hope you die out here, you bitch," I said. And so I surrendered, resorting to simple name-calling, the basest of retorts—and one that played on her womanhood as well. Mother would have been ashamed of me.

And yet it found its mark. "I told you what I'd do," Sally said, and she stepped toward me with her arm cocked for a backhanded blow. I braced for it, but there was no need. Watson, moving with a speed I did not think him capable of, lurched forward and interposed himself between Sally and myself. He inched forward, his huge metal bulk pressing Sally backward.

"Desist," he said.

Sally retreated a few steps, and Watson kept pace. After about five feet he stopped, allowing her to create some distance between them. She stared at him with a kind of grim acceptance. I, on the other hand, felt both terrified and elated; I had not thought Watson capable of anything like this. Joe rose from his place by the stove, the coffee cup still in his right hand. They both looked more affected by this development than they had been by the glittering centipede of the night before.

"You'll refrain from laying hands upon Miss Crisp."

"You don't talk to me," Sally said, her tone diminished.

She fixed a baleful glare first on Watson, then on me. The moment stretched. I felt compelled to offer an explanation, even an apology, for this unprecedented behavior; but there was no explanation. And she deserved no apology.

She turned away from us and finished packing her tent. After a moment, Joe followed her cue. He tossed the rest of the coffee into the sand and started breaking down the stove. I stood beside Watson, unsure how to feel about anything. The world had slipped its tracks and was careening in a dark direction.

Soon, we were packed. Sally led us off without a word. The rest of us fell in behind her.

16

Mars is ghost country. I know this better now than I did then, of course, but on that journey I began to get my first true sense of it. The cavalier attitude Sally took to the centipede unnerved me. I could have accepted it if they'd been as dismayed as I was, but the fact that they took it in stride suggested to me that the desert was haunted ground, that the spirit of an extinct animal was no more cause for comment than seeing a family dressed for Sunday service.

As the day wore on, I saw more of them. I'd catch glimpses from the corner of my eyes. I'd turn my head subtly, hoping to catch them unawares, only to find nothing there.

Even Joe started to react after a while. His attention would be snared by something and his whole head would whip around; I could tell by his increasing distress that he had no better luck than I did. He'd end up squinting into the distance, as though something was hiding from him just around the corner of the sky.

One likes to think of ghosts as residents of darkness, but they teemed in the rusty sunlight. Figures appeared distantly, usually alone but sometimes in small groups, too far away for me to note any particular features. Occasionally I would see the peaks of towers or long, hulking structures larger than any building I had seen in my life; a kind of awe would overcome me, and then these structures would be gone, as though blown away by a gust of wind. Once, as we crested a tall dune, we saw what looked like a caravan a mile in length, made up of lumbering, many-legged beasts of burden hauling carriages of multiple tiers, or strapped with what looked like small wooden buildings on their backs, spangled with glittering baubles and long tassels, topped with covered platforms on which strange figures reclined while attended by servants waving great fans. I couldn't make out much detail, except to know that they were not human beings. The caravan was visible for so long that I became sure it was real, and that we had stumbled across evidence of a living alien civilization. But I turned my head once to see if Sally and Joe saw it, too, and when I looked back, it was gone.

Only one set of phantoms came close to us. For a solid hour, two figures walked side by side in tandem with us, only a hundred yards off. They wore the heavy, clumsy coats and crossed bandoliers of the United States Martian Brigade, from the time the US skirmished with Germany for control of the Peabody Crater. I recognized their uniforms from our history textbook. That engagement had been settled in 1896; that should have made them middle-aged men, but they looked only a few years older than I was.

I felt a curious absence of fear. I broke off from the group and headed toward them. I wanted to talk to them; I wanted to see if they were capable of talking, to see if they knew what they were.

Sally called to me. "Get back here."

I continued walking. The men took no notice of my approach.

A hand grasped my elbow, and I wheeled around to confront Joe Reilly. I tried to wrench my arm away, but he held fast.

"Let go of me!"

"Come back, Anabelle."

"I said let go!"

"Will you please come back?"

Behind him, Watson turned on his treads and began to close the distance between us. Sally remained where she was, watching to see what transpired.

"Watson's almost here," I said. I knew it rattled him.

"So what? He's a dishwasher."

I didn't have to say that something had changed in Watson, the way it had changed in the very landscape we crossed. We'd passed into a new territory, into wild Mars, and new rules applied.

Watson came closer. He did not call out as he normally did; he came in silence, and I was surprised to find that this unnerved me, too. "Let go," I said again, and this time when I pulled my arm, Joe released it.

Joe turned to face Watson, his hands held up in front of him. "Ease off, can opener. I let her go."

"Are you all right, Miss Crisp?"

His orange eyes seemed bright, even in the midday sun, as though something was on fire inside him. I was uneasy, and I did not want to feel that way around my friend. "I'm fine, Watson."

Watson ignored me. "You'll refrain from laying hands upon Miss Crisp." His new mantra.

Joe bristled. "You're a goddamn Engine," he said. "You're a tool, nothing more. You open your mouth to me again and I'll strip that cylinder down to basic functions."

"Joe!" Sally's voice carried like the crack of a whip.

Joe glanced at her. She shook her head. That seemed to be enough. To me, he said, "If she calls you back, it's because she's trying to save your fool life. You don't go wandering off out here. Are you crazy?"

I looked back toward where the soldiers had been; of course, they were gone now. Nothing but empty sand in every direction. "I wanted to know if they were real," I said. "Don't you want to know?"

"No," he said. "I sure don't. Let's keep on."

He glared at Watson and turned his back to us. He kept walking, trusting us to follow.

We did. "Are you all right, Watson?" I asked, keeping my voice quiet.

The sand in his gears cracked and ground as he trundled along. "I seem to be somewhat out of sorts," he said.

"Should I be worried?"

He looked at me, the glow of those eyes casting light on my face. "Never you, Miss Crisp."

Somehow that did not put me at ease. Once we had all gathered again, Sally continued on, offering no commentary on what had just occurred.

One thing troubled me about the ghosts. We were told in school that they were manifestations of our thoughts and dreams, that the Strange somehow affected what we saw. *They're mirages,* Miss Haddersham had said. But if that was true, why was I seeing things I'd never even imagined before? And why were we all seeing the same things, creatures that hadn't existed on Mars for thousands of years?

Who exactly was doing the dreaming?

• • •

LIKE THE NIGHT before, we began to set up camp about an hour before nightfall. None of us had spoken much since I'd tried to interact with the phantoms, except Watson, who had taken to muttering what sounded like rhyming couplets. I'd felt a chill when I first realized it. When I asked him what he was saying, he seemed surprised, and claimed he didn't know what I was talking about. Engines weren't supposed to lie, unless it was part of their cylinder's programming. It certainly wasn't part of his.

Until that point, Sally had been the dominant presence in our little group; our attention turned to her when it came time to make any decision, and when she spoke, it carried the authority of a judge. I didn't like it, but I couldn't pretend otherwise. She cowed my rebellious nature in a way no one else had managed to do. I think it was because I believed her capable of any action. Her threats—all unspoken, transmitted through her eyes—were not idle.

But Watson had changed that. His threatening posture against Sally this morning, his warning to Joe this afternoon, and his odd behavior since then had shifted the dynamic. Now all our apprehensions were directed toward him.

Not him, I thought. *It.* I felt bad for thinking that, as though I were betraying him. But Watson was an *it*. Any personality he displayed was a function of the cylinder installed in his head. I had to remember that.

It was an Engine. That was all. And something was going wrong with it.

Once Joe had the fire going, he slopped something out of a tin can and into a skillet. In a few minutes I smelled ham and kidney beans. The wind carried that scent across the desert. My stomach growled. We hadn't eaten since breakfast. Sally pushed us too hard.

"Come by the fire, Anabelle," Joe said. "Get some grub."

I went eagerly, Watson in tow.

"The Engine can stay where it is," Sally said.

For once, I was grateful for her input. "Wait by the tent, Watson."

"If you like," he said.

Soon enough we were seated around the fire, its dancing light playing over our faces, shoveling food into our mouths. We wore blankets draped over our shoulders. I watched the smoke rise into the darkening sky, where it seemed to carry all the way out to the stars, dissipating into the dark wash of space. I could see a few familiar shapes in the stars, but I couldn't recognize any of their names. I regretted not paying attention in school.

Joe gestured at me with his bowl, speaking around a mouthful of beans. "What's wrong with your Engine?"

"Nothing," I said.

"Bullshit."

"He just don't like you, I guess."

"He's haunted," Sally said.

Joe looked from me to her. The firelight reflected in his eyes and made them look big and scared. I wanted to be glad about that, but it only made me feel scared, too. "Bullshit," he said again.

"It ain't bullshit. Ghosts run wild out here. We seen it all day. They can get caught up in the Engines. I seen it more than once. You'll see it, too, when we get to where we're going."

I looked at Watson, standing sentry by my little tent. His eyes shed an orange light, but the rest of him was cast in darkness.

He looked like a creature from a fairy tale—something stumbled from a dark wood, lured by the moon. I felt cold inside.

As if summoned by an invocation, ghosts appeared around us in the darkness, too: phantoms curling in the wind with the sand from the dunes, rising up in breezy spirals, coalescing into the suggestion of a form, and then dissolving into the wind like blown seeds. They seemed capricious, dancing just outside the light of the fire, teasing us with half shapes and almost sounds.

"You see them?" Joe said. His voice was a whisper.

I nodded.

"Of course I see them," Sally said.

"I don't like that they're paying attention to us. They weren't doing that before."

Sally shrugged, finishing off what was left in her bowl.

"Is that bad?" I said.

"It's why I'm pushing us so hard," she said. "They'll get bolder."

"But they're not even real!" The illogical nature of the whole thing infuriated me. It was ridiculous to be afraid of figments.

And yet I felt the stirrings of real fear. Sally was the one among us who had been out here many times, and there was no mistaking her apprehension. She tried to hide it, but I could see it there nonetheless, coiled behind her eyes and behind all the muscles in her face.

"It's not them that's the threat," she said. "It's what follows them. Too many of them ghosts around and they might as well be a beacon for the things that live out here."

"Like what?" I said.

She cast a dark look at Watson. "Things like him. Engines with cylinders gone feral."

"Watson's not feral," I said weakly, avoiding her true point.

"Not yet," she allowed. "But there are others have been out here a lot longer. War Engines left over from the conflicts with Germany. They have ghosts in their heads, and engaging in any way with these phantoms tends to bring them out. It's like they can hear each other. It's best you don't get them worked up."

The War Engines. I'd managed to forget about them somehow, caught up as I was with the spirits, and with Watson's odd behaviors. I felt a different kind of terror begin to build, this one much more immediate. War Engines were not figments.

"Well, what are we supposed to do?" I tried to ask it in a reasonable tone, but I seemed to be well past that now; I could hear the fear in my voice, I could feel it crawling up my throat.

Joe kicked my foot with his own. He smiled at me. "The fearless Anabelle Crisp, ready to soil her britches over some shapes in the wind."

I looked at him like he'd just slapped me, and for a moment anger occluded the fear.

"I'm just messing with you, kid," he said. "Don't hurt me. And I mean that, by the way. My pride's taken enough of a beating these last few days."

I took some long breaths, settling myself. Sally lit up one of her cigarettes, ignoring the both of us, finding her own peace.

"I saw you looking up at the stars a few minutes ago," Joe said. "You know the constellations?"

I looked up at them again. The longer I stared at them, the calmer I felt. It was easy to let your mind drift out there with them, riding up on the smoke from this cooking fire to sail out into the gulf; free from this cold planet, the ghosts in the desert, the feral Engines, the neighbors who smiled to your face and ransacked your whole life when you were knocked down. Free from the whole madhouse.

"No," I said.

"Too busy skipping school, hanging out in spaceships?" He was still smiling at me; he was trying to be my friend. It made me sad in a way I couldn't put words to. When I didn't answer, he said, "I had to learn to navigate by the stars to be a pilot. In case our systems went down, and I had to steer us with nothing but the naked eye. Those names were pretty dull, though. Some were just strings of numbers as long as your arm. I always preferred the names of the constellations."

"Well, do you know them?" I asked.

He looked a little sheepish. "Not many. Mostly I just know the strings of numbers."

Sally pointed to a pattern of stars a few inches above the crater's distant edge. "That there is the Big Dipper. You see how it looks like a pot?"

"Everybody knows about the Big Dipper," I said, trying to keep my voice even. "That's the only one everybody knows."

She scoffed. "Well, did you know it's just part of a constellation called the Big Bear?"

"Ursa Major," Joe said.

"Which means Big Bear, right? The ladies are talking, Joe. You just button it for a little while."

I smiled despite myself.

"Over there, that's Cassiopeia. And over there is Orion, you can tell by those three stars that make his belt. What kind of stars would we see if I yanked down his britches, what do you think, Joe?"

Joe turned away so I couldn't see his face.

Sally was already back to me. "You know about Chauncy Peabody, right?"

"First man to land on Mars," I said, suddenly bored. If she was going to try to play Miss Haddersham, I was going to bed. It was getting cold enough that it might be the best idea for us all, anyway.

"Sure. Everybody knows that, too. Do you know where he landed?"

"Let's see, could it be Peabody Crater?" I said. "Could that be it?"

"Goddamn right. Smashed right into a rock all loaded up with the Strange. I bet you don't know what happened to him."

"Yes, I do," I said, feeling testy. "He got lost and died of dehydration, and his ship was tracked by some dumb friend. This is little-kid stuff, everybody knows it. It's cold and I'm going to bed."

Joe seemed to think this was a good idea. He grunted his concurrence, breath clouding in front of his face.

But Sally wasn't done. "You think he landed in the Strange and what happened to him was he just didn't drink enough water? You better believe that's little-kid stuff, smart-ass. You want to know what really happened?"

I watched her across the dwindling fire. She smiled at me, her teeth dull and crooked, but she looked angry somehow. Like something boiled inside her and caused her a pain that wouldn't abate.

"How would you even know, anyway?"

She leaned back and smiled for real, satisfied. I'd asked the question she'd been waiting for. "I asked him, that's how."

I'd had enough. Peabody had landed on Mars in 1864; even if he hadn't died of thirst, he'd be dead of old age by now. I stood up and walked back to the tent. I was tired of adults thinking I was stupid just because I was still a kid. I decided I wouldn't argue with them about it anymore, especially not these two idiots; I would just turn around and leave. And anyway, it was cold and I was tired. It was time for sleep.

"Go on and walk away then," she said. "You *are* a little smart-ass. You'll see soon enough."

Joe said, "Sally—"

"Squeeze some more juice into that fire, Joe."

"It's cold, Sally."

"We got a little while yet. I'm thirsty, aren't you?"

Something was going on between her and Joe—that much was obvious. I was still a child, but I knew enough about the jittery energy between men and women. Though my own parents' relationship had always seemed sedate to me, I'd seen enough calamities of the heart from other people around town to recognize the tension here.

I'd never felt it myself, not for any of the boys in New Galveston, nor the girls either. It wasn't a thing I missed or wished I felt, mostly because I only ever thought about it when I had to listen to Dottie or Brenda back at school get all moony over one of the fool boys around town. I wasn't conscious of its absence at all.

Maybe that's why I was so curious about the dynamic between Joe and Sally. It seemed different, too.

Joe sighed and went to get the fuel canister. He came back with a flask of whiskey, too. As the fire flared to life again, I saw a phantom retreat to the darkness beyond its light: a shimmering, flowing whiteness, there and gone. Another behind Sally did the same. They rose and fell at the firelight's edge, dozens of them, dipping farther into the distance and returning, like curious feral dogs.

AT SOME POINT in the middle of the night, Watson woke me up. He was whispering so as not to wake the others.

"Miss Crisp. Miss Crisp, can you hear me?"

I blinked, staring through the small plastic window that afforded me a view outside. It was deep night. The stars were a crystalline field overhead, Deimos a cold flare among them. The interior of the tent was warm; the blanket wrapped around me felt like protective arms.

"What is it, Watson?"

"I'm frightened."

I wanted to go back to sleep. Not because I was tired, but because I didn't want him to say any more. It was impossible that an Engine should be frightened. He didn't even understand the concept.

"Why?" I said quietly.

"When I entered conservation mode, I was in another place. And yet I was here at the same time. It was a mushroom garden, and it went on for many miles. It was full of floating green stars. How is it possible that I can be in two places at the same time?"

I turned over, tears in my eyes. I wasn't frightened exactly, and I wasn't sad. But I had begun to mourn something. I didn't know what.

"You just had a bad dream, Watson," I whispered, my voice quavering. "Just a bad dream."

17

The War Engines found us the next day. We'd been traveling untroubled by spirits or even arguments since wrapping up our tents and setting out, and I had begun to allow myself the hope that we would continue that way for as long as the daylight lasted. Joe and Sally walked beside one another, talking quietly and amiably. I noticed, however, that Sally walked with her rifle unslung, held loosely in her left hand.

"You plan on shooting phantoms?" I asked her once, and she ignored me.

Watson would not leave my side, and his presence kept the others at a distance. He didn't mention the midnight conversation we'd had, and I didn't bring it up. I was trying to convince myself that I'd been the one who was dreaming.

A ragged hole erupted in Watson's chassis below his shoulder, and what sounded like several fat insects whizzed by my ear. A split second later I heard a heavy *thumpthump-thumpthumpthump* echoing from the dunes. I stood stock-still, looking around like a rube. A part of my brain had figured it out, but my body just couldn't catch up. Somebody shouted something and then Joe tackled me from behind.

The breath went out of me and my face dug into the sand.

"Goddamn it, girl, I said get down!"

I heard another series of *thumps*—it was a heavy gun, of course. I knew it, I *had* known it. "Get off me!"

Joe paid me no heed. I spat sand from my mouth and tried to get a look around. His forearm was pressing down on my back and it was hard to breathe.

Sally's voice came from behind us. "She hit?"

Joe's breath was hot in my ear. "Are you hit?"

"No!" I yelled. "Who's shooting at us? What the hell kind of gun is that?"

"One of them War Engines I was telling you about last night," Sally said. "They have Gatlings. I should've seen the bastard. He must've been coming out of the sun."

Relics of the war with Germany for the control of Mars in the late nineteenth century, War Engines were massive machines designed for traveling desert terrain and eliminating human beings in as efficient and ruthless a manner as possible. They were supposed to have been decommissioned thirty years ago and dismantled for parts, their cylinders melted, as part of the peace treaty with Germany, but the will to see the job done waned after a while. And the US government didn't seem to mind as long as they were confined to the crater and only shooting cultists.

"They're supposed to be destroyed!" I said helpfully.

Joe said, "You want to break it to him or should I?"

Another series of bullets cut through the air.

Watson hadn't moved. He stared in the direction the shots had come from. The echoes didn't confuse him the way they did us. Or me, at least.

I was worried for my friend. Those bullets would tear through his chassis like paper. The one hit he'd taken left a hole I could reach my arm through. I struggled against Joe, but he held me down easily.

"Watson! Get out of the way! Go hide!"

"I'm quite safe, Miss Crisp."

"No, you're not!"

I watched Sally crawling through the sand toward us. She pushed herself forward with her knees and elbows; her teeth were bared in an animal rage. "All of you, shut up!" she hissed. "It's over a rise, it can't see us if we're low."

"It can see Watson!"

"I said shut up!" She came abreast of us, then stopped, listening for a sign. For the moment, there were no more shots.

"It don't want to hurt an Engine," Sally whispered. "It wants us. So let it fix on Watson for a minute. You follow me over that ridge ahead. We have to be quick. It'll be on the move."

I looked to where she indicated. The sand formed a hillock not ten feet from where we sprawled. It was a small mound, but from this vantage point and under these conditions it seemed like it might as well have been the face of a cliff.

"Girl," Sally said. I looked at her. She must have seen the fear on my face. "I'll go first, and you follow. Joe will come behind you. Don't stand up and run, you hear me? Stay crawling. You'll be okay. Just make sure you keep moving."

I nodded. Joe shifted off me, and suddenly my lungs could fill again. The urge to leap to my feet and charge that mound as fast as I could was profound. It took great concentration to keep it smothered.

A voice carried over to us, from the shooter's position. "Anabelle?" It sounded bereft, tear-choked. *"AnabeeeeeeEELLE?"* The word escalated into a shriek.

It froze me. I looked to Sally and Joe: their faces had drained of color. Why was he calling for me?

"It's not an Engine, it's a man," Joe said, incredulous. "Is it one of Silas's goddamn cultists? What the hell is he shooting at us for?"

"Hey!" Sally called. "Stop shooting, you goddamn fool! It's Sally! I got Joe here with me! For chrissakes!"

She was answered with a wail of anguish and another burst from the Gatling gun. Sand showered onto us from the top of the dune.

"Who's coming after you who would shoot at us?" Joe said.

"I don't know," I said, panic speeding my blood. But I did know. The miners. Charlie and his friend. They must have been tracking us all this time. I couldn't understand it. It would take more than anger to drive them all the way out here, more than rage. This was madness.

And where would he get a gun like that?

"We're sticking with the plan," Sally said. She scuttled ahead, her whole body pressed flat. I wanted to wait and see if she made it before I tried for it myself, but when she was about halfway there, Joe started prodding me. I eased forward, my blood loud in my ears, my breath coming in quick gasps. My body felt enormous, as conspicuous as some engorged fly crawling over a porcelain dish. I waited for the slugs to hit me, to punch holes through me and into the sand. I imagined my blood pouring into them, all my life spilling away, Mars gulping it down like some carrion feeder.

Sally reached the apex. I heard more shots, but they went wild. I was next.

This seemed foolish. If we passed over this small hill, there would only be more hills, an endless stretch of them. This deranged cultist had only to follow our obvious tracks as we crawled from dune to dune, until either he got a clear shot or exhaustion decided the issue for us.

I must have stopped. Joe hissed: "Go!"

The grumble of rotors sounded close behind me; Watson had positioned himself between me and our predator. He was a massive metal edifice, glinting in the low sunlight. Encouraged, I crawled faster, until I reached the little summit and practically rolled down the other side.

"Anabelle!"

"You want her, you dumb shit?" Sally yelled. "Come on and get close!"

Watson followed. I waited for another fusillade to rip him apart, but nothing happened.

Sally was waiting for me. She ignored Watson, watching for Joe. In another moment he was over as well. No further shots followed.

"Did you get a look at him?" she asked.

"I wasn't really keen on sticking my head up."

"Watson?" I asked. "Did you?"

"A glimpse, Miss Crisp."

"Well, why the hell didn't you say so?" Sally spat.

"Don't yell at him. He don't just volunteer stuff, you got to ask him things. Ain't you ever had an Engine before?"

"Hell no I haven't, and I wouldn't, either."

"Ladies," said Joe. "Maybe another time?"

Ignoring them both, I turned to Watson. "What did you see?"

"I believe it was a War Engine, as Miss Milkwood suggested," he said.

"I don't get it," Sally said.

"Why is it chasing *me*?" I said. The fear and the frustration threatened to overwhelm me. The urge to flee was physical. Again, I had to will my body still.

"Like I said last night, some of these things get haunted. It's not the Engine itself, it's the cylinder inside it. Ghosts move in. Some of them get nasty. Don't know why, don't really care."

"Anabeeeeeeeeeeelle! Oh Jesus, it hurts! You filth!"

Joe grabbed her arm. "Listen to that! That's a human voice!"

Sally looked unhappy. "Something ain't right. I'm going to head over there a ways," she said, gesturing along the base of the dune. "When I give the sign, you get your Engine to poke his head above the ridge. Draw the thing's attention. I got to lay eyes on it."

Without waiting for a response, she hustled in the direction she'd indicated, trusting I'd do what I was told. I was not at all happy about volunteering Watson's body to draw more fire from this thing, but I didn't know what other option we had. Except just to keep running. I exchanged a glance with Joe; he looked as confused and panicked as I felt.

When she was satisfied, Sally crawled halfway up the dune, then gestured at me.

"Go on, Watson," I said. "Don't get hurt."

"I shall be fine, Miss Crisp." His treads turned and he rolled up the dune's side, his scuffed metal shell glinting dully in the morning sunlight. I was struck by a feeling of separation from myself, an awareness of being in a situation I'd read about in my pulp magazines or watched on the movie screen. It was a lot less fun than I might have hoped.

Watson's head breached the line of exposure at the dune's top—nothing happened. Soon his whole body was perched at the apex, like some shining monument to our presence on Mars. A dozen yards away, Sally lay pressed into the sand, flicking her gaze from Watson to me, waiting for something to happen.

I prompted him. "Do you see it?"

"Yes. He's standing still. He's staring at me."

"Shit," Joe said. "Well, is it an Engine or not?"

Watson didn't answer.

Sally scrambled the last few feet to the dune's apex and trained her rifle on it, hoping that Watson had sufficiently captured the thing's attention. She stared for a moment. "What the hell," she said.

I couldn't resist. I had to see for myself. I crawled up the slope, kicking away Joe's hand as he tried to restrain me. Carefully I peered over the top, my nerves jangling, ready to duck back down at the slightest hint of motion.

A hulking Engine—the biggest I'd ever seen—stood atop a dune some distance behind us, a human figure dangling from his right arm. It was Charlie, one hand grasping ineffectually at where the Engine clasped his head, the other arm—the broken one—out of its sling and hanging crookedly at his side. His feet kicked gently, as if he were swimming. Green light stuttered at the place where the Engine held him, providing him a kind of malfunctioning halo. Charlie called out again. Electric light sparked from his open mouth.

"Filth!"

As I absorbed this, the huge Engine lifted its left arm—the Gatling gun.

A rifle shot cracked, but it came from my right. Charlie lurched as if he'd been punched. His limbs jerked strangely—each independent of the other, as though receiving conflicting signals—and then he sagged from the War Engine's limb. The Engine made a quarter turn to the left, and its Gatling arm lowered several degrees. It seemed confused.

"Let's go," Sally said, sliding from her position.

I didn't need any extra prodding. I told Watson to follow, and slid down to where Joe was waiting.

"Did you get him?" he asked.

"Yeah, I got him. For whatever that's worth. Let's get a move on."

Sally was moving fast, and we had to hustle to keep up. Watson ground along, gamely keeping pace. As we ascended the next dune, we all looked behind us, muscles tensed for more gunfire. But we saw only the unbroken, rippling sea of sand, and far behind it the outline of the crater's ridge. Beyond that, out of sight now, were New Galveston and Dig Town; they seemed dreamlike to me now, silly childhood visions. This was the new reality.

"What was it?" Joe finally asked.

"War Engine," Sally said.

"How can those things still be functional?" he said. "Even if they didn't get scrapped—who's maintaining them?"

"Don't know," she said. "But it seemed pretty functional to me."

"What about the man?"

"Let's keep moving."

Joe was bewildered. "Sally? Tell me!"

Sally didn't answer him. When he turned to me for illumination, I shrugged. "It was one of the miners from the restaurant. Sally shot him."

"I said, let's get moving," Sally said. "That thing is still out there, and it's fixed on us."

We fell in behind her. I kept looking back, seeing nothing but desert.

SALLY DROVE US without mercy. We scaled dune after dune, breath heaving from our lungs, sweat stinging our eyes. Watson labored to keep up; despite his new treads, he was getting too much sand and dust into his gears. He started to fall behind.

I slowed down, too, dragging the others' momentum in turn. At last Sally turned on me in a fury. "What's the matter with you, girl? I thought you were tough. Is this pace too much for you?"

"He can't keep up! We're going too fast!"

"You know who else is going too fast?" She didn't have to tell me. "If your little dishwasher can't keep up, then I guess he's going to have to figure out his own way forward."

A little way ahead, Joe was gripping his knees, taking advantage of the respite to catch his breath.

We were nearing the center of the crater; the rocky perimeter encircled us, making every horizon dark. We were beginning to encounter protrusions of rock, remnants of one of the millions of meteorites that had slammed into Mars throughout its long, dark life. Sally regarded the one closest to us—a triangular wedge, like a massive door stop—and gestured to it. "Let's make it that far," she said. "It'll allow us to get a look behind us and you can clean that thing's treads. Maybe that'll help."

In a half hour we were there, the shadow cast in its lee a cool reprieve. I felt the sweat drying on my face. Watson drifted to a halt, the sand in his treads sounding like ground glass. Even though I knew he couldn't feel pain, I cringed.

"I'm going to climb up and take a look," Sally said. "You stay down here in the lee. Joe, come with me."

That set off an alarm in my head, but I was in no position to object. They had to go up, and I had to clean Watson. I watched them ascend, Sally lurching with an absurd power, almost like an Engine herself, while Joe slipped and scrambled behind her.

Watson opened the hatch on his chassis, and I retrieved the brushes and the oils. The gaping bullet hole was horrifying up close—twisted metal, the stink of oil—and I felt my lower lip tremble. Crouching beside him, I set to work—first digging the biggest chunks of rock from the treads, then spraying them with a solvent that loosened the sand and dust.

"How are you doing, Watson?"

"I am mostly functional, though the bullet has compromised movement in my left limb. This cleaning will improve my ability to travel. I trust this will please everyone."

"Yeah, well. I'm not too worried about pleasing them. They're the ones who ought to be worried about pleasing me. I have all the power here."

Watson did not respond. Of course he didn't; there was no prompt. And yet I couldn't help but consider his silence a judgment.

"I could turn them both in to the sheriff. They're both helping the cultists, and she's with the Shank kids, who're making moonshine. One visit from me and that's two diseases cut out of our town. Right, Watson?"

"I'm sure you are correct."

I watched the dirt on his treads start to bubble and fizz. Another minute and I could get to the real work.

"You ever wish you talked like the rest of us?"

"I don't know what you mean, Miss Crisp. Are you having difficulty understanding me? Perhaps a fuse has been jostled loose."

"No, I mean . . . how our voices sound. The words we use. You speak with a British accent. It's one we chose for you. It was a joke. Does that ever bother you?"

Watson turned his head, as though he were staring into space. "I'm a joke?"

"No. But your voice is. Or it was. I mean there's nothing wrong with it, it's just—you didn't have a choice."

"Perhaps I need a new one."

"What kind would you like?"

"I'm sure I have no preference, Miss Crisp. I am an Engine, after all."

I didn't want to look at him. Instead I took the picks and the rags and started working on his treads. The solvent had done its work; the grime came away easily. After a few moments of this a thought occurred to me. I sprayed the solvent across his chest, careful to keep it out of the hole in his shoulder.

We weren't exactly negligent about cleaning Watson back home, but we weren't really on top of it either, especially since the Silence began. A layer of grease had accumulated over his chassis; it caught the blowing sand so that he looked like he was covered in a pink fuzz. I watched that whole carpet of filth start to hiss. After a moment I passed the rag over it, and I was astonished at the brightness of the yellow paint underneath.

"You had a dream last night, Watson," I said as I continued to clean.

"That isn't possible, Miss Crisp."

"I know, but you did. You dreamed of a mushroom garden and floating green stars. I was in a mushroom garden just a few days ago. In Widow Kessler's cellar."

"Were there stars?"

"No."

I sprayed more, wiped away more. I was wasting the solvent, which was designed for hardier work, but I didn't want to stop.

"Father once told me about fireflies on Earth. How they look like floating stars."

"I think I would like to see fireflies, Miss Crisp. Perhaps one day we'll all be able to go back."

My Kitchen Engine wants to see fireflies.

It didn't take long to finish cleaning him. Another fifteen minutes and Watson's metal facing gleamed in the waning afternoon light. I wrapped another cleaning rag around the wound in his shoulder; it would help at least a little in keeping dust and sand out. I oiled his treads as best as I was able. He looked like someone new: someone he should have been this whole time, had he not been subject to the indifferent attentions of my father and myself. We had imposed our own identity on him, and he'd had no choice but to carry it with him his whole life. I felt a tide of guilt, even though some part of me still wondered if it was akin to feeling guilt over an unwiped counter, or a coffee maker clogged with grounds.

"You look beautiful, Watson."

"Thank you, Miss Crisp."

I put the materials back into their place inside his chassis, this time taking care to snap the plastic bands securely around them, folding the soiled rags and tying them into the netting where they should have been this whole time. Neatly. Cleanly. Treating him like he mattered.

"Anabelle!"

Sally's voice, coming from above.

"Come up here. Leave the Engine where it is."

THEY WAITED FOR me at the top of the outcropping. They were lying flat, oriented so that they could see the land ahead of us. When I made it to the top, Joe beckoned me over, motioning for me to keep low. I got onto my belly and crawled beside them.

Beyond the wedge, the rocky debris became more plentiful: a vast scattering of massive rubble formed a ripple of broken earth that scarred the otherwise perfect emptiness of the Strange, stretching across both dunes and hard desert. Although I knew it was the broken remnant of some enormous meteorite, it seemed much bigger than that. Like the wreckage of a moon.

"I thought you were looking to see how close that War Engine is," I said.

Sally pointed ahead. "Look there."

There were more of them. I counted six, including the one we'd already encountered. It had outpaced us, maneuvered around us, and we hadn't had any clue. As hard as Sally had pushed us, it shouldn't have been possible.

Three of them were accompanied by miners. I couldn't make out any details from this distance, but I could see that two of them moved erratically, their limbs jerking as though gripped by some manic impulse. From this vantage point I could see that the Engines weren't simply holding them; they were brutally interfaced with them, something in their metallic hands breaching the miners' skulls and extending into their brains. The third miner—Charlie—slumped from the Engine's hand, limp as a rag doll. The War Engine shook the body once, as though to coax it back to life. Charlie swung heavily. I could see the bullet hole in his chest, put there by Sally's rifle.

"How did that one get ahead of us?" I said. "Engines don't move that fast."

"These are a different breed," she said. "They're not like the models we know. They're fast. They're made to hunt in the desert."

Not one anymore. Six. Six War Engines, all of them looking for us.

One of the miners called out: no word could be pulled from the sound it made. It was just a mangled attempt at language, the will of something alien—something cold and mechanical—being pushed through a throat made for warmer expression.

"And now they're hunting us," I said.

"They are for the time being," Sally said. She looked at me. "I'm worried about Watson."

I think it was the first time she'd used his name. It set off a warning in my head. "Why?"

"Is that a serious question?"

"There's nothing wrong with him."

"There's something wrong with *all* of them. He's going to change, girl. He's changing already."

Joe put his hand on my arm. I yanked it away.

"Belle," he said. "We can't take him with us."

"We're not leaving him behind," I said.

Sally hissed her exasperation. "He ain't in no danger. Those Engines don't hurt each other. Yours got hit by accident. You saw how he wasn't struck again. Those monsters will roll right on past him without a second look."

"You don't know that for sure."

"I'm not saying we abandon him," she said. "We need him to get their attention so we have time to get past them."

"We're not leaving Watson," I said. "That's just the way it is. I need him to run my mother's cylinder. Without him, this is all for nothing."

Sally turned on her side and grabbed my shirt, pulling me close. "If they catch us, we will die. You need to understand that." Her hot, foul breath washed over my face.

I resisted the urge to flinch. Instead I pressed my face even closer. "You're here because I determined this would get done," I said. "Nothing is changed. If you're too scared to go, then I guess you better turn around and run home. Help the cultists and the moonshiners while you can. I promise you it won't be long."

Sally recognized a threat when she heard it. Her eyes went flat. It was like the soul retreated into its cave, leaving the body behind to do its dark work. I'd pushed her too far, and I knew it. Would she cut me open right there, on the high rock, like some sacrifice lifted to the sun? Or would she just choke the air from me with her bare hands?

Watson felt very far away.

"Sally," Joe said. *"Sally."*

She was there again, she was present in her body, and I knew I would live at least until the night.

"Have it your way," she whispered.

We descended the outcrop, and she got her first look at Watson in his new and improved condition. She paused to take it in, and then she proceeded around him, keeping her judgment to herself.

18

We moved into the maze of rubble.

Sally guided us away from the gathering of Engines, the sounds of the shrieking humans and the growling treads fading behind us. She didn't say it, but I suspected the Engines were forcing us to diverge from the path she normally traveled. That might not have worried me, except that the afternoon grew late. One of the moons was a thin white crescent in the golden sky. I found myself staring at it, trying to determine whether it was Phobos or Deimos, panic or dread.

Behind us, Watson's treads clamored and clacked, the sounds bouncing off the rocks, traveling ahead of us and returning as multiplied echoes. I was jumping out of my skin, and I knew the others must be, too.

Soon, other sounds joined the echoes: the heavy squeaking of rolling wheels—a heavier and more sinister sound than Watson's treads made—and an occasional deep-throated, metallic syllable of one War Engine speaking in code to another. Most disturbing were the high wails of human beings, carried on the wind like wisps of blood-dipped lace, a half-articulated cry for help or a lover's name, or simply a howl of anguish. The War Engines were closing in.

The sun failed. The night deepened, lengthened, approached the lethal cold. The air turned brittle, our breath froze. We shivered as we lurched along, our arms wrapped around our bodies, trying to preserve our core heat. My teeth clattered like rolling dice.

Joe trudged at my side, breathing heavily, hoarsely. My hair hung over my face, tinkling with ice. I raised my head to say something to him and realized it was not Joe at all but a ghost that kept pace with me, a tall and emaciated human being with black gulfs for eyes. It turned its face to me and smiled, its mouth an emptiness that stretched until it melded with its eyes, until its entire face was an unlit hole, a doorway into an unknowable world. I could sense something alive in that hole, something hidden and curious watching me. A different kind of chill fixed my heart, and I might have screamed if I'd had the breath for it.

"What are you?" the ghost said. Then the hole in the face widened until the ghost seemed to swallow itself and I was only staring into the night sky.

"Belle?" Joe's voice.

"I'm coming." When I caught up to him, I said, "It talked to me."

If he had an opinion about that, he kept it to himself. Maybe he just didn't have the energy for any more speech. I was running out myself. Somehow Sally kept ahead of us, a living reservoir of will, as inevitable as any machine.

I started to slow. I had nothing left, no reserves of my own. I was too cold, my brain too sluggish. The sounds of the War Engines occluded everything else: the sound of our feet in the sand, the sound of our breath, even the sound of my own blood pounding in my ears.

This was death. It had arrived at last.

Watson paused at my side. "Climb onto me, Miss Crisp."

I did, planting my feet on the fairing over the treads. "You're my friend, Watson."

"Yes."

I tried to clutch onto him but my fingers barely moved. My breath frosted on his chassis. "It's no use."

He wrapped his clumsy working arm around me and inched forward. I nearly toppled off, but he kept a tight hold. The crook of his arm was pinching my flesh, but I couldn't feel it. I leaned my head into his shoulder, watching the stars above us. They looked like a river of glimmering silver above the towering walls of rock, and we were carried by its current, bound for a strange new country.

Atop one of the distant outcroppings, as if crawled from the river of light, was a deep-sea diver from out of Jules Verne, waving to me. I raised my hand and waved back.

"Look, Watson. It's Captain Nemo."

"No, Miss Crisp. That is an astronaut."

I blinked, lifted my head. He was right. It was an old-fashioned space-walking suit, of the kind that serviced early saucers in mid-transit, or that occupied the German deep-space stations fired like cannonballs into the void soon before the Great War. It even had a thick umbilical connecting it to some unseen fixture behind it. I hadn't seen a suit like that ever in real life; I knew them only from my history books.

They were large, ungainly contraptions, rudimentary Engines in and of themselves. They were designed to perform simple maintenance functions in space with or without a human inhabitant, making it easier for single-pilot vessels to make trips between Earth and the moon.

I still assumed it was no more real than that glowing centipede crawling through thin air, as if it were swimming in the ghost of a sea, until Sally stopped in place and raised the rifle to her shoulder.

Joe staggered to a halt a few steps behind her. He cast an uneasy glance back toward Watson and me, then at the cliffs of rock surrounding us.

"Is it one of them?" I asked, meaning the War Engines.

"No," she said. "Now just hush a minute."

I fought down the urge to snap at her. "You can't shoot a ghost," I offered.

"This one you can."

When she didn't fire, I realized that she hadn't intended to; she was staring at it through the scope. She lowered the rifle and turned back to us. "It's all right," she said. "Let's go."

I looked to Joe to see if this made sense to him. He caught my look and shrugged. "Don't look at me, kid. I don't know shit."

Sally guided us to a crevice in a slab of rock so massive it seemed, up close, like the side of a mountain. The ground inside descended into a cave, and I could see light reflecting off a wall at the bottom of the slope. The walls were so close that we had to turn sideways to fit. Sally forged ahead. Joe started to follow but stopped when he realized I wasn't coming.

"Watson can't fit," I said.

He opened his mouth to say something, and closed it again.

"I'm not going."

"Belle, this is it. This is why we came."

"I'm not leaving him behind."

I could see the frustration mounting in his eyes. "He'll be okay."

"How do you know?"

He looked around for assistance, but Sally hadn't slowed. It was just the three of us for the moment. "I guess I don't know for sure. But Sally said they wouldn't hurt him, and I believe she knows what she's talking about. Anyhow, I don't see as you have any other choice. You want to turn around and go home, now that you're finally here?"

"No," I said. I couldn't do that, and he knew it.

"Then let's go. Let's go before those things get here. You're going to have to trust Sally about this."

"Do you?"

"Yes, I do. She's the only friend I got. She can be one to you, too, if you just let her."

"*Watson* is my friend."

"Watson is a machine. Please! She hasn't steered us wrong yet."

"She steers you like a mule, Joe Reilly, and you let her. I don't know that right or wrong has anything to do with it."

"Maybe I need that, Belle. Maybe that's none of your business."

"Fine, but I ain't like that. I make my own way."

He sighed. "I know you do. So you figure out which way you're going to make it. Come down here where it's warm and light, or go back out there with those War Engines and see if you can find your way back home empty-handed in the cold. Me, I'm going with Sally."

With that he turned around and descended into the cave. He was illuminated briefly by lantern light before disappearing around the corner. His shadow played over the wall for a moment, and then I was alone.

Watson waited at the mouth of the crevice. The wind howled through the rocks like a screaming spirit. I wanted to go out to him, but the cold was too strong. I huddled just inside the crevice, trying to figure out how to solve this.

I couldn't see a way.

"Watson!" I had to shout over the wind. "I don't know what to do!"

"Go with the others, Miss Crisp. I shall wait out here. I'm not troubled by the cold."

"I won't leave you alone!"

"You won't survive the night, Miss Crisp. I'm afraid I must insist."

I felt tears freeze in my eyes. It wasn't fair. Nothing was fair. "Don't go anywhere! I'm coming back as soon as I can!"

"I will remain right here. Dream well, Miss Crisp."

I turned and left him. He was just a machine. But it felt like a betrayal.

I ROUNDED THE corner at the bottom and came up short as I bumped into Joe. He hadn't left me after all; he'd been waiting just out of sight. He could see the distress on my face, I suppose, because he put his arm around my shoulder and squeezed me briefly in an awkward hug. He released me before I could react. That warm human gesture slipped past the bulwarks of anger I'd maintained and settled over me like a blanket. It reminded me of my father, and I almost broke into sobs.

"Come on, kid. Let's go see what we've gotten ourselves into."

The passageway was well-trod and relatively flat. We didn't have to go far before it opened into a larger cavern, the source of the heat and light. Lanterns were suspended from hooks fixed into the stone, and a heat lamp—much smaller than the municipal-grade models used in New Galveston, but effective nonetheless—hummed quietly in the center. The room appeared to be the central point of a network; tunnels branched off in three directions. Five people loitered here, three men and a woman— and Sally. They were seated around the heat lamp, eating dinner. Their eyes all flashed green in the lantern light. The smell of cooking beans made my stomach complain.

One of them climbed lazily to his feet and walked out to meet us halfway. He was tall and thin, little older than a boy. He carried a rifle with him, its barrel pointed to the ground. He did not call out to us or address us in any way.

Joe stopped, and I stopped with him. "Percy," Joe said.

"Joe. You're not supposed to come out here."

"I know, but it's important. I wouldn't have come otherwise." He looked past the young man toward Sally, who watched the proceedings with apparent indifference.

"Don't look at her. Look at me." Percy gestured. "Who's that with you?"

"Sally didn't tell you anything?"

"I'm asking you."

"Yeah, okay." I could hear fear in Joe's voice. He hadn't expected to be challenged like this by someone he knew. "This here's Anabelle Crisp."

"Am I supposed to know that name?"

"Nope. Just answering your question, is all. Look, can I talk to Silas?"

"What's she doing here?"

I'd had about enough of this. "I'm here because Silas Mundt stole something from me. I'm here to take it back."

"Stole something? You're gonna have to be more specific than that."

"My mother," I said. I knew she was near, and the word seemed like a talisman in my mouth. It gave me power. "He took my mother from me."

Percy seemed surprised to hear it. He turned to face Sally. "What's she talking about?"

"A cylinder," she said. She sounded dismissive, as though she was trying to reassure the man that nothing terrible had really happened. "Silas took a cylinder with her mama's recording on it."

Percy looked back to me, an incredulous grin on his face. "Tell me that ain't true. Tell me you didn't come all the way out here for that."

"I'll peel that smile right off your face, you condescending son of a bitch. Take me to Silas."

The humor on his face curdled. I watched his hands tighten on his rifle. "These ones might think that attitude is cute, kid, but it'll get you hurt out here. You hear me on that."

Joe took a step forward, shielding me. "Calm down, Percy."

Sally called out from the fire. "Stop showing off, Perce! We all know you're the biggest and the meanest and the toughest! Unless you make me haul my ass off the ground, then maybe it's a different story."

Percy looked about as intimidating as those whey-faced Earthers who used to visit before the Silence hit us, so I knew she was just giving him the same treatment she gave everybody in her life. It seemed to deflate him, though; he relaxed his grip on the rifle and his posture eased. He headed back to join the others. "Silas is with the boss," he said. "Come get something to eat, I guess."

Joe moved to join them. If he was still nervous, I couldn't tell—though I guess it's possible that he lived his whole life in a state of low-grade fear, and that the threat he faced now was no worse than the usual. He ambled over and took a seat beside the heat lamp, as if he knew them all well. Maybe he did.

As he helped himself to the beans simmering in the pot, I examined the rest of them, trying to figure if one of them had been present at the robbery. I couldn't be sure. They were dressed warmly, for outdoor work, wearing the same heavy-weather jackets Silas Mundt had worn when he came in that night, complete with the moth sigil branded onto the sleeve. Though their faces looked clean enough, their clothing bore the dirty pink stain of Martian dust worked into the grain. It had probably been years since they were washed. I was not surprised that these were a filthy people.

Joe nodded at the space beside him. "Come sit down."

"I don't think I will."

"Suit yourself."

My stomach cramped with hunger, and my skin shivered in the chill, but I would be damned before I'd accept their hospitality. I found a place beneath one of the lanterns and sat there, staring into one of the dark passages leading deeper into the rock.

The others talked amongst themselves, untroubled by my separation from them. I felt an unreasonable sting, though I had manufactured this alienation myself. I hated them for who they were and what they'd done to my father and me, yet I wanted them to pull me into their fold, to feed me dinner, to assure me that there were no horrors dwelling in the darkness I stared into. No mysteries. Only love, warmth, a solid and knowable ground.

Something stirred in the hollow throat of the tunnel, a thing venturing up from the cold center of this place. It resolved itself into Silas Mundt, who stopped at the edge of the light and stared at me, his green eyes reflecting like a cat's. I stared back. He glanced at the others, who had not yet seen him. He smiled at me, and in that moment of vulnerability I welcomed it. I don't think I smiled back. But I did not rebuff it, either, and maybe he could understand the significance of that.

He approached the others, who greeted him and made a space for him to sit.

He didn't take it. Instead he filled two tin cups with the beans, grabbed some spoons, and came to sit with me beneath the lantern.

I was cold and hungry and exhausted, and I took what he offered gratefully. We ate together.

HE PLACED HIS empty cup on the ground beside mine. "So," he said at last. "You come here to kill me?"

It sounded ridiculous to hear it out loud. I remembered my earlier ambition to destroy this place and everyone here. Now here I was accepting the man's hospitality. I was too tired to contemplate anything else. "You know why I came."

"I don't, actually. I know I didn't kill your dad, and I cannot figure what else it could be. Are you mad I took the steak?"

"You took my mother's cylinder. I want it back."

"Oh." He worked a fingernail between his teeth, seeming to think about things for a minute. "As I recall, you said your mama was on Earth. What's it got on there, a recording? A personality imprint?"

"A recording." I didn't like hearing it put so clinically. It made it seem trivial. "It's all we have left of her. At least until she comes back."

"Listen to you. No one's coming back, little girl." He picked up a rock from beside him, turned it over in his hands. "But I guess you know that. I guess that's why you came all the way out here to get it."

"Are you going to give it to me?"

Instead of answering, he pointed at the people gathered around the heat lamp. "I got strict rules on who can come here. I'm known for being a hard-ass about it. Sally's allowed, Joe's not. And even Sally can only come on certain occasions. You know you put those two in danger, dragging them out here?"

"I didn't drag nobody. Joe Reilly got his own self into this mess by his association with you. And if you think anybody can drag Sally anywhere, you don't know her too well."

"Nah. I know her better than you do. She talks rough, but she's all soft inside. She must like you. Joe, though . . . Joe's spent his whole life in over his head. It's kind of amazing to me, we spent so much time thinking our ability to get off this big red tomb depended on a guy like that."

"I guess we found something to agree on," I said. "Are you going to hurt them or something?"

"No. We're past that now." He looked at the rock, turning it over and over in his hand. Little green flecks flashed in the lantern light—the Strange. It must be shot through these caverns, too. They weren't breathing in its pulverized dust like those who worked in the mine, but the whole crater was rich with it.

"Yeah," Silas said. "I'll give you the cylinder tomorrow."

"No. I want it now."

"There's no point. You can't leave until the morning anyway. It's too cold, and them War Engines that followed you here are still out."

"What are they, anyway?"

He considered for a moment, then chucked the rock to me. I caught it.

"You know what that is?"

I knew he meant the green striations. "It's the Strange."

"Why do you think it's called that?"

It seemed an absurd question, considering all I'd seen the past few days. "'Cause it brings out ghosts. 'Cause it makes people's eyes change color, makes them act crazy. Turns them mean."

He stared at me a moment. I noticed, too, Sally and Joe sneak the occasional glance this way. I suspect it surprised them to see me talking amiably to Silas Mundt as much as it surprised me to be doing it.

"No," he said. "It don't do none of those things. Except maybe the eye color. Can't argue with that one."

"I saw all of it," I said, bristling. "Everybody in Dig Town is crazy with it. They're moving underground!"

"That's what you think you saw. What you really saw is Mars, trying to speak with us." He reached over, traced his dust-grimed finger along the stripes in the rock. "The Strange is Mars's thoughts," he said. "That's Mars's dreams. That little vein right there might be a wish for love, or it might be the memory of a barge coming down a river ten million years ago. It might be a dream of Earth."

I wanted to be irritated by the silliness of what he was saying, but I wasn't. I couldn't be. I was exhausted and scared, and that made me vulnerable to his unusual theories. I listened.

"We call it the Strange because it's something new, it's something we don't understand. But it's not new. It's old. It's Mars's consciousness, and we're digging it up, breathing it in, putting it into our machines like oil. And it's trying to express itself through these things. You put it in a War Engine, it's going to see us through a War Engine's understanding of the world. You put it in an angry or a desperate man, same thing."

Or a town full of abandoned people, I thought, *who've lost the will to go on.*

"Mars changes us. We change Mars. Whatever comes from that will be something alien to us both."

I put the rock down, watching the lantern light play along its colors. "I have a friend who says she knows about you. She says you grow ghosts. She said that's why you call yourselves the Moths."

He smiled at that. "'Ghosts.' She ain't far wrong. We have a garden down below. You can see it soon."

"When you give me my mother's cylinder back?"

"That's right."

"I thought I'd have to fight you for it."

"No more fighting for me, girl. That's finished now." He leaned against the cavern wall and closed his eyes, drawing in a deep breath. He looked both tired and peaceful, the way you look sometimes after completing long and difficult work. "Anyhow, it's the right thing to do, and I know how god-awful important that is to you. Which reminds me." He leaned over so he could reach into a pocket in his trousers. He pulled out a dime, grungy with dust and oil, and pressed it into my palm. "For the coffee."

I stared at it on my hand. It felt almost holy: a symbol of my strike against injustice. I felt a powerful satisfaction, far out of proportion to its worth. My fingers closed over it. "I thought you said it didn't matter."

"It matters to you, don't it?" Silas climbed to his feet and extended a hand to me. "Let's go get warmed up and be social for a little bit."

I took it. He pulled me upright with an easy strength—the same strength that he'd once turned against my father. We joined the others around the heat.

THE OTHERS MADE room for us around the heat lamp. Sally and Joe watched me, trying to get a sense of how the conversation had gone. My thoughts were too murky to pay them much attention just then. I was trying to process what Silas told me, trying to figure what he meant by his garden of ghosts.

Sally said, "Your numbers are low. Where'd everybody go?"

The four cultists exchanged quick glances, then looked to Silas to field the question. He helped himself to some more beans before answering. "Some left. Some got taken by the War Engines. You know, the same ones you brought with you."

Joe bristled. "Same ones that chased us, you mean."

Percy spoke up. "We never had a group that big bunched up outside! We know how to keep hidden. That's why we don't want outsiders like you bumbling around!"

"We didn't—"

Silas held up his hand. The others quieted. "It's okay, Percy. It doesn't matter anymore." Turning to Sally, he continued his point. "The work is about done. A lot of my people dispersed into the desert, looking for somewhere to land. I expect you'll see some of them in Dig Town soon."

Sally seemed surprised. "The work is done?"

Silas nodded. "About."

"I didn't know you were that close."

"Why would you? As you keep saying, Sally: you ain't one of us."

I watched their faces. "What work?"

"All of it. The ship. Our little garden of ghosts," Silas said.

Sally scoffed.

Silas shrugged. "I like it. I'd have called it that the whole time if I'd thought of it."

"You got a poet's soul, Silas. Soft and squishy. Too bad you never learned to read."

"Now don't be mean, Sally."

"What ship?" I asked. I looked at Joe, who stared at the ground between his feet.

"You'll see," Silas said with a grin.

You'll see, again. Silas was a carnival barker, and as much as I was warming to him, this streak of showmanship irritated me.

A distant, percussive sound rolled down to us through the cavern we'd entered by, like thunder from a faraway storm. All eyes turned in its direction.

"How long's that been going on?" Sally said.

Silas shrugged. "A few days. It's new, just like their experiments with the puppets. Mars is trying to figure us out."

Joe looked outraged. "Those people they've taken. You call them puppets? Those are human beings out there."

"They ain't people no more, Joe. What would you like me to call them?"

Joe didn't have an answer. He glared into the glowing coils of the heat lamp.

"They're gonna get in here pretty soon. We can't stop them. I wish we had a little more time, but it is the way it is."

"Sounds like they might get in here tonight."

"Maybe. With six of them here at once, maybe." He paused. "Your coming here tonight is a stroke of luck for us, though, believe it or not. We were about to come to you."

"Oh?"

"We need the fuel from the *Eurydice*."

Another *boom* rolled over us. Little trickles of sand and grit streamed down from above.

"I think I might have you all wait in the ship tonight," Silas said. "We might have to leave in a hurry."

I didn't know what he was talking about—what work they were completing, what ship we were going to wait in (wasn't there only the *Eurydice*?)—but one concern overrode all others. "Watson's outside. We have to get him in!"

"They won't mess with him. They don't hurt their own."

"Watson isn't one of them."

He shook his head but didn't pursue it. "Let's get on down there. I'll introduce you to Peabody, and you can get settled in. We'll leave in the morning." He looked at me, offered me an olive branch. "You'll get your cylinder, and we'll even pick up your Watson on the way out."

He stood, brushing the dust from his trousers. Sally, Joe, and I stood with him and followed him down one of the dark tunnels. The rest stayed where they were, sitting in silent communion in their little island of heat, while the thunder of heavy guns grumbled intermittently outside.

19

Silas led us down the same tunnel he'd emerged from. It descended steeply. Joe and I followed him, and Sally brought up the rear. There weren't any electric lights set up down here, and the meager light behind us disappeared after we turned a corner. We followed the beam of Silas's flashlight; he swept it back and forth in constant motion, so we could tell where the walls were, when the passageway narrowed or the ceiling dropped close. The temperature fell precipitously. It occurred to me that the sun had never touched these walls, not once in all the long Martian years. Until the Moths moved in, perhaps nothing living ever had either.

I glanced behind us, fancying I sensed a presence keeping pace. But everything behind was darkness. I imagined something large there, with a hard metal wall where a face should be and a cold algorithm for a heart. I thought of poor Watson keeping to his station by the crevice in the bitter cold, the War Engines circling like carrion birds. I prayed Silas was right, and that they would leave him alone.

We continued to descend for some time, until at last we saw a bloom of light on a distant wall. We stepped into a vast chamber, open to the sky; above us was a silver spray of stars. The flashlight had limited reach, but a luminous green mist covered the cavern floor, which stretched for many hundreds of feet. Rising from it were rows of translucent crystalline structures of various heights, flickering like film projections, steaming like organs wrested from a butchered pig. They were at once organic and mineral, at once solid and spectral. Maneuvering among them, a farmer tending his demented crop, was the bent figure of the astronaut I'd seen waving at us from the precipice. His suit was degraded, rotted and torn in various places. Sparks occasionally spit from behind a bent metal plate on his chest, and a network of heat coils glowed from one arm where the fabric had entirely melted away.

To one side of this garden stood a spaceship. It was much smaller than the *Eurydice*, a large sphere with a viewport in the front and a short ramp extending from its belly to the ground. It was old, battered, and scratched; it looked like something excavated from the ground rather than descended from the clean corridors of space. I recognized it from our discussions in Miss Haddersham's classroom: the *Lamplighter*, the vessel piloted here nearly seventy years ago by Chauncy Peabody, the first man on Mars.

The astronaut straightened, seeming to observe us as we approached. The light was too dim to make out his features behind the faceplate, but I detected movement there: a kind of dark-winged fluttering, as though he were not a man but a spirit made of feathers. Mushrooms were attached to one side of the faceplate's interior. A chill rippled over my skin.

Silas guided us between the weird structures. Sounds came from some of them: weeping, laughing, hints of faraway voices.

Other kinds of sound, too: long, nearly inaudible grinding; frequencies of noise that vibrated against the interior of my skull like continental tremors, the musings of earth and stone.

At the base of each of these strange, insubstantial structures was a cylinder affixed to a metal rod pounded into the ground. I knelt to look more closely. Each cylinder had been cracked open on one side, exposing the receptacle that housed the granules of the Strange, making them vulnerable to the influence of the ground-clinging mist. Breached and exposed this way, each functioned as a kind of seed for the apparitions rising from them.

A garden of ghosts, grown from the receptacles of the Strange contained within the cylinders.

Mother was down here.

Sally touched my shoulder. "Get up, Anabelle."

I couldn't. My muscles wouldn't work. I felt light-headed, nauseated. "Mother?" A whisper at first, then a shout. "*Mother?*" One of these ghosts must be hers.

"Silence the child," said a new voice: an older man with a cultured accent, a kind you didn't hear much in New Galveston.

Sally knelt beside me. "You stop your caterwauling. We don't know nothing yet. Let's figure it out before we start raising hell."

Too dazed to argue, I let her haul me to my feet.

"Thank you, Mrs. Milkwood. I'm obliged." The voice belonged to the astronaut, who knelt to continue his work. He was pulling the cylinders from their rods and placing them delicately into round slots on a metal tray, like rows of test tubes.

I could see then what seemed wrong about his head. Behind the astronaut's faceplate was a skull, its forehead resting against the cracked glass, utterly inert. Crawling over it, fluttering against the faceplate, were several fully grown black moths. I noticed then one or two occasionally crawl out of a rent in the suit, a few more clinging to the exterior. He was infested with them.

I felt as though I was looking at a child's Halloween drawing. The skull's mouth did not move when it spoke. The voice coming from the external speaker sounded somehow inhuman, like a thing that had never had warmth or breath behind it.

Joe had half a smile on his face, but his eyes held terror. He looked like he wanted to run. "What the hell is this?"

"Watch your mouth," Silas snapped. "Mr. Peabody don't care for harsh speech."

"Especially not in the presence of a lady," the thing said. Looking at me, it corrected itself. "*Two* ladies. How do you do, miss? My name is Chauncy Peabody. Forgive me for not extending my hand. Time does not allow me the luxury of formalities, as I'm sure you understand."

"That's all right," I said weakly. "My name is Anabelle Crisp."

"And you, sir?"

". . . Joe Reilly."

The thing turned toward Silas. "The pilot. I don't need a pilot. Why did you bring these people here?"

"I didn't. They came on their own. The girl there wants to take one of these cylinders back home with her. I figured she came all this way, why not."

The thing looked at me again. The skull jostled as it turned, making a dusty sound. I noticed a tether drooping from the suit, trailing off into the mist, in the direction of the *Lamplighter*. It served as an umbilical, meant to connect the suit to the ship's oxygen and to its motherboard. This suit was a crude Engine with a corpse trapped inside.

Chauncy Peabody's corpse: the first man on Mars. This talking monstrosity had once been a man with a complicated legacy, celebrated by our textbooks but spoken of darkly by my mother.

Chauncy Peabody—the living one—had been a professor of astronomy at the University of North Carolina, where he had served with distinction for the first ten years of his career, until Jefferson Davis called him to duty in service to the Confederate States of America upon the outbreak of the Civil War. Peabody refused. The history books will tell you that he cited as justification his belief in the equality of all men under God, and as a corollary his opposition to the institution of slavery. According to Mother, this wasn't true. In fact, he cared little for the plight of the slave in America. He cared only for his research on Mars, which he had come to believe was not only habitable by human beings, but reachable in a relatively short trip. Hoping to avoid conscription so he could continue his work, he wrote a letter to the president, underscoring the importance of his studies and even suggesting the potential of the red planet as a new home for the Confederacy.

Jefferson Davis was appalled at the notion of ceding any ground to the Union—let alone the whole of the Earth—and proved unsympathetic to the professor's arguments. Peabody was discharged from his position, and though the history books will not say this either, he was forced to leave in haste under cover of night, lest the morning find him hanged as a traitor. Peabody did not like his chances crossing through Virginia, so he fled west, where he trusted that a more indifferent population would cause him less trouble. Eventually he found himself in Galveston, Texas, the city from which he eventually launched the *Lamplighter*. He landed on Mars, sent one transmission home, and was never heard from again.

Or so I had thought.

"They're not yours to give, nor hers to take," he said. "They're mine."

"The hell they are," I said. "You stole everything down here. And you can keep it all, as far as I care. I only came for my mother."

Silas put his hand on my shoulder. I shook it off.

"Mr. Peabody," he said. "We ain't gonna be able to take them all with us anyway. You know that."

Something about the astronaut changed. I couldn't see it, but I could feel it; it was akin to a sudden temperature drop, or a charging of the air before a sandstorm. It radiated like a dark star, a terrible, malignant energy, a brutal intelligence. The moths in the helmet careened in agitation, fragile wings pressed against the glass, frantic bodies hurrying in and out of the skull's mouth, eyes, a fissure in its head.

The others felt it, too. Even Silas went pale.

"Come away," he said, and turned quickly toward the *Lamplighter*, not troubling to see if we followed.

We did.

"What's happening?" I said.

"It's Mars—what you call the Strange—alive in him. When the *Lamplighter* crashed here, it crashed right into one of those veins. It went all over the ship, into the circuitry. What happens to the cylinders we make on Earth happened here, too. It came to life. The *Lamplighter* is alive. And since the suit is tethered to it, it uses the suit to walk around, to talk to us. Like Sally said: sometimes he thinks he's Peabody, sometimes he knows he ain't. It's those times you got to be careful."

"What do you mean it came to life?" I said. "The cylinders aren't alive!"

"They are, though. That's what I'm trying to tell you. They are alive. How do you think you can give the Engines such convincing personalities? There's life at the root of that. They're all little fragments of the same being. It's just that the amounts used in the cylinders are too small to do anything. Mr. Peabody here, in this garden, he's nurturing them. Like plants. Exposing them to more of it, allowing them to grow." Silas spoke with an intensity I didn't like. "He's a new kind of being, and he's shepherding a new species into existence. The real Martians."

The idea rocked me back on my heels. That was why Watson was starting to dream. He was out in the crater, and all that sand laden with the Strange was working its way into his body. Feeding what was already there. Who was he turning into?

Joe said, "Where the hell does that leave us? We have a huge, insane Engine in here and deranged War Engines out there." I could hear the barely contained panic in his voice.

Silas gave him a brilliant smile. Despite myself, I was reassured by it. He radiated confidence. "He's not insane. Remember how I told you Mars interprets us through the vessel it's in? This one sees us through Peabody and his ship. He's an explorer. He's a leader. He wants to go back to Earth. He wants to see what's there." Gesturing toward the garden of ghosts, he added, "And he wants to bring as much of Mars with him as he can."

Going back to Earth will end the Silence, I thought. The realization numbed me.

"All he needs now is the *Eurydice*'s fuel, Joe. He'll fly you back there to get it."

"Sally and Anabelle, too," Joe said.

"Of course. And myself, too, to make sure it gets done. Let's just not agitate him before then, okay?" He looked at me. "You can have what you came here for. It won't make a difference to him, or to anything else. It probably won't make a difference to you, either. It ain't the same as it was before."

I knew it, but I didn't want to hear it spoken aloud. The thought of what being exposed to the Strange might have done to her made me feel sick. But still, I was finding it hard to stay angry at Silas. I was warming to him, despite the rage I'd been nurturing since the robbery. He was, after all, giving me exactly what I wanted. And he was the only one on Mars actively working to go back home. "I understand why you're helping him outfit the ship," I said. "But why the garden? Why are you helping do that?"

Silas smiled, his eyes unfocused. "Because it's beautiful. And because we're not."

THE *LAMPLIGHTER*'S HULL was painted a creamy white, and the ornamentation over the rivets indicated that the ship was of nineteenth-century vintage. A fluttering tarp—once part of a brightly colored tent—had been fashioned into an awning over the entrance. I had a vision of Peabody reclining in a chair underneath it, watching while the living people in his thrall labored in his weird garden.

Within, a hallway stretched in both directions. One way terminated in a ruin of twisted metal beams and plates; the other, though buckled, turned toward the ship's dark interior.

The hallway canted steeply downward. Sand had blown or trickled in over the many years the ship had been stuck here. A narrow path had been forged through it, but I slipped more than once as I followed Silas down. Absolute darkness soon overwhelmed us. Silas flicked on his flashlight and reached for a switch on the wall. A series of yellow lamps lining the ceiling stuttered into life. One flickered and went out. A few others hummed and sparked but managed to stay lit.

The corridor made a curving circuit around the vessel's central portion, where I assumed the engines resided. Small storage compartments along the way held oxygen generators and cans of preserved food, most of them ruptured and spoiled. The hallway leveled out and terminated at the main cabin, an area about half the size of my hab back in New Galveston. The sand had filled the chamber once, and though Silas's people had since removed most of it, small drifts still rested in corners and under control panels. Hanging loosely from the back wall was a foldout cot, one strut snapped, the blankets stiff with sand. What I had first taken to be solid wall, glinting oddly in the dim light, was in fact a bubble of hard glass, built to weather the occasional strike of small meteors and random debris. It had done its job well, withstanding the force of impact when the ship crashed into Mars. Through it we could see the garden, and Chauncy Peabody carefully collecting his cylinders.

The interior walls were made of wood, now dry and cracked. Brass railings were fitted along the circumference of the room. Curtains had once been hung on runners bolted to the ceiling over the window, so one might draw them and indulge in a fantasy of life at home. They had long since rotted away, hanging in black tatters on either side of the glass. A smashed bookshelf reposed against one wall, its spilled contents—treatises on astronavigation, geology, agriculture; biographies and journals of great explorers; as well as a variety of popular novels— mostly buried in sand. Broken china suggested a tea set or dinnerware. A star chart hung from one wall, the portrait of a handsome woman beside it. Papers and charts had been blown all over the room, most of them torn and crumpled beneath the astronaut's trudging feet. As Joe and Sally took it all in, I stooped and picked one up. It looked like a partial manifest: so many pounds of salt pork, so many jars of preserved tomatoes, so many gallons of water.

Weariness threatened to overwhelm me. The day had held too much: I couldn't take it all in. Mother was here, somewhere: promised to me, yet still not in my hands. Watson was outside: ostensibly safe, yet surrounded by hostile entities, and alone. War Engines patrolled the entrance to the cave, trying to get in, some already ghoulishly integrated with human bodies. Peabody's corpse patrolled his macabre garden. Mars itself was alive.

And then there was Silas: the man I'd come here wanting to kill, become my willing ally.

I needed to sleep.

But first there was work to be done, preparing for departure. We put some effort into making the cabin habitable for the short journey to Dig Town, focusing first on returning the heating system to working order. Peabody (not really Peabody, I reminded myself: it was the *Lamplighter* that was alive; like the War Engines outside, it was using Peabody's corpse as a kind of puppet) had apparently devoted a considerable portion of his energies into self-preservation, bowdlerizing the parts of the ship that had been crushed or broken in the crash and repurposing them into maintaining the integrity of the cabin, which Silas claimed was the home of his true consciousness. I stared with macabre interest at the bank of cylinder receptacles, just like the one I'd seen on the *Eurydice*, where the ship's power center was maintained. Peabody's consciousness was housed there: self-awareness as either a miracle or a disease.

Silas left us on our own at one point, returning about twenty minutes later. He had a little canvas bag with him, which he opened for me.

"I didn't know which one it was," he said. "So I brought 'em all."

Inside were four cylinders; I recognized them as the ones he'd taken from our diner. My heart beating, I carefully retrieved the one with Mother's recording. It was cracked, like the others. Dull metal, smudged with oil and gritty with sand. Ugly, clumsy, decidedly mundane. Not like any grail, nor any jewel of Opar.

But it was hers, and I had it again.

After all this, I'd only had to ask, and it was returned.

"Where were they?"

"They were planted in the garden. I just pulled them while Peabody was loading others into the hold. He didn't know. No reason he has to."

It was a quiet, profound moment. Joe and Sally watched me, and Joe looked pleased. Silas crouched beside me, strong and confident. Without hesitation or complaint he quietly provided me with what I needed when I asked it of him, shoring up the foundations of a life I'd thought utterly collapsed. I clutched the cylinder tightly, anticipating the look on Father's face when I brought it back to him. I knew it was Silas who had caused all this in the first place—I hadn't entirely lost my faculties—

but so much more had gone wrong since then that this victory felt profound.

"Thank you," I said.

"Sure, kid." He gave me a friendly chuck on the shoulder. "Anyway. Back to it."

While we worked, Peabody would occasionally come in, each time carrying a tray of cylinders, covered and fastened. He would walk between us, unspeaking, and secure them in a storage closet with several shelves. The closet was too small to accommodate his full garden. I asked what would happen with the rest.

"We're gonna have to leave a little earlier than we'd planned, thanks to them War Engines," Silas said. "We were gonna place the ones we couldn't take in Engines, like your Watson. Since we can't do that, we'll leave them where they are. We're connecting the cylinders with wire in the hopes that the entities that grow will be able to communicate with each other. Or maybe they'll become one entity. Who knows? In any case, we're just giving them a boost. They'll do whatever it is they do. They're the real Martians. Not us."

"Why not us?" I said. Everyone in New Galveston was so fixed on getting us all to identify as Martians—especially since the Silence—that it seemed almost heretical to hear a contrary opinion.

"'Cause we're a disease. We never should have come here."

Joe scoffed.

"What, you don't think that's true? Everywhere we go, we lay waste. We take and take and take, and leave nothing behind us. Look at them War Engines outside; that's how Mars knows us. Killers. Ruiners."

I remembered what the War Engine had called us. *Filth.*

"There's good things here," Sally said.

"Name one."

"The tribes."

This caught me off guard. "You mean Indian tribes?"

"I do. Out past Brawley's Crossing, which I imagine you believe is the farthest outpost of human life, are the Cherokee and Lakota Nations."

"What?"

"Didn't know about them, did you? New Galveston might be the first official colony, but people have been moving back and forth between Earth and Mars for over sixty years. You really think you're it?"

Brenda had said as much back at school. I never thought for a second she could be right. Were there really that many more people here?

"How many?"

Sally shrugged. "I couldn't say."

"I don't believe you. I've never seen them."

"You think they came all this way to shake the white man's hand? You ain't seen them because that's how they like it." She watched me try to reckon with this news, and so I know she took great joy when she said, "And that's just the ones I know about."

"Well anyway," Silas said, eager to regain the floor, "let them have it. They won't last long. Nobody who stays here will, thank God. We need to get back home, and we need to stay there. Peabody's how we do it."

Conversation slowed after that. The lights were turned low. As we arranged ourselves around the small room—Joe and Sally lying atop their heat tents instead of inside them; Silas leaning back in the pilot's chair with one leg crossed over the other, a cigar burning in one hand—I felt a weakening of some resistance inside me. Resistance to what, I couldn't have said at the time, though now I know that it was to everything. To my companions, to my circumstance, to the dissolving order around me. I allowed myself to feel cradled in this warmly lit bubble of safety. With that feeling came a rising sadness, as something I had ignored or fought to suppress saw its chance for a reckoning.

I clutched my mother's cylinder in my hand, unable to believe I had it at last, and with no need for argument or struggle. The rest of New Galveston could stew in its cowardice, in its pettiness and greed. The Silence had broken them, and it was clear to me then that they would stay that way. But it would not be silent in our home. It would not be silent in my father's broken heart.

I'd rescued my mother's voice, and I was bringing it home.

And, maybe, I was bringing home the answer to the Silence itself.

20

It was still dark when the War Engines broke through. I'd drifted off to sleep, and I'd been dreaming: a raging sea, untold tons of water moving like muscle, a sight I'd never seen in life. The waves crashed into a cliffside, shaking the earth, rumbling like a world-spanning storm. Someone screamed. I opened my eyes, and the rumbling was real.

The others must have been sleeping, too. We were all sitting up, our eyes adjusting to the low light, trying to understand what we were hearing.

Peabody was with us. He stood in our midst, silent and still. A single black moth perched on his tilted, ruined skull, wings beating like a slow pulse.

Silas leapt off his chair and rushed down the corridor. "They're in! They're in!"

My first thought: "Watson's out there."

I looked at the others, expecting them to launch into action. Joe and Sally stared back at me, their faces blank. They didn't move. Peabody's reaction, if he had one, was unknowable to me.

Another scream floated down to us, a ghost on a dark current. I pushed myself to my feet, and against every instinct in my body I made my way to the mouth of the corridor. Sally's rifle leaned beside it; I snatched it up and raced down the hallway. I felt the cold pulse of wind waiting at the far end.

"Stay here!" Sally called, but I ignored her. As far as I was concerned, they were once again displaying cowardice in the face of a true threat. If they were worried enough about it, they'd follow me.

I arrived at the door to see Silas pulling it closed and spinning the seal.

I felt the hum of the *Lamplighter* as Peabody brought the engines to life.

"No!" I raised the rifle, aimed it at Silas. "Open it!"

He looked at me as though I'd lost my mind. "The War Engines are inside! Can't you hear what's happening? We're getting out of here!"

"Watson! If they came in, then he would have come in with him! He's looking for me!"

Silas took a step closer, anger contorting his face. "Put that goddamn gun down! You idiot! We're leaving!"

There were other cultists out there. People he'd been living with and working beside for God knew how long. People who'd stayed with him as others fled, people who believed as much as he did in the chance to send the *Lamplighter* home and solve the greatest mystery, the direst calamity, that the Martian colony had ever faced. And he was prepared to leave them all behind, without even attempting to save a single one.

He took another step and I fired the rifle. I was aiming above his head, and by some stroke of luck I did actually miss him. The bullet struck the metal wall behind him and ricocheted past my own ear. His face was almost comical with shock.

"Open it!" I screamed.

He spun the wheel and hauled the door open again. As he did so I slammed the button that extended the ramp. The wind was howling, and an icy spray stung my face. A wedge of light spilled from the hatchway onto the cold ground. The green mist of the Strange clung to the ranks of the unharvested cylinders, their weird crystalline ghosts shivering in the night.

Some of the Moths were here, having been pushed back into the garden by the advance of the War Engines. They'd arrayed themselves in a defensive position in front of the corridor, waiting for the Engines to make their appearance. A couple of them turned to look back at the ship, their drawn and haggard faces lighting with hope. The others kept waiting, their rifles and their pistols ready, prepared to sacrifice their lives to aid in the *Lamplighter*'s escape. It was a remarkable, doomed act of courage, and I couldn't help but wonder how different things might have been if the people of New Galveston had shared even a quarter of that bravery.

Screams cascaded from the tunnel's yawning mouth, as if Mars itself cried out. I walked to the bottom of the ramp, the rifle dangling uselessly in my hand, looking for any sign of Watson. But no Engines had made it into the garden yet.

A percussive blast of gunfire overlaid the screaming, calm and unhurried.

Thumpthumpthumpthumpthump.

Thumpthumpthump.

One of the Moths started firing into the tunnel.

And then there was Watson, that dear old Kitchen Engine, that stupid bucket of rattling parts, frustrating and helpless and reassuring and safe, rolling quickly out of it, his useless dishwasher arms sticking comically out, his head peering this way and that as the rifle rounds *ricocheted* off his chassis.

"Watson! Over here!"

He heard me and altered his course. The Moths let him go, concentrating their fire at whatever was coming down the tunnel behind him.

The *Lamplighter* vibrated with energy. Its big engine hammered and rolled, an old horse eager for another run. Every impulse in my body urged me back inside. The ship was moments from flight.

Watson made it halfway and stopped. He was saying something to me, but I couldn't hear him over the *Lamplighter*, the wind, the gunfire, the screams.

I jumped off the ramp and ran to him. I wasn't dressed for the temperature. The wind was already making my body shake, my fingers numb. I'd forgotten how bad it could get, without the heat tents, without even a heavy-weather jacket to block the wind. The cold was a killing thing. Keeping low, I hustled across the small open space separating me from Watson. I spared a quick look at the mouth of the corridor.

A War Engine filled it. It was one of the Engines with a dangling human being, a puppet, as Silas had called it. He twitched like a hideous living doll. His hands were black at the fingertips, as were his nose and his cheeks. Frostbite, in its dark flourish. The machine's other limb was a Gatling gun, and it spun in a red heat as it spewed bullets across the garden like a swinging scythe.

"Watson," I said, arriving at his side. I positioned myself so that he was between me and the War Engine. "Watson, what's wrong? Let's go!"

"My treads have come loose," he said. I looked down and saw

that it was true: the right tread had separated and lay uselessly in the dirt.

"Watson, no. Can't you move anyway?"

He made an effort, inching forward.

"I'm afraid not, Miss Crisp."

"Try!" I ran behind him and threw my whole weight against his body. It was like trying to push a fully loaded wagon, but he crept forward again.

I glanced at the *Lamplighter*. To my horror, the ramp had been retracted. Silas stood at the door; he locked eyes with me once before swinging it shut.

"NO!"

The *Lamplighter* lifted off the ground.

It was like seeing Death raise its head. I stood in the middle of this maelstrom of blood and terror, the frozen wind slowing my brain, the ghosts in the garden winking out as the cylinders were shattered by stray bullets of the firefight, and watched that little sphere of warmth and possibility start its journey into the starry sky, as removed and peaceful as an illustration from one of my books.

I was suddenly aware of my mother's recording, still in my pocket. If I didn't make it out, Father would never hear her voice again.

"I'll protect you, Miss Crisp."

He pushed me until he stood between me and the War Engines. He rotated his position so that he faced them. It was everything he could do. It was all he could do. I rested my forehead against him.

What Moths remained made their final stand. Though a few had taken up positions behind the odd crate or a recess in the cavern walls, most of them had nowhere to hide. They stood lined up in the open, like the soldiers from the Civil War I'd seen pictures of in school. They fired a volley at the War Engines and lowered their rifles to reload.

The War Engines fired their Gatling guns, and the bullets flew, thundering hammerblows with a noise so loud it was almost physical. People came apart like toys. Limbs flew every which way, blood leapt and arced, misting the air. The Moths screamed. Some of them fired back, their bullets pinging off the Engines' hides or landing with dull wet thuds into the dangling puppets' bodies. I fixated on Percy, the arrogant kid who'd wanted to stand up to Joe until Sally backed him down, crouching on one knee and bracing his rifle against his shoulder, firing futilely at our encroaching doom.

A voice sounded behind me: "Anabelle! Get inside!"

It was Joe Reilly, standing in the opened hatchway, his jacket flapping in the wind. The loading ramp had been extended again, though since the *Lamplighter* was still airborne, it hovered a foot off the ground.

"Come on, Watson!" I started pushing him again.

Rage colored Joe's face. "Goddamn it, forget him and come on!"

Watson tried again, making it another six inches before lurching to a stop. A stray bullet caught his head, just under his left eye. A shower of sparks and metal flew out like a small geyser. "I think, Miss Crisp," he said, "that I would prefer to stay."

The War Engines released another volley of hell, and the sound and the stink of human destruction was too much. I dropped to the ground, terror short-circuiting everything else; I curled around myself, arms over my head. I think I was screaming.

A small point of stillness in my head, an embattled fortress of reason, told me that I had to get up and go. That I would be killed for sure if I stayed even another moment.

"Anabelle! It has to be now!"

All right, I thought. *All right. There's another way to save him.*

I pulled myself up to Watson's side. "Bluebonnet," I said.

Watson's eyes went dark and his cylinder tried to eject from his body. It caught; the bullet to his head had warped the metal. I tried to grab it with my fingers, pry it out. "No, no, no, no, no, no."

It wouldn't come.

I turned my head in time to see bullets shred Percy's head and shoulders into gaudy ribbons of blood and bone, the flesh of his face ripped away by a hurricane of metal, the teeth in his skull briefly visible before they dissolved into splinters and dust.

I felt a crushing horror. These people were giving up their lives so that Peabody and the *Lamplighter* could escape, and by delaying that escape I risked turning their sacrifice into a useless, gore-strewn waste.

Watson sat inert like a stone. I tried to shove the cylinder back in, to wake him again. So he could hide, so he could come home on his own.

It wouldn't go back in. It was completely stuck.

"Watson," I sobbed, turning toward the ship and running. "Watson, I'm sorry! I'm sorry!"

I reached for Joe. He grabbed my forearm and hauled me onto the ramp, nearly pulling my arm from its socket. I felt a surge of relief at his strength, at the way his grip brooked no argument. I was a child still, and he illustrated this by lifting me off my feet and carrying me to safety.

"Go go go go go!"

Bullets punched into the *Lamplighter*'s hide and into the open port as the hydraulics labored to pull the ramp closed. I saw Joe's coat flare out on one side as the bullets pinged and spanged around us. The ship pitched hard to one side, tumbling us painfully into the damaged corridor. I slammed into the wall, breath exploding from my lungs. The whole world tilted and spun, and I knew that the bullets must have ruptured some necessary pipe or reservoir, or smashed through the motherboard that housed Peabody's consciousness.

But the *Lamplighter* quickly leveled, and the inertia of a fast ascent pressed me into the floor.

The ramp hadn't closed completely; one of the struts had been damaged, and it stalled out with a gap several inches wide, beyond which the cold night air roared like a banshee, and flashes from the firefight could be seen dropping swiftly away.

Watson was down there among them.

Joe climbed to his feet, examining a large hole in his jacket. Remarkably, the bullet had missed him. I felt a vast relief, even underneath the grief I felt for Watson.

"I almost died," he said. "I almost got killed for your piece-of-shit Engine."

I stared at him, stunned. He looked calm, but it was the wrong sort of calm: all animation in his face had ceased. It was like he'd been wearing a mask, and it had come loose in the violence, and now just hung there like dead skin.

I was scared all over again, and I didn't even know why. "I had to do it," I said. I looked around for my anger, but I couldn't find it. I needed it and it wasn't there. "I had to try to save him."

"No," he said. "You didn't. You risked every single one of our lives for something that isn't even real. In fact, that's Anabelle Crisp in a nutshell, isn't it? That's what you do."

He leaned against the bulkhead, his eyes unfocused. He seemed to think about things for a minute. Maybe he was looking for something, too. Finally, he said, "Get away from that door. If you slip out, I don't want to have to go fetch your corpse." He walked away, toward the main cabin.

I pressed myself against the wall, staring through the gap in the broken door, into the darkness where I had left my only friend in the world. Where I had left a field of slaughter.

I wrapped my arms around myself, clutching my mother's cylinder to my chest. I closed my eyes and imagined that my head was in her lap, her fingers stroking my hair. *It's not your fault,* she said. *Everything's going to be okay.* For the first time since Silas had broken into the diner, I cried.

part three

the consequences thereof

21

The *Lamplighter* rattled like a can of nails. The walls shook and the floor threatened to buck me off my feet. Sand still filled much of the main cabin. It was heated, at least. Joe had set up our camp in a corner as far from the pilot's chair, where Peabody had stationed himself, as he could. He retreated into himself, his heat tent furled beside him, the cookstove set up but as yet unlit. He had a bottle of whiskey in his hand, and for the moment it absorbed his full attention.

Sally sat on a crate nearby. She watched me as I came in, her face still and unreadable. The overhead lamps reflected from her eyes and gave her an unearthly aspect.

Silas had placed himself on the other side of the cabin. I didn't know what to expect from him; an anger similar to Joe's, no doubt. But he regarded me levelly, without emotion. "Glad you made it," he said.

The thing that thought it was Peabody was apparently oblivious to us all. The suit slouched in the pilot's chair, inert. I had the sense that it had been parked there, like an unoccupied automobile, and that whatever force steered it roamed through the *Lamplighter*'s circuitry for the time being.

Still, his voice crackled from the suit's speakers. His normally genteel manner had disappeared; in its place was a taciturn brooding, a contained energy that seemed to radiate . . . not a threat, exactly, but an alienness that delivered the same effect. He spoke softly, not to any of us but apparently to himself, muttering ruminations involving equations and words I had never heard before.

"What's wrong with him?" I said.

Sally shrugged. "He gets like this sometimes. The part of him that's Chauncy goes away, and the part of him that's something else comes in instead. Whatever it is, it don't like to talk to people. Best to leave him alone when he's like this."

Silas said, "What you see before you is the closest thing to a god you'll ever know. You wouldn't poke God in the shoulder when he was thinking, would you?"

"That ain't no god," I said. Whatever goodwill Silas had built up with me had burned away when he slammed the door on me in the cavern. I knew his true heart. I wouldn't forget it again.

"That's Mars itself, sitting in that chair."

I remembered my lessons. Mars was the god of war.

I thought of all those cylinders exposed to the Strange, what Silas had said about the consciousness of Mars taking root inside. If he was right, what had it done to the *Lamplighter*, steeping in it for over sixty years? This thing that sometimes thought it was Chauncy, a long-dead pioneer, and sometimes remembered it was something else. It would have to be mad. Absolutely, apocalyptically mad.

"It doesn't know what it is, does it?"

"How can it?" Sally said. "For that matter, how can anybody? Whatever it is, it's something new." She took out a cigarette and dragged a match across her shoe. "Anyhow, no point worrying about it. Whenever it thinks it's Chauncy, that's when it uses the suit. That's when it's safe to talk to it." She took a long drag from the cigarette, her attention drifting.

She'd known all those people.

"I'm sorry, Sally," I said. My eyes were still raw from crying. I didn't care that she saw. I wanted her to.

"Ah, this is what they wanted." She tried to smile, but it died fast. "Just came a little faster than they'd planned is all." She nodded at my coat. "You got your mama, though, right?"

I nodded, patting the pocket where the cylinder resided. It made me think of Watson again, and I felt my eyes tearing up.

"He'll be fine," Sally said, intuiting my thoughts. "They don't hurt their own."

"He's not their own," I said.

Joe scoffed. "Oh, enough," he said. "Enough of that bullshit." The bottle he was drawing from was over half-gone already. He was drinking it like it was water. I'd never tried liquor myself, but I'd seen enough people do it to know that it generally kicked on the way down. You couldn't tell that, watching him in action.

"Enough of what?" I said.

"Enough pretending that your stupid kitchen utensil is real. Enough pretending that recording you have in your pocket is your mother."

"Easy now," Sally said quietly.

Silas just watched.

Joe glared at her but took a break from his guzzling. He clutched the bottle in his hands, sitting cross-legged under a bank of knobs and switches, like a little boy. Staring at me.

Something sizzled and spat behind his eyes, and it made me nervous. "What are you looking at," he said.

"I don't know." I didn't want to fight him. The slaughter still played out behind my eyes, the stink of blood still roosted in my nostrils. Everything was too much. Too big. The thought of any more conflict made me want to collapse. *Please stop,* I thought. *Please, please stop.*

"No? You had all kinds of opinions on it back in New Galveston. What happened since then?"

"Joe," Sally said. There was a warning in her voice.

"No, Sally. No. You weren't there. You didn't hear the things she called me, all the threats she made. She was going to get me hanged, do you hear me? *Hanged!* She wasn't joking, either!" He took another few furious swallows. "So high and mighty, this little brat. Such a princess. She's a fucking monster is what she is."

"Please stop," I said. It came out in a whisper.

"That's enough," Silas said.

"You shut up. You have nothing to say. You tried to leave her behind back there."

"Yeah, I did. But I did it because I'm in service to a cause greater than myself. I'm here to get Peabody back to Earth. And then *all of us* back to Earth. The one thing you're supposed to do, Joe, that you're too chickenshit to do. Because all you're in service to is your own cowardly hide." He looked at me, still talking to Joe. "She may not forgive me for it, but I guarantee you she understands me."

Joe took another swig and continued listing his grievances, as though Silas hadn't said a word. "And now here I am, chased by a War Engine, trapped in some goddamned antique, on the way back to a town full of people who hate me, and almost *shot . . .*"

It was clear he had more to say but emotion overwhelmed him. He put the bottle down and pulled the edge of his coat into view, examining once again the bullet hole that had perforated it, front to back. The bullet must have missed him by a centimeter. His hands shook as he pushed a finger through.

Sally watched him, lighting up another cigarette. "Joe," she said quietly. "Go to sleep."

"I could have been gutshot," he said. "You ever seen that happen to somebody?"

"As it happens, I have. It was a near thing, but you weren't hit. A lot of other people were. You need to let it go now."

He took another drink. It was a smaller one, though; the fight seemed to have left him. He gave me a sullen look, and I was surprised to see a rime of tears in his eyes. "I didn't ask for any of this," he said. He lay down and pulled a blanket over his shoulders, turning his back to us. The bottle was clutched in his right arm, his shoulders shaking. He stifled a sob: a difficult sound, something he was ashamed of and tried to hide.

Sally sat beside him. He put his head in her lap, and she stroked his hair, like a mother consoling her child. I wanted to turn away but I was helpless to. Instead I watched with a heavy feeling in my heart. Everything inside me hurt.

She kept petting his hair even after it was clear he'd gone to sleep, the smoke from her cigarette curling over her head. Without looking at me, she said, "You got to make some allowances. The Silence messed people up all kinds of ways. Whatever was bad in us just got worse."

Hearing her say the words—*the Silence*—reminded me that she'd had a life before it. Though obvious, it struck me as a revelation. I'd only ever thought of her as a creature of Mars, as much a part of its landscape and its ecology as the storms that swept over us every couple of years or the strange insects that hatched each monsoon season and died off when the world went dry. That she'd had a life on Earth before coming here seemed impossible somehow.

"How old were you when you came here?" I asked. Although I was asking her about herself, posing the question made me feel vulnerable. But the rules felt different now; barriers hadn't exactly come down, but they seemed temporarily crossable.

She squinted at me through the smoke. She took another drag from the cigarette before she decided to answer. "I was about twenty, I guess. I came when New Galveston wasn't much more than a bright idea. They had all kinds of plans for it."

"What did you do back on Earth?"

"What do you care?"

Embarrassed, I dropped my eyes. "I don't know. I thought I might try being civil."

She huffed a laugh and gave me a full view of her ruined teeth. "I think running for your life agrees with you, kid." She stubbed out her spent cigarette and fetched another one. "I worked on my family's farm. We were poor. No school for me. I found me a sweet old boy and married him, and was all set to go work on his farm, keep doing the same damn thing I'd been doing, until the idea of going to Mars came up. For the first time in my life, somebody from the wide world needed people like me. Hard folk, ready for hard work. For the first time I thought maybe I could be part of something important."

I was too busy trying to process the idea of Sally Milkwood being married to register the sadness in her voice. "Where's your husband?" I said.

"Dead. Red lung."

She said it matter-of-factly, like she was talking about a dog she might have been fond of. It was easy to imagine the life that followed, the desperate struggle to survive in a world not designed to accommodate impoverished widows. "I'm sorry," I said.

"You might as well be sorry for the sun going down. It's just what happens."

A score of slaughtered dead lay behind us as proof of that. My mother and perhaps the entire population of Earth was proof of that, too. And so was that dead stupid miner bleeding out at my father's feet.

"I had a cart and I had a good mule. I took to hauling goods, 'cause that's a skill I had from back home. I'd trade anything to anybody, including the Shanks's moonshine. Met Joe that way. Joe has a weakness—he has more than his share, maybe— but he's my friend. That's why I came out here with you. I'm protecting my friend."

"That's a sweet story," said Silas. I'd almost forgotten he was sitting there. "Is that why you helped us? 'Cause you wanted to be our friend?"

"I helped you because you paid me," Sally said mildly. "That's the beginning and the end of it. So you can go to hell."

It's funny how quickly the mood can turn, with just the wrong syllable, the wrong inflection. Silas's voice soured the atmosphere. He was right: I did understand why he'd been prepared to leave me back there. He was motivated by a singular purpose, which was something I understood. But he was exhausting in a way I hadn't encountered in a person before. Every action he took provoked an extreme reaction from me: the robbery, the return of my mother, leaving me to die in the slaughter. I hated him and I respected him. I didn't know how to reconcile those truths.

I took my mother's cylinder from my coat pocket and cradled it in my lap, staring at it. I felt Silas's eyes on me, but I didn't care. Nor did I care, in that moment, about the price that had been paid, and had yet to be paid. Heat flushed my face and stung my eyes, but I beat it back. The Moths had stolen from me. New Galveston had stolen from me. Even Joe Reilly. If he'd been brave enough to fly us home, maybe we'd all be safe right now. Maybe nothing was wrong on Earth, and we were here fighting and dying for no reason at all. Considering all of that, I figured a bill was due. And it was my job to make sure people paid what they owed.

An image of young Percy's bullet-scored body filled my mind. One of the bullets had carved a runnel through his head above his left eye, exposing his brain to the air. That house of mysteries, that garden of dreams, just a spilling pile of riven, bloody meat. Grosser and uglier than the clean metal device that held my mother's last words to her family.

"I guess he got to shoot his gun after all," I said, and tried to laugh. It came out sounding different, though.

Sally either didn't know what I meant or didn't care. She was stroking Joe's hair again, lost in her own thoughts. Maybe it was her husband's hair she was petting, maybe it was his face she saw.

Well. She could tend to her own dead. I was busy trying to raise mine.

THE NEXT MORNING we were still flying. It seemed shockingly slow to me; I couldn't figure why the ship wouldn't have access to the same speed it used when traveling between planets. Leaving the others to stew in their own miseries, I walked down the corridor to where the ramp shuddered and groaned in its incomplete closure. Sunlight flared painfully through the gap. Blowing sand flowed around the ship's hull, sounding like a soft, granular rain. In the bulkhead around the entrance, big black craters showed where the bullets had punched through.

I laid myself out flat on the floor and crawled closer to the edge. The wind whipped my hair and thundered in my ears. The smell of Mars filled my sinuses with a clean, metallic tang. I was surprised to find it good. My eyes adjusted quickly to the light, and I beheld scrolling below me the same difficult landscape we'd traversed over the past few days, rendered majestic by distance, a beautiful tapestry of russet, gold, and pink. Strewn boulders, shattered remnants of an ancient meteorite, were from on high an elegant alien scrawl, or the features of an unknowable face. Choking dust became lovely wisps, like the ephemeral skirts of the ghosts that crossed those fields every day and night.

The ghosts I couldn't see from up here, and I wondered if maybe they only appeared when there was an eye to behold them. How could there be a memory, without a mind to conjure it? To feel ashamed by it, or to ache for it?

If Silas and the Moths were right—if Mars was itself a sleeping mind, stirring to consciousness through our presence, grasping for understanding through our Engines and even our own bodies—then these apparitions were just figments of that memory, and walking across this world was like walking through the cobwebbed hallways of an ancient brain.

And now we were stirring that brain awake.

The trouble was, it could only understand us, speak to us, through our own filters. Instruments of war. People abandoned and terrified. Rage, fear, loneliness.

Furthermore, if the War Engines were attacking the miners and laying siege to Peabody's cave, that suggested each manifestation of the Martian intelligence was operating at cross-purposes to the others. Was there no self-recognition there? Had we made Mars alien even to itself?

We're a disease, Silas had said. *Ruiners.*

Was that, then, what had happened to Earth? All those cylinders made from the Strange we sent there, from a whole industry devoted to harvesting the fossilized memories of a world, to containing them and shipping them home like weird batteries for our frivolous conveniences, for our governments and our vehicles and our wars. Had it awakened there, as it had here? Had we driven it insane?

It was a desolating thought, and it careened through me like a wrecking ball. I imagined all the Engines on Earth, in their terrible multitudes, exerting the will of this dark intelligence upon a soft and unsuspecting people. I imagined a ruined world, stalked by spirits demented by both time and bewilderment.

What good would going back there do now? What hell would we find?

Regardless of those questions, my own journey felt completed. I'd become the hero from my stories: I'd ventured out when others had been too afraid, I'd descended into a pit of horrors, losing someone dear to me in the process, and I'd rescued the one who needed rescuing. And now I was going home: aloft, triumphant.

First I would see Father, and return him to himself. Then we would repair the diner, and then we'd reclaim our lives. We would put things back together. We would restore order.

I knew difficulties awaited the others, but I couldn't bring myself to worry over them. The relief was too intense.

I had won.

22

By late afternoon, we were approaching Dig Town. We were all in the control room. I sat atop some piled crates, facing Peabody, who was animating the suit again. Through the scratched window behind him I could see the Martian desert drift slowly by. The sky eased into an amber afternoon glow, the sun a small disc on the horizon. Dig Town came into view as a dark tangle of shapes atop the plateau. The network of unlit sodium lights around the Throat looked like the fingers of a great hand reaching toward the heavens.

Joe and Sally sat some distance away. Joe was still lost in his funk, and Sally had ceased trying to coax him out of it. They passed a bottle back and forth between them, whatever exchanges they had pitched too low for my hearing. I tried not to think about it. I had what I needed. What they did or thought should no longer concern me.

Silas leaned over the controls, staring through the window. He'd resolved that we would land a short distance outside Dig Town in an effort to evade attention. The last thing he wanted was a crowd of hope-crazed citizens fighting for a place on board.

I felt removed from these discussions, which was fine with me. Whatever they did wasn't my business anymore. Even the idea that the ship was going to leave for Earth didn't excite any strong feelings in me. It was that particular absence of enthusiasm that troubled me; why didn't I care? It was our chance to find out the answers to all our questions. My chance to talk to Mother again.

What you see before you is the closest thing to a god you'll ever know.

I couldn't shake that thought from my head. I'd dismissed it at first as just more of Silas's sideshow bluster, but the more time I spent in Peabody's presence, the more gravity that pronouncement assumed.

Peabody rarely spoke on the journey. When he did, it was always to inquire politely after our comfort, or to lament the shortsightedness of the people on Earth who had failed to recognize his genius.

"They'll understand when I return, with all the glories of Mars in tow," he said.

And how will they receive you? I wondered. *What will they say to the dreadful apparition that walks down that ramp?*

I wondered this especially when the Peabody persona receded and the other intelligence held sway. It shriveled something in my heart. It was dark, cold, hungry. I fancied I could feel its curious fingers sliding over my brain. On these occasions the suit would remain inert in the pilot's chair, moths slipping into and out of the rents of his decayed suit and crawling across his dead skull. It did not seem impossible then that this was a god after all, the physical embodiment of the Silence coming to claim his throne at last.

• • •

I DOZED, AND was awakened from a fitful sleep by an argument.

"No," Sally was saying. "That's foolish. No."

Silas was looking at me, leaning on a bank of knobs and buttons beside his master. Peabody was stationary, the skull leaning to one side, grinning. "It's not negotiable, Sally."

"What's not negotiable?" I said.

"I'm gonna keep you here with me while the others get the fuel," Silas said.

My stomach dropped. "No, you're not. I'm going back home. I got what I needed. You all can do your own thing."

"I can't risk you running your mouth about the *Lamplighter*. You could have the whole community on our heads before we're ready to fly."

"She ain't gonna do that, Silas," Sally said.

"Says you."

"That's right, says me. Since when has that not been enough for you?"

I looked to Joe to back her up. He was slumped on his bunk, only half-conscious. I guess he'd drunk himself into a stupor.

"Look," Silas said to me, trying to sound reasonable. "You just sit here with me until they get back with the fuel, and someone to repair the ramp. Then I take off, you go home, everybody gets what they want. I don't see the problem with that."

"The problem with that is it makes me a prisoner," I said. "You came into our diner and did that once. I won't let you do it again."

"Oh, you won't let me?" he said, standing up.

Sally shoved him hard in the chest. He lost his footing and fell back onto the bank of controls, scrabbling to catch himself, then slid onto the floor. He landed on his elbow and cried out, cradling it against himself.

"Don't you ever," she said. "God damn you. Don't you ever."

Peabody stood. We all froze, watching him. Even Sally seemed frightened, though she didn't retreat from where she loomed over Silas. The skull rolled against the faceplate, the moths' wings made little tapping sounds in their disquiet. The presence we felt at all times surged like a tide, occluding our thoughts, filling us with fear and awe.

From the floor, Silas laughed weakly. "Watch yourself, Sally," he said.

I took Sally's hand and pulled her away. She did not resist.

"It's okay," I said. "I'll stay."

"No, you won't." She didn't acknowledge Peabody; she kept the full weight of her attention on Silas. "She's coming with me. If you don't trust me, after all the work we've done together, then I guess you'd better do something about it right now."

This roused Joe from his apathy. "Sally, hold on now. . . ."

"Be quiet."

Silas pulled himself to his feet, flexing his bruised elbow a few times. He wore that same mean little smile he'd shown me all that time ago, when he left me in the diner with the still form of my father.

"Compromise," he said. "She goes with you, fine. But she leaves her precious cylinder here. With me."

"No!" I said.

"Just to keep her mouth closed about the *Lamplighter*. You all come back with the fuel and with someone who can fix the ramp, she gets the cylinder back, and we all part as friends. That's the deal."

I looked at Sally, desperate for her to resist, but she only gave me a flat look. "Fine," she said.

"I ain't leaving it with you! Not again!"

"Kid, I don't *want* it!" Silas barked. "I want it, you, and everything about this place left behind me forever. But I also don't want to fend off a bunch of city folk who'll want to hitch a ride home with us. So this is how I make sure that doesn't happen."

"I'll stay, then."

Sally shook her head. "No, you won't. We'll need your help. You're coming with us."

I turned my back to them all. Hate and fear filled me, emotions I was growing very tired of. I only wanted to sleep in my own home, with my father in the next room, and with the sound of my mother's voice. I wanted Watson back. I wanted to be in touch with Earth again.

It was the possibility of all those things that let me make peace with the compromise. I would do anything to see them realized.

Still, I felt unsure. I thought of the cavern full of people who believed in the absolute rightness of these endeavors, each one of them now butchered and cold. I feared that I was not traveling through the air in an old spaceship, but rather in the belly of some terrible beast, and that I was guiding it to my own home.

"Okay," I said.

• • •

WE TOUCHED DOWN about fifty yards outside Dig Town, the thrusters pushing up a corona of dust that settled over us again like an unseasonable light rain. The damaged ramp struggled to extend, filling the chamber with the sound of grinding metal. I peered through the window, fearing I'd see a train of people coming to greet us. Nothing had flown in a Martian sky since the Silence began, and I couldn't fathom that a working spacecraft wouldn't bring them out in droves. Sally had assured Silas that that wouldn't happen, though, and she proved to be correct.

The ground remained empty, the few shacks I could see from here remained quiet and still. I should have been relieved; my hope of getting the cylinder back home rested on the success of Silas's plan. And I was, mostly. But it was a sinister portent. I was afraid to get out of the ship.

Night was close. The repairs and the transference of fuel would have to wait until morning, when the temperature was warmer. Silas wanted us all to spend the night aboard the *Lamplighter*, but none of us would have it. Not when we could see home through the window.

Unable to force us, Silas conceded. He took the cylinder from me. Putting it back into his hands hurt. My eyes misted over and a hook dragged against my heart.

"Come back with Harry Wickham first," he told us. "While he works on repairs, retrieve the fuel from the *Eurydice*. Don't waste time."

"You'll see us in the morning," Sally said.

We gathered our supplies—lacking Watson's help, we had to leave the heavier camping gear behind—and disembarked.

Dig Town waited for us, another empty skull.

• • •

DIG TOWN WAS not completely devoid of people after all. A few still perambulated the streets, senses dumb to the world. They displayed no interest in the *Lamplighter*, nor in any of us. Some slumped in doorways or against walls; I was reminded of stories of indigents on Earth. A year ago such a sight would have been unthinkable. Occasionally one would lift his head as we walked by, as if he'd heard a noise from another room. But this glimmer of curiosity never lasted.

Sally broke away first. "I'm gonna check on Laura and Billy."

The Shank kids. I'd managed to forget that she stayed with them. Her concern for them now seemed almost offensive to me, considering what we'd all just been through.

"Those two are tough as nails," Joe said.

"That ain't no protection from what's happening to this town. You both should come."

"The hell with that," he said. "I'll sleep in my own bed tonight. You two can handle Harry in the morning. He won't hear anything from me anyway."

Sally looked at me.

"No," I said. I didn't want to share a roof with the Shank kids, but I didn't want to go home to New Galveston, either. It was hard enough sleeping there without Father home; I couldn't imagine what it would be like without Watson, too. "We still have light in the sky. I'll talk to Mr. Wickham. Then I can stay with Widow Kessler. She put me up last time."

I wasn't worried about being chased through the streets, like last time. Not now that Charlie's corpse dangled from the grip of a War Engine out in the crater.

Sally didn't look pleased about this, but she offered no resistance. She knew Silas having the cylinder kept me on a tight leash. "Okay then. If you get Wickham to help tonight, you let me know in the morning. Then we'll both join Joe at the *Eurydice*."

It was a plan. Sally left us, Joe watching her go with sweat beaded on his face.

"Guess it's just us now," I said. He didn't respond. We continued in uneasy company through Dig Town.

Our route took us by the center of town, and the Throat. There were more people gathered here—maybe a dozen, in discrete assemblies. Some stood on the catwalks surrounding the hole, more gathered directly on its perimeter. Their attention was fixed on the abyss, their bodies inclined delicately toward it, like subterranean flowers toward a cold, dead sun.

I recognized the path that led to Widow Kessler's home; I remembered what she'd told me—*the gardens are calling them down*. I recalled the presence in her basement, the wild explosion of mushrooms and the skull nestled within. The events in Peabody Crater had pushed all of that from my mind, but it seeped back in now, a nightmare stirring back to life.

By the time we arrived at Mr. Wickham's shop, the sun's rays were nearly horizontal, spearing over the hills and through the rough buildings in golden planes. Lamplight filled one of the windows, indicating that he had not gone into the Throat yet. The white paint of the word "Parts" shone in the evening light as if lit by electricity.

Joe stopped a few yards short of the door. "You go on," he said. "He doesn't like me."

I stepped up to the door and knocked. "Mr. Wickham?" I waited a moment and called again. "Mr. Wickham, it's Belle Crisp."

Still nothing. The sky was bruising on the horizon. I wondered how long it had been since Sally had left us; not as long as it felt, surely.

"Open the door, Belle," Joe said.

I looked back at him. "I can't . . ."

"It's a place of business, for Christ's sake. It's what you do. Open the door."

"Easy for you to be brave standing so far away."

"What is it you're scared of?"

There was no need to answer that.

I opened the door.

"Mr. Wickham? We need your help. Can I come in?"

The light inside came from a lantern hanging from the rafter, and it illuminated a work space largely unchanged from the last time I'd seen it. Parts of Engines were stacked on workbenches and leaned in corners everywhere you looked, tools hung from a series of hooks on one wall, buckets and cans of screws and nails and God knew what else lined shelves on walls like books. The air still smelled like oil and woodsmoke. I felt a pang of loss when I noticed Watson's legs placed carefully on a shelf.

And there was Mr. Wickham, seated at a table near the back of the shop, where he'd arranged his living space: a kitchen, a cot, a picture hanging from the wall. He sat in profile to the front door, hunched as though over a dinner plate, though the table was empty. Although he was as large as ever, he seemed somehow diminished—as if he were trying to fold into himself.

I stayed in the doorway for a moment, unsure of what to do. Joe asked a question behind me, but I didn't hear it.

"Mr. Wickham?"

He raised his head and blinked, then looked at me. His eyes shone green in the lantern light, more deeply and more brightly than before—that green luminescence that exploded from the crushed mushrooms in the widow's cellar, that animated the moldering bones of Chauncy Peabody, that lit the metal hearts of the War Engines. The light that Silas claimed was Mars itself staring back at us.

"Belle," he said. "You shouldn't be here."

"I—I came—I need your help."

He rested his forehead in his hand and seemed to be thinking hard about something. "You went out with the others," he said. "Did you get what you wanted?"

"I did. That's why I'm here."

"You ready to put your Kitchen Engine's legs back on?"

"Watson—Watson didn't make it back."

"Oh." Everything he said came out slowly, like it was hard for him to think. "I'm sorry about that, Belle."

I took a step into his workshop, encouraged by the fact that he still seemed well-disposed toward me. "It's okay. He's still out there. His cylinder is jammed. He's not dead."

"Cylinder. That's right. You were looking for the cylinder with your mother's recording on it, weren't you?" The more he spoke, the more he sounded like himself. He passed a hand over his face. "What time is it? I'm starving. Are you hungry?"

I wasn't until he asked, and then food was all I could think about. I suddenly saw myself sitting across the table from a friendly face, eating a good meal and not worrying about feral Engines or shivering ghosts or the hostilities of my companions. I imagined, too, listening to my mother's sweet voice speaking to me from one of Mr. Wickham's spare Engines while I ate—

tomorrow night, it would be a reality tomorrow night—and it bent my heart so much I could hardly stand it.

Without my saying a word, he got up from the table and moved toward his little stove, stumbling a little as he got his feet working again. His movements were sluggish and tentative, as if he were trying to remember how to use his body. A pot fell from his hand and clattered across the floor.

A board creaked behind me and we both turned to see Joe Reilly standing in the doorway. He had one foot in the store and one on the bare ground, his head peering around the corner as if he might need to duck away quickly. "Everything okay in here?"

Joe's presence stirred Mr. Wickham to a greater display of energy than anything I'd yet said to him. "I told you to stay out."

"I know, Harry, and I'm sorry, but this is important."

Mr. Wickham hurled the pot he'd retrieved against the wall. *"What do you want from me! There's nothing left! I have nothing left!"*

Joe and I watched him in stunned silence. Breathing raggedly, he put his hands onto his face again, pulling at the flesh as if at a rubber mask. I took a step backward.

"Harry," said Joe. "We came back with a ship. It's the *Lamplighter.*"

Mr. Wickham looked at him directly for the first time I'd ever seen. "I don't understand."

"Yes, you do. The original ship. We found it. It's here, Harry. It still flies. It needs your help."

Mr. Wickham walked toward Joe, suddenly unaware of my existence. "You're lying."

Joe stepped back outside, holding the door wide. "No. It's real. This is our chance, Harry. This is our chance to go home."

It was the wrong thing to say. Upon getting close, Mr. Wickham grabbed Joe's shirt and hauled him into the workshop. He shoved him hard against a table; Joe flailed to keep himself upright, sending tools and the outer carapace of a dismantled Rockhauler Engine clattering to the floor.

"You were our chance," he said.

Joe scrambled to get out of his way. Mr. Wickham kept advancing on him. I ducked away, too, putting the kitchen table between myself and the two men. I didn't know what to say to calm him down. The air stank with hurt and malice; I wished more than anything that Sally hadn't left us alone.

"You were our chance, but you were too weak!"

"Mr. Wickham, stop!" I shouted.

He gave no sign of hearing me. "They went into the *Eurydice* while you were gone, did you know that?"

Joe stopped inching away, his face going slack. He seemed suddenly unsure of his footing. He put his hand against the wall to stabilize himself, no longer trying to avoid the beating he knew was coming. "What?"

"That's right. They were looking for Anabelle. When they couldn't find her, they went looking for you. Went right up into your ship. Guess what they found?"

I felt my stomach clench. They would have found its guts ripped out, its fundamentals harvested and taken away. They would know the ship would never fly again, that it couldn't now even if Joe changed his mind. The thing I'd threatened him with had become real, simply because we'd left town.

"I see," Joe said quietly. "I see."

"There's a gallows waiting for you." Mr. Wickham smiled, his shining eyes giving his expression an eerie cast. "I helped build it." He reached Joe, who'd stopped trying to move altogether. He put his big hand on Joe's cheek, cradling it in a strangely intimate gesture. "The world is dying. But knowing I get to watch you hang makes it almost okay."

I felt my lip trembling. If I hadn't forced him to come with me . . .

"But Mr. Wickham," I said. "The *Lamplighter* is really here."

Mr. Wickham kept Joe pinned with his own proximity, but I had his attention again.

"That's where all the *Eurydice's* parts went. Its ramp is broken. It's got a few bullet holes. It needs to be fixed. It needs you."

He remained still, thinking. "Who's going to fly it?"

"It's going to fly itself. It's . . . alive."

He stared at Joe, tears in his eyes. "It's too late," he said. "The widow is coming."

"What?" Joe shook his head. "No, Harry. It isn't too late. Please go out there. You'll see. Someone's there who'll tell you all about it. His name is Silas. You can even stay overnight on board. You'll see. You'll see."

Mr. Wickham peered through the open door like someone staring into a dream. "Where?"

"Other side of the Throat, a little beyond the town limit," I said. "On the northern decline."

He stepped toward the door, then stopped himself and pointed his finger at Joe. "I would tell you not to leave. I'd tell you not to try and run. But the truth is there's nowhere for you to go. Stay, or run off into the desert. Your reckoning's coming, whatever you do."

He stepped out into the waning light, heading for the *Lamplighter*.

Joe stayed silent. There was nothing to say anyhow.

"YOU SHOULDN'T GO to your ship," I said. "Go to Sally. Or you can even come with me."

Mr. Wickham's revelation of the gallows had me reeling. I felt physically sick. He'd been gone about ten minutes. I wanted to give Joe time to rouse himself from his stunned condition, but it only seemed to be getting worse. The wick on the lantern needed turning; the workshop was growing dark, and the various large metal pieces took on a hulking, malevolent aspect.

"No, I don't guess I will," he said mildly. "I guess you and me are done. You got what you wanted. All the way around, you got what you wanted."

I lowered my head. I wanted to tell him that I wasn't the one who decided to sell off the *Eurydice*'s guts to a deranged Engine cult in the desert; I wasn't the one who let a whole community suffer in a protracted state of deluded hope that he might change his mind. He'd done all that himself; that's what they were going to hang him for. And all that was true, but it was also true that they might not have found out about it if I hadn't played my hand—at least not for a while yet.

"I'm going to see my father at the jail tomorrow. I'll talk to the sheriff while I'm there. I can change his mind."

"They ransacked your diner, robbed you blind. Your father's either going to precede me to the noose or walk up right behind me. Did you forget all that? They don't give a damn what you have to say. I just wish I hadn't, either."

"Fine," I said, angry again. "You just go back to your shack and get drunk. I know that's what you want." Not having anything else worthwhile to say, I headed for the door.

"That's what I like about you. Straight to the heart of things. And you know what—you're right. What an amazing, insightful human being you are. How special. How unlike the rest of us."

Everything he said cut. Everything felt like a whirling blade in my chest.

I pushed the door open. I needed to be out of there.

"Hey, Belle. How does it feel to be the hero of the story?"

I walked away.

23

Twilight settled over Dig Town. I made my way along the paths, trying to remember where I'd been before, which turn would take me to the widow's home. It was no good. Last time, I'd been too busy concentrating on avoiding being caught to pay attention to any landmarks. Even now, though Charlie was dead, I was careful to tread quietly, to peer around the corners of buildings so I didn't blithely stumble across someone who wished me ill. Those I did see still wandering were headed to the center—to the Throat. Their eyes were little green lamps in the gloaming, and they were not dressed for the night. It was this, even more than their eyes, that unsettled me; they were walking in the growing dark in their shirtsleeves or their work clothes, loose and light. Though not deadly yet, the night was dangerously close. If they didn't feel the cold on their skin, how could I know they felt anything human at all?

I didn't intend it, but my searching took me into an alleyway that opened straight onto the Throat at its far end. I looked, despite myself.

A green particulate dusted the air like a fog. It hadn't been there last time. It turned the frozen steam a sickly green color, swirling and eddying under the lights strung over the hole. It looked demonic, like a ceaseless, blighted breath from the center of the world. Four people climbed onto a large platform designed for supporting heavy machinery and lowered themselves down. The sound of the massive, turning chains filled the night. I stared at the huge links, overcome with the feeling that I was seeing the machinery of Mars laid bare, watching it lower us into hell.

Pulled by a perverse curiosity, I climbed the nearest stairs, until I stood on the wooden catwalk surrounding the Throat. From here I could see directly into it.

Like the last time I peered into that gulf, I experienced a vertigo beyond a simple physical disorientation; I felt an unbalancing in some fundamental part of me, in my heart or in my soul. I felt the attraction of the abyss, the allurement of extinction. I could imagine every ache and every fear laid to rest. Tears stung my eyes.

The Strange.

I was struck by an image of Mars as a vast haunted house, its interminable tunnels infested with ghosts, the very rock of which it was made deranged by malignant intent. We'd made our little stations here, planted our foolish flag, and sent fragments of that evil rock back to Earth to fuel the Engines there—quaint Kitchen Engines like Watson making dinners, big work Engines building cities, delicate vanity Engines serving us tea in our homes so we could pretend we were little kings and queens. Feeding our obsessive need to tread where we were not wanted and turn the world in service to us. We'd sent this phantasmal rock to Earth, and the Silence fell over the world.

The vision made me sick. I turned away from the Throat, leaning against a wooden railing and breathing heavily until I got my equilibrium back.

I felt the dust coating my own throat. We were all breathing it in. Not as quickly or in as concentrated amounts as the miners, but we were doing it nonetheless. How long until all our eyes shone green? Until we all lowered ourselves down that awful well?

I descended the stairs again, putting the Throat behind me, returning to the narrow Dig Town roads. The temperature was plummeting. I had a jacket, but the heat tent was on the *Lamplighter*. I did not want to go back there, though. I'd had my fill of madness. I only wanted to sleep, and then to go home.

By the time I found Widow Kessler's house, another fifteen minutes had passed. My fingers had gone numb and it hurt to breathe. When I knocked on the door, I felt the wood distantly, as though under a layer of insulation.

When the door was opened to me, I was greeted by more madness.

"COME IN, CHILD."

Widow Kessler turned away from the door, leaving it open. Cold air rolled into her little home, so I hurried in and shut it behind me. The potbellied stove in the kitchen corner radiated heat and provided the only light. I headed for it immediately, without thinking to ask permission, and thawed my hands. Manners belonged to another era.

"It seems we're caught in a pattern," she said. "You come here seeking shelter in the night, and I make you tea." She busied herself at the stove, doing just that.

"At least no one's chasing me this time," I said. I took a seat at the small table. My eye went to the cot in the partitioned section of the hut. It had been moved from its position over the trapdoor leading to the cellar. "And if you let me stay, I'd rather not sleep down there again."

Widow Kessler chuckled. She turned to me at last. The stove light painted the left side of her face in oranges and blacks. Her right eye, cast in shadow, burned like a green cinder. I pulled in on myself, hugging my elbows.

"What is it, Anabelle? You're not frightened of me, are you?"

"No," I said, without conviction.

"There's no reason to be." She stood beside the chair opposite me. Shadows leapt and danced behind her. "There's no reason to fear any of it."

I didn't know what "it" was, and anyway, I didn't believe her. To my way of thinking, there was plenty to fear. More, in fact, than we had any notion of.

"Did you find what you were looking for?"

"I did." I didn't know what more to say about it.

"Is it enough?"

The question surprised me. "I don't know. I haven't listened to it yet. I didn't really get it for me, though. I got it for my father."

"So you say."

"It's true. Once he hears her voice again, once he can talk to her, he'll be better. He'll be like he was before."

"Before what? The murder? The robbery? Or the Silence?"

I didn't know which I meant. There were so many stages to his descent. When was the last time he or any of us felt normal? When was the last time any of us could remember what that even meant? The widow's question called into clarity all the doubts I carried with me, all the guilt I'd acquired, all the anger that still remained unanswered.

The anger, especially. There was still so much undelivered justice.

The tea prepared, she brought both mugs to the table and sat across from me. It was warm and good, and made me think of home. I felt a sudden vast sympathy for her, despite her eeriness. I felt protective. How could she not have become frightening, living in this horrible place, the darkness pulling at her like a tide?

"The Silence is almost over," I said quietly. I was breaking a confidence, but I didn't think she was about to run all the way to New Galveston. I wanted her to know. I wanted to light a candle in her dreams again.

She looked at me quizzically.

"We came back in the *Lamplighter*. The original ship. It's a secret. But it's going back to Earth."

She received this news quietly. Instead of the excitement or disbelief I'd expected, her face clouded over, her eyes unfixed from me.

"Maybe you can go back soon," I said.

"Go back where?" She seemed very far away.

"To Earth," I said. The word—such a simple syllable—felt alien on my tongue. It sounded like the name of an imaginary kingdom, as unanchored to reality as Atlantis.

"Earth is a dream."

"No, it isn't," I said, a strange terror stirring; I had the irrational thought that if I didn't challenge that, it might become true. I remembered Earth, of course, but only in slivered images. My father driving us along a narrow road through dense Appalachian woods. My grandmother's house, dark and warm, smelling of nutmeg. A rocking chair by the hearth. Snow on the evergreens. These things existed. They were not a dream.

"Don't say that, Mrs. Kessler. You were born there. You lived most of your life there. You met your husband there. Don't you want to see it again?"

"Zachary," she said, lost briefly to a memory. She reached across the table and took my wrist in her hand. Her thumb pressed into my palm. She was striving for intimacy but couldn't quite manage it; she was speaking from across a gulf I couldn't see. "You'll grow up in this new place, and things that are strange to us will hold no mystery for you."

"Where does the tunnel in your cellar lead to, Mrs. Kessler? Who's down there?"

"It's nothing to be afraid of, Anabelle."

I pulled my hand free. I felt suddenly tired. Her reaction unsettled me, her evasion unsettled me, and the prospect of returning home was oppressive. Despite all that had happened, the resolution to all of this still seemed so far away. The thought of joining the widow, all the people of Dig Town, and moving early into my own grave suddenly seemed a peaceful alternative.

"Can I sleep here?"

"Of course, Anabelle. Use my cot."

"What about you? Where will you sleep?"

"I'll be in the cellar this time." She paused. "You might hear some activity. Don't come down."

That was the last thing I wanted to hear. But it was too cold outside to go anywhere else. I was stuck here, and would have to endure whatever came.

I left my tea unfinished and went straight to her cot. After several nights of sleeping in a heat tent and in the rumbling hold of an antique spaceship, her simple canvas cot felt like an outrageous indulgence. My body suspended over empty space like a cloud, no hard ground to compromise with. She closed the grate on the stove, and the light became an orange outline, narrow beams angled across the wall and the ceiling. A warm darkness filled the rest, and I recalled again the fragmented memory of my grandmother's house. I closed my eyes, breathing deeply; I could almost smell the nutmeg. The room succumbed to a profound silence. I felt the dark hollow of sleep opening beneath me.

The last thing I saw before falling was a ray of orange light catching the widow's eye, staring into the darkness above her in beatific ecstasy.

A SOUND AWAKENED me. There was no swimming into consciousness; I was launched into high alert. My attention skittered around the room, looking for a threat. The fire in the stove was down to embers, filling the room with a red, seething darkness. Widow Kessler was nowhere to be seen. The trapdoor to the cellar was shut. Whatever was wrong in this place resided below, and I stared at it, waiting for something to push it open. I became aware of a shuffling sound in the cellar—not one person this time but several, shifting quietly, as though milling in directionless ambulations. Whispering rose through the floorboards, filling the widow's little home like smoke.

I sat up, breathing heavily. Ready to run.

I heard the widow's voice; whoever else was down there went quiet.

She continued to speak, but I couldn't make out the words.

Despite the fear, I had to know what was going on. Everything in my life seemed to be an unanswered question, and here at last was an opportunity to settle one of them. I swung my legs off the cot and crept the few steps to the trapdoor. Wood squeaked, but not enough to carry. I pulled the handle, and the trapdoor creaked open.

The room immediately below me was empty. I could tell because lantern light bled through from the adjoining room, the one where I'd found the skull and the field of mushrooms. The one where I'd seen the figure retreating down the long tunnel.

The widow's voice became clearer.

"It's nearly over. It's going to be all right."

She must be telling them about the *Lamplighter*. I felt both apprehension and relief: the former because the secret I'd promised to keep was getting out, the latter because what was going on down here was reassuringly mundane.

I put a foot on the top rung of the ladder, less afraid of making noise.

"You don't have to be lonely anymore. You don't have to hurt anymore."

In a moment I was standing in the cellar, among the rows of preserves, canned goods, and stacked boxes. Lantern light bloomed from the small archway leading to the adjacent room. From my angle I couldn't see into it, but I could see some of the mushrooms that carpeted the floor in there curled around the entrance, like the seeking tendrils of some vast fungal beast. Eventually, I imagined, it would fill her cellar and come creeping through her floor.

"We came here because we were called. We came here because it needs a voice. We will be that voice."

I hesitated. She wasn't talking about the *Lamplighter*.

"Eat," she said. "Eat, and then follow me down to the gardens."

Something cold filled my chest. I crept toward the opening, as quietly as I could. The ground here was packed earth, which made it easier. I pressed myself against the wall and peered into the room.

The lantern was resting at the mouth of the tunnel, backlighting Widow Kessler, who seemed a black shadow carved from the light. Arrayed before her were eight residents of Dig Town, miners who'd been here too long, miners who'd spent far too long breathing in the Strange. They sat with their backs to me, but their scooping hands and the wet gulping sounds made it clear that they were eating the mushrooms that crowded this room. Phosphorescent green clouds erupted from the mushrooms they split in their teeth. A crescent moon of light reflected from the pale white bone of Zachary Kessler's skull at their feet.

I bit my lip to keep from making a sound. She was nothing but a dark shape, but I could swear Widow Kessler was staring right at me.

"It's time," she said. "It's waiting for us."

She turned and started down the tunnel. The Dig Towners slowly got to their feet, never once looking back, and followed her.

I went back upstairs, shut the trapdoor, and lay down on the cot. I had nowhere else to go. I shivered despite the heat, pulling the blanket up over my head: the childhood defense against monsters.

Somehow, eventually, I slept.

24

When I awoke the next morning, Widow Kessler had not returned. The fire had gone out in the stove, but warmth still lingered in the shack. A mug and the preparations for coffee had been set out for me, as well as a small bread loaf. I climbed off the cot, wrapping the blanket around my shoulders.

The trapdoor was open. I knelt by its side and called softly down.

"Mrs. Kessler?"

There was no answer. After a brief hesitation, I retrieved a candle from her table and lit it with a match. Then I dropped the blanket and climbed down the ladder. The candlelight intruded feebly into the heavy darkness. Even though sunlight filtered into the room upstairs, down here it was still midnight.

"Mrs. Kessler? Are you down here?"

I passed by the canned foods and the water, the crates of supplies, and proceeded into the side room where I had witnessed part of her strange service. The carpet of mushrooms had been partially trampled here, but was still thick enough to cover most of the ground. I crossed slowly, careful to avoid Zachary Kessler's bones. I stepped to the lip of the cavern and peered down.

A passageway descended steeply, the mushrooms continuing along its length, even growing up along the sides. Tentatively, I continued walking. Faint, luminescent spores puffed around my feet each time I stepped on a mushroom. I knew I couldn't help but breathe some of it in, but after passing through Peabody Crater, it seemed foolish to worry about that now.

The tunnel began to curve rightward, its angle of descent increasing. A trail had been trampled through the fungus from the night before—and probably from before that, too—and I did my best to follow it, assuming it provided the most reliable footing. I slid my hand along the wall to keep myself steady.

I began to feel like I was floating. There was a powerful sense of crossing into a dream.

Whispers drifted up from below, carried on a light breeze that shivered the candle flame. I paused.

"Mrs. Kessler?" I said, barely audible.

I stared at the wall ahead of me as the tunnel continued its rightward arc. My heart hammering, I resolved to continue a few more feet, and then turn around. I had to get back to Sally's place to continue the work. But I was light-headed, curious, carried by a dark enchantment. I had to see.

Another bend, and the tunnel stopped at a precipice. Standing at its lip, I found myself looking out into the Throat. It was a vast well of darkness. A dozen feet away I could see one of the metal elevator shafts—one of the smaller personnel carriers—stretching from the disc of sunlight above to the glittering abyss below.

The abyss, glittering with hundreds of green flecks lining the walls, more drifting like snow in the air.

Not drifting; they were fluttering, hitching through the air in erratic patterns. They were moths. Hundreds upon hundreds of moths, their feet shining with the residue of the Strange.

I looked more closely at the green flecks lining the mine below me; my body convulsed with a horrified shudder.

They were the open, staring eyes of the miners. Their bodies cemented against the walls by the fungal growths, the moths flying into and out of their mouths, tending to their macabre business. They should have all been dead—the moths nested in the dead—but their eyes were lit and the whispering I'd heard rose like wispy ghosts from their mouths.

It's waiting for us, she'd said.

The bleak intelligence I'd sensed before, standing on the catwalk surrounding the Throat, radiated from below. Not something locked in the world's core, like some pulp monster, but the world itself, the pale, staring eye of Mars, felt here because this was where we'd cracked directly into the Strange.

We will be that voice.

"Go."

I yelped. Looking around wildly, I finally saw Widow Kessler, her body affixed to the wall like all the others. The mushrooms had covered both arms and were already growing along the skin of her face.

"This is your world now."

I dropped the candle and it went end over end into the Throat. I ran back up the tunnel without it, the only illumination coming from the clouds of the Strange released by my own trampling feet.

•   •   •

WHEN I WENT outside, I discovered to my dismay that it was nearly noon. I'd slept too long and too hard. Sally had known where I was staying; why hadn't she come to get me?

By this time I'd come to know enough of the town's layout to find Shank's place quickly. Though I was moving through a ghost town, my skin prickled as though I was being watched, or stalked. I peered around every corner before turning it, examined every path before taking it. I saw no one. I imagined them all underground, mushrooms growing from their mouths and their staring eyes, moths flitting over them like anxious housekeepers.

My head felt clearer in the open air, so much so that I wondered if what I'd seen had been a dream or a hallucination. The farther I walked, the less real it seemed. I resolved not to tell the others about it; at least not right away. We had bigger problems at hand.

Finally, I arrived at the door of their dilapidated little shack. I pounded on it, hesitant to call out.

After a moment, the latch was undone. I pushed the door open to see Sally retreating into the interior, her back to me. I slipped in and shut it behind me, feeling moderately better.

The place looked just as it had the last time I'd been there, except that Sally was alone. She found her bed and collapsed onto it. Two empty jugs of moonshine stood close by. The place stank of it. I made an effort to hide my disgust.

"Did Joe come back yet?" I said.

She put a hand over her eyes. "Christ, my head."

"Well?" It was a stupid question—the answer was evident— but I was angry at her for compromising herself. I wanted to punish her for it.

"Do you see him here? No, he did not."

"What's the matter with you?"

"It's called a hangover. It's what happens when you get drunk. Why don't you try some of it and find out."

How dare she. My mother's cylinder was up as collateral. I never would have believed that Joe Reilly would be the responsible one and that Sally Milkwood would be the one to jeopardize it.

"Get up. We have work to do."

"For Peabody? For Silas? They can both go to hell. Maybe I'll send 'em there."

"No, for me! For my parents! Get up!"

That got through to her. She pulled herself to a sitting position, squeezing her eyes shut with the effort. When she looked at me finally, I couldn't read her expression. Something between anger and pity. "Your folks," she said. "You can't save them, Belle."

I had a retort loaded like a bullet, but it was then that I realized the significance of her being alone here. Laura and Billy—the Shank kids—were gone. My eyes roved over the other two beds pushed against the far wall, rumpled and used. Dirty clothes were piled in the corner. A worn book lay by one bed, a spray of playing cards by the other. But no sign of them.

"Yeah, they're gone," she said. "They were gone when I got here. I guess they went down the hole, just like every other idiot in this town."

"Maybe . . . maybe they went back to their father."

She laughed; it sounded ugly. "That man ain't fit to grow a plant. They didn't go back there."

"But maybe—"

"They didn't. I know it for a fact. Now leave it."

I almost did. I wanted to. But I had to tell her. "I think it's Widow Kessler," I said. "I think she's leading them down there."

She looked at me for a moment, then turned her gaze to the floor. "Sadness is a contagion in this town," she said. "It'll kill you if you let it."

There was more bad news to deliver. "Mr. Wickham said they built a gallows for Joe."

Her eyes caught fire. Joe might have been the last person left in the world she cared about. If anything was going to get her up and moving, it would be the fact that he needed her still. She swung her legs off the bed and hauled herself to her feet. "Why the hell didn't you say that first? Why did you let him go?"

I remembered Joe's last words to me: the meanness in them. They'd slammed the door on any chance we might ever get along in the future. He was done with me. I was too ashamed to confess, in the moment, that I didn't want to stop him. I didn't care what he did. "I'm sorry," I said, and I was.

She went to her closet and pulled her rifle out. She strode to the door, her face hard. It looked like it would splinter into pieces if it moved at all. "Let's go," she said. "I'm done with this bullshit. If anybody tries to harm any one of mine in any way, I'm going to blow them to bloody ruin. Let 'em come find out."

FROM AFAR, NEW Galveston looked just as it always had. The habs of the town center were arranged in sensible square patterns with a perfectly navigable network of roads, in stark contrast to Dig Town. The Taproots—that neighborhood of houses built from Martian stone and Martian wood—extended to the south and the southwest. From a distance I could see people milling about, conducting the ordinary business of life. Whatever sickness infected Dig Town had not yet touched New Galveston.

The place was not without a sickness of its own, though. I was reminded of it quickly enough.

After having spent time in the *Lamplighter*, the *Eurydice* looked larger and grander than ever. This was a ship meant to shift a population, bringing not only the people but their means to build homes, to plant crops, to husband animals. The roots of life itself.

Nearby, where Joe Reilly's shack had once been, stood a gallows. They'd used the wood of his own home to build the instrument of his execution. Tall, gaunt, spare, it stood in the afternoon light like the skeleton of one of the strange ghosts that haunted the crater—a harbinger, a death animal.

The leftover wood was piled neatly a dozen feet away, in the shadow of the saucer. Amidst the detritus was a small table, a smashed chair, shelves from which books spilled like viscera.

I stood transfixed before it. Here was the manifestation of my wish: the very engine of retribution. Here was where the guilty would climb to meet the justice they'd called down upon their own heads. Here was the junction between deed and consequence; the verdict I'd passed to Silas Mundt, the threat I'd delivered to Joe Reilly.

I was paralyzed by it. I felt sickened and elated at once, galvanized and broken—a delirious feeling. In retrospect I recognize that this was a kind of holy awe, the sort one must feel when staring into the inscrutable face of an angel. The kind I felt peering into the Throat, spangled with hundreds of staring eyes.

I looked for a sign of Joe. A wagon was parked nearby, a mule hitched to it and standing with his kind's characteristic moroseness. The *Eurydice*'s ramp was extended.

"He's in the ship," I said, but Sally wasn't convinced.

"Go slow," she said. "Stay behind me."

We were just about under the saucer's shadow when a voice came from the *Eurydice*'s interior. "Hey, folks." A woman's voice. "Drop that rifle."

It was Deputy Mae Ackerman. She was lying prone inside the ship, aiming a rifle of her own at us. More specifically, at Sally.

"I don't think I want to," Sally said. She didn't raise it just yet; I think she knew she wouldn't be fast enough, and Ackerman had plenty of cover.

"Don't make me force the issue. I know who you are. You're Sally Milkwood, the moonshiner. We knew you were holed up in Dig Town somewhere. Believe me when I tell you I would not lose any sleep over putting you down right here."

I stepped in front of Sally. "Would you shoot me, too?"

"Move aside, Anabelle."

"Where's Joe?"

"He's in jail, where he belongs. Move aside."

I wasn't about to, but Sally shoved me away, and I found myself with a mouthful of sand. "I won't hide behind no child," she said. She threw down her rifle. "Come on then, Deputy. Come see if you can do it."

Deputy Ackerman stood, the barrel of her rifle as steady as the needle of a compass. She came down the ramp slowly. "Anabelle, I need you to back away."

My heart galloped in my chest. I liked Ackerman from what I knew of her, but she was going to ruin everything. I couldn't let her take Sally. And I needed Joe. I stood, still ready to argue. "What if I don't?"

She didn't hesitate. "Then I'll shoot Sally in the gut. She'll live or she won't, but it'll put her out of commission. And then I'll take you both to jail." She let me think about that. "If you stand aside, though, I can just cuff her."

I glanced at Sally, who offered no opinion on the matter. Her attention was on Ackerman, and it didn't waver.

I backed away, despairing. I couldn't stop this. We'd lost.

"Good girl." To Sally: "Get on the ground."

Sally said, "Belle, put that gun down."

I didn't have a gun, and I was about to tell her so. But Deputy Ackerman whipped a glance at me, her eyes narrowed, and Sally charged at her. It was only half a second. Ackerman realized the gambit right away and fired, but Sally was already on the move, a freight train. She collided with Ackerman and they were both airborne for a strange, drawn-out second, the gun flying from the deputy's hand.

They crashed to earth and breath exploded from Ackerman's lungs with a pained cry. I thought I heard a rib crack. Sally was a big woman and she used her physicality like a weapon. The deputy fought hard, twisting her body to get free, jamming her thumbs into Sally's throat, but Sally cracked the side of her head with her clenched fist three times, and Ackerman went limp.

It all happened in the space of a few seconds. I don't even think I breathed.

Sally pushed herself off the deputy, checking herself for a bullet wound.

"Did you get hit?" I managed to ask.

"I don't think so. Guess I'd feel it by now." Her voice sounded hoarse, and I could already see bruises forming on her neck. She kicked the dropped rifle away from Ackerman and removed the revolver strapped to her waist, too. She shoved it into the waist of her pants, pushed up against her belly. "Check the wagon. Did he load any fuel in it before they caught him?"

I walked over to it. The mule watched me forlornly. Four heavy canisters were loaded into the bed. I told her so.

"I'll go bring down what's left. We won't have time to stop here on the way back."

"On the way back from where?"

"We're gonna bust Joe out. I'll be damned if he'll swing at their hands."

I paused, stunned by the audacity of it. At last I said, "My father, too."

She nodded, staring back in the direction of Dig Town and the *Lamplighter*. "While we're at it, why not, I guess." She handed the revolver to me. "Hold this on her. If she wakes up, you holler for me. Can you shoot it?"

"I practiced with a gun before."

"That's good. What I'm asking is, can you shoot it at her?"

I swallowed. "I don't know," I said.

This seemed to satisfy her. "That's all right. Shoot it in the air if you have to. I'll come running."

"Hurry," I said, worried.

"I will."

I sat on the back of the wagon as she ascended the ramp, the gun dark and heavy, incongruous in my hand. My mind was filled with the stink and the bloodshed of the massacre in the crater. I felt effervescent with a sense of terrible power.

WE KEPT THE deputy hog-tied and laid out in the wagon bed between the fuel canisters, below the line of sight of anybody in the road. We drew attention anyway, though: big Sally

Milkwood and me, pulled along the main thoroughfare by a laboring mule, on our way to the sheriff's station. We must have stirred a lot of conversation.

Most of those who recognized us just stopped and stared. One shouted my name, and another—a regular customer at the diner—came running up to me, her arms outstretched as though she were prepared to pull me into a hug; we rolled on by her and I did not meet her eyes. I saw her freeze in bewilderment behind us. It was too easy to see her as part of the mob, smashing windows and hauling a bag full of cans from our pantry. I knew it might not be fair, but I was beyond such considerations. If it were up to me, I would march the whole town to the gallows.

We passed the Mother Earth Diner on the way, affording me a glimpse of that dark shell, and though I tried not to look, I couldn't help but stare. To my horror, the door yawned open, and people were moving things out of it. What hadn't been stolen from us was now being stacked haphazardly out in the sunlight: damaged chairs and tables, jugs of frying oil, the grimy fans of our air vent, dismantled and spread out like innards. My breath caught in my throat. I felt the blood rush to my face, pound behind my eyes.

At that moment Fenris Dunne, that well-intentioned, oafish farm boy who'd tried to walk me home after the robbery, came strolling out the front door, wiping his grimy hands on the back of his trousers. He saw me in the wagon and froze in place.

"Anabelle!" he called, but by that time we were past him. I turned away from it all, facing resolutely ahead, willing my composure still with every bit of strength I had left. I heard him call once more, but that was all.

Sally didn't say a word. She acted like she hadn't seen or heard a thing, and I was grateful for it.

As we got nearer the sheriff's station, Sally said, "Let's talk about what we're gonna do."

I nodded, dizzy with mounting fear. We'd already crossed into a new kind of life by capturing Deputy Ackerman, yet what was coming up would cement our fates as enemies of the law.

"I'm gonna need your help in there. I'd rather leave you safe outside, but the situation won't allow it."

"Okay."

She looked at me. "Are you up for this?"

I nodded. All the fire and bluster I'd used to get by this whole time had abandoned me. Since the massacre in the crater, I'd lost confidence in my ability to bring war to all who stood opposed.

She must have seen it on my face. "They got your daddy in there, do you recall that?"

"Of course I do."

"Okay then. Just remember that when you start having doubts."

"They might have Jack in there, too," I said, voicing my chief concern.

"Who's that?"

"Their Law Engine."

She stayed quiet. Finally she said, "I'm just going to have to improvise when it comes to him."

I was not reassured.

• • •

WHILE SALLY DROVE, I rolled a tarp over the back of the wagon. Ackerman was still out, but we gagged her in case she woke up while we were inside. The doubts Sally referenced were already starting to flourish. What if the deputy didn't wake up? Or what if she was hit so hard she'd be simple for the rest of her life? I knew of a teamster who was kicked in the head by a horse and lived like a little child from that day forth.

Sally pulled to a stop in front of the sheriff's station, and I came back to the moment. It was midafternoon; the street wasn't exactly crowded, but it wasn't empty, either. A few faces hovered behind the glass of the bank across the street, curious about what was going on.

"We're not going to hurt anybody, are we?"

"Nobody will get hurt unless they ask to get hurt." She checked on Ackerman once more. Satisfied, she grabbed her rifle and the deputy's gun, then tilted her head for me to follow. I climbed down after her, my heart pounding like a war drum.

We entered the building. I knew the sheriff kept two deputies on staff—Ackerman and the younger man whose name I'd never learned—plus there would be Bakersfield himself and maybe Jack in the offices. My hands were shaking. There was no way this could work.

The other deputy was there. He was leaned back in his chair with his boots on the desk, an adventure novel held open in his right hand, a big grin spread over his face. On the cover of the novel was an unclad woman whose modesty was protected by her flowing hair and rising flames. I recognized the novel from my own reading: *She*, by H. Rider Haggard. This caused me an unaccountable spike of embarrassment.

He straightened into a more professional position just in time to see the barrel of Sally's rifle level itself a foot from his chest. "Steady, boy," she said.

He fumbled for the sidearm at his waist. Sally stepped forward and pushed the rifle hard against his ribs. He yelped and went still.

"I said steady. Calm and quiet. Who's in back?"

His eyes flicked back and forth from Sally to me, lingering on me once he recognized who I was. "Sheriff Bakersfield," he said. "Jack." His voice sounded weak, and I felt bad for him.

"You're going to hang with your daddy," he told me, and my sympathy vanished.

Sally handed me the rifle and switched to the revolver instead. "Get up," she said, and he did. She pressed the gun's barrel hard into his temple, causing him to wince. "You'll live through this if you do what I tell you. But if you call out, I'll dig a tunnel through your brain. Do you doubt it?"

"No."

She stood behind him and wrapped a rope quickly around his wrists. The binding wouldn't hold up for long, but it served the purpose now. She hooked her left arm around his neck and pressed the gun's barrel against the side of his head. "Let's go in," she said.

Inspiration struck me. "What's Jack's command word?"

Watson's had been "bluebonnet"—the word that ejected his cylinder and rendered him inert.

When the deputy didn't answer, Sally encouraged him with some pressure from the gun barrel. He sighed and said, "Sidewinder." He hung his head. "Shit."

We proceeded through the door into the office, the same spacious room in which I'd received so much terrible news in what seemed another age. Sheriff Bakersfield was sitting behind his desk, staring in surprise as Sally and the deputy made their way in first, her gun to his head, followed by me with the rifle. He stood up, but made no further move.

Jack was there, as expected. He rotated toward us, the port in his arm already sliding open to reveal the gun barrels.

"Sidewinder," I said, and he stopped. His eyes went dark and the port for his cylinder slid open. Just like that, he was neutralized.

Bakersfield watched this all happen without a word. Then: "Anabelle. Thank God."

"Lift your hands," Sally said.

He did as she told him, but he kept his attention on me. "We were worried about you, Anabelle. Are you hurt?"

I was confused by this approach. Did he not see what was happening right in front of him? "No, I ain't hurt," I said testily.

The deputy spoke. "Sheriff, I'm sorry, they just—"

"That's all right, Boyd." Bakersfield looked beyond him. "Mrs. Milkwood, am I right? You mind telling me where Deputy Ackerman is?"

"I do mind. I'll tell you she's alive, though. And until I get what I came here for, that's all I'll tell you."

"I suppose you want Joe Reilly."

"And my father," I said.

Sheriff Bakersfield nodded and sighed. "I figured."

"Is he downstairs?"

"He is. I won't tell you he's all right. He hasn't been eating much, he hasn't said two words to nobody. At least, nobody who lives in this world."

Sally shoved the deputy into the nearest chair. He cried out as his hands twisted underneath him. To Bakersfield she said, "Give her the keys to the cells."

"Anabelle," he said. "This isn't the way to do this."

"Sheriff, do not make me repeat myself."

"All right. They're in the drawer here. Don't shoot me for doing what you asked."

"Don't make it necessary then."

He opened the drawer slowly and withdrew a set of keys, which he placed on the desk. Cautiously I crept closer to him, then snatched them up. While I was there, I pulled Jack's cylinder from its socket, too. I didn't want it sliding back in and reactivating while our attention was elsewhere. Bakersfield watched this and closed his eyes in disappointment. "Don't do this, Anabelle. Don't become one of them."

"One of them?" I said, the rage flowing back like lava. "You mean like my father, who was trying to protect me and his livelihood? Or do you mean like the people who ransacked our diner and didn't have to account for a single thing? Or maybe you mean the people stripping it bare right this minute? You goddamn hypocrite!"

Bakersfield's face went red. "Now hold on! Those people are stripping it with the town's sanction! There's not going to be any more diners now! We're not gonna go on making livings by charging people money for what we all need to survive! As far as your daddy goes, he killed a man. Don't you understand that? I'm sorry for how it happened, and I'm sorry for what they did to your place after. I tell you, there will be an accounting for that. But we have got to have justice in this town or we'll lose everything. We'll lose everything."

Here was my argument being thrown back at me. *There has to be justice.* It threw me off-balance.

"Shut up," Sally said. "Let's all go downstairs." She nudged Boyd. "Get up. You first. Sheriff, you after him. Anabelle, you bring up the rear."

We proceeded down the stairs as she directed.

"And as for Joe Reilly," Bakersfield said.

"I told you to shut up."

"You want me to stop talking, you're going to have to shoot me, Milkwood. You ready to do that? Anabelle, are you ready to let her?" When no one said anything, he kept on going. "After you left, we remembered you mentioned Joe's name. So we went to pay him a visit. He wasn't there, but guess what we found? The *Eurydice* was gutted. Permanently grounded. Reilly took away our last chance. Not just mine, not just yours. Everyone's. Can you understand what that means? Your daddy murdered a man, but Joe did something worse. He murdered hope. He's got to account for that. He's got to."

I wanted so badly to tell the sheriff why I was doing all this. I wanted to tell him about the *Lamplighter*, about the end of the Silence. Maybe he would stop fighting us. Maybe he would help. But I knew what the cost of telling him would be. Silas had made that clear.

We reached the bottom of the stairs.

Joe Reilly stood behind the bars of the nearest cell. Two down from him stood my father. Unable to help myself, I ran to his cage, smiling, the keys jingling in my hand, truly lighthearted for the first time since before the robbery.

He looked at me with an expression of horror.

25

Anabelle—what have you done?"

Behind me, Sally ushered Bakersfield and Boyd into an empty cell. The exchanged threats between them faded into a subliminal hum. My whole attention was on my father, and the look on his face that broke my heart.

"I found it," I said. "I got Mother's cylinder back. I did what I said I would."

I wanted him to be proud of me. Why wasn't he proud of me?

"But—you have a gun."

"I'm saving you," I said.

"No. Anabelle. You can't do this. Who is that woman?"

"Dad. They're going to hang you!" I heard tears in my voice.

"I know."

"I won't let it happen. I'm breaking you out."

He grabbed my shoulders through the bars. "Belle. You're going to ruin your life. That's the sheriff, for Christ's sake! What do you think you're doing here?"

"The hell with the sheriff. He just sat on his ass when we needed him!"

"Now they're going to hang you, too."

How dare he, I thought. How dare he be weak when I needed him.

Sally moved me aside. "Come on out, Crisp. I didn't risk my life for you to play martyr."

Father said, "Who the hell are you?"

"I'm the woman putting some muscle behind your daughter's intentions. Now get up those goddamn stairs." When he didn't come out right away, she hauled him out by his collar.

"Hey!" I said.

"No time to be sweet. All of you, get upstairs. We got to get moving."

He did as he was told. It troubled me, in a way: he was so much reduced from his former self. He seemed small and weak, pushed about by larger personalities. And one of those personalities was me. Although he was doing exactly what I wanted him to do, exactly what he needed to do, I felt a nettle of shame. I tried to banish it, but I couldn't. It seemed to indicate a more fundamental problem.

Joe led the way, taking two steps at a time. My father went next, considerably slower.

"You made a bad mistake," Bakersfield said from his cell. "Before you were just a nuisance we figured we'd get to sooner or later. Now you're my number one target."

Sally turned. "Then maybe my big mistake is not killing you right now."

"Sally," I said. "No. Please don't."

My father stopped halfway up the stairs, terror on his face. "I won't allow it," he said, but everyone knew he carried no power to stop it.

"Joe, get his sorry ass on the wagon, will you?" She looked at me, then at Bakersfield. "Your lucky day, Sheriff. But you come on when you're able. You'll find me ready."

Outside, my father and I climbed into the wagon. He watched with a sorrowful countenance as Sally and Joe dragged the groggy Ackerman from the wagon bed and hustled her inside, to deposit into another of the cells. "My God," he said. "My God."

When they were back, Joe flicked the reins and we lurched into motion.

The door at the bank banged open as we moved away. A voice called, "Hey! That's Joe Reilly! Hey, stop!"

Joe whipped the reins again, and the poor mule did its best. We maintained a decent pace, but if someone went for a horse, they'd get us easy. Sally held her rifle in the crook of her arm, an open warning to anyone thinking to try it.

We watched behind us. Whoever it was who'd yelled at us was standing in the middle of the road, his hands on his hips. If we were lucky, he'd just go back in the bank where he'd come from. But I knew that was unlikely. He'd be going into the sheriff's office next, demanding to know why they'd cut the nefarious Joe Reilly loose. And why they'd cut Sam Crisp loose, too: the man who'd accidentally killed his aggressor in defense of his own daughter; the man who'd waited on them and served them old-fashioned Southern cooking for the last ten years.

Sally said, "We need to get, Joe."

"I know it! We only have the one damn mule."

"Where are you taking us?" Father said. As though I were an unwilling passenger here just like himself.

So I answered before Sally could. It was important he knew my place here. "We're going to the *Lamplighter*. You and I are going back to Earth."

Joe and Sally exchanged a look. Father gaped at me like I'd started speaking in tongues. I could hardly believe what I'd said myself. But the idea came to me as clear as an angel, haloed by light. We didn't have a place to go here, not anymore. Mars was rotting beneath our feet. All of New Galveston had turned against us for no reason that made sense to me. What's more, the nest of horrors Widow Kessler was tending in Dig Town seemed ready to hatch; I didn't know what that would mean for us, but I didn't want to be close by when it happened.

So we would go home. We'd go back and find Mother—the real one, not just a recording. Of course I knew it was a risk, but we weren't like Joe Reilly; we'd risk death for the chance of something real, for the chance to reunite under green trees, where the nights were warm.

Father did not react. He seemed to be lost in a doleful rumination.

Over her shoulder, Sally said, "Can't wait till Silas hears this."

"I just gotta convince him, that's all," I said, more to myself than to her.

We carried on in silence.

WE MADE IT back to Dig Town by late afternoon. Sunlight streaked across the outcroppings of the crater, sending rays of light and darkness across the untraveled road. We passed through the deserted outskirts, toward the center of the mining town.

Father didn't acknowledge any of us. It hurt me grievously. He kept his back to us, instead watching the distant landscape of Mars roll slowly by. I don't think he yet believed in the reality of the *Lamplighter* and what it meant for us. I suppose it was all too much for him to accept. He was trying not to face what I had done, the cost I'd incurred to my own future on his behalf.

As if the cost of doing nothing would have been any less.

I followed his gaze into the horizon—into the great, hungry maw of the crater. I knew the ghosts were moving out there now, strange shapes unknowable to the human eye, geological memories of an entity beyond language. I imagined the War Engines moving among them, lost and wrathful, their cylinders crackling with an animosity without source or reason. Algorithms of hate.

And I imagined Watson, stalled amidst strewn corpses and ghosts nailed to the ground, his own cylinder absorbing the Strange, growing thick and heavy with dreams.

What a vast system of nightmares surrounding our little village. We were nothing more than a guttering candle in a dark world.

We passed the Throat, the scaffolding of work lights dead and black in the cool air. The green-tinged sediment rose from it in a silent geyser. The catwalk was empty of people. I supposed they had all gone down by this point. There was no one left for Widow Kessler to take. Father stared at the open mine with an expression I was afraid might be longing. It was too easy to imagine him a willing member of the widow's deranged congregation, submitting himself to her weird garden. Even as we traveled past it, he turned and watched the green plume recede.

I tugged his sleeve. "Dad," I said.

He turned, and I pointed.

The *Lamplighter* awaited us. It looked like a small round jewel against the backdrop of the long desert, reflecting a late afternoon sky scudded with chalky pink clouds. The damaged exterior looked much improved. Mr. Wickham had already finished his repairs and departed. I felt a pang of loss: he'd always been kind to me, and I'd wanted to tell him what I'd seen in Widow Kessler's cellar. To try to steer him away from it, though I knew it would have been futile. At the very least, I'd wanted to tell him goodbye.

Silas emerged from the ship, standing atop the mended ramp.

"I was starting to get worried," he called.

"None of this has come easy yet," Sally said. "No reason this should be any different."

Father tensed. "That's the man who robbed us."

"Stay calm," I said.

"Are you helping him?"

I flushed. "It's more complicated than that."

Joe pulled the wagon close to the ship and brought it to a halt. We all disembarked, except Sally, who positioned herself so she could keep watch behind us. She lit a cigarette.

"Whatever you need to do, do it quick," Sally said. "The law will be here soon, and we stirred 'em up good."

While Joe started pulling the fuel canisters from the wagon bed, Father approached the *Lamplighter,* his eyes bright with wonder.

"I can't believe it," he said. "I thought there weren't any other ships."

Taking advantage of the only chance I might get, I walked up the ramp to stand beside Silas. He leaned against the bulkhead, arms folded, waiting for me.

"I need something from you," I said. I had to stand to one

side as Joe mounted the ramp, hefting one of the canisters up with him, past us, and into the interior.

"I know," Silas said. "You can have the cylinder once I'm fueled up and ready to go."

I bristled—the deal was when I got the fuel here, not once he got it loaded—but I let it go. "I need you to take us with you," I said quietly.

His eyes narrowed. "Say again?"

"If he stays here, they're gonna hang him."

"I'm sorry to hear that, but I don't think I'll be taking anybody else along."

"Please." It about killed me, begging this man.

He stared at me for a moment, then leaned over and watched my father, who was still fawning over the ship. "No. This was built to be a one-man vessel. There ain't enough air for two, let alone three. Sorry."

I was crushed. I had no argument against that. I knew the *Lamplighter* was designed to be a one-person vessel, but after spending time inside, I'd convinced myself it was spacious enough for more. I hadn't thought to account for the oxygen.

Joe came back out, headed for another canister. "This'll go faster if you help," he said as he brushed by.

I walked down the ramp, slowed by despair. After all this, nothing. A calamitous end. The noose for my father, and now likely for Joe and Sally. Maybe for me, too, if the governor could see his way to hanging a kid. From the way we'd been treated so far, I believed he could.

And Silas Mundt, of all people, triumphant. With my help.

I stopped at the wagon, staring at the remaining canisters of fuel. Sally watched me from her perch, cigarette smoke curling around her face. "Why, Sally? Why did we help him only to be executed ourselves?"

"You planning on getting hanged?" she said. "Not me. We're getting the hell out. I told you, there's other places out here than this one. Places the sheriff don't know about. I ain't worried."

"And Silas gets to win?"

She shrugged. "Who cares about him? I don't reckon that ship is gonna make it all the way back to Earth anyhow, after being buried so long. Let him choke out there in the deep."

I care, I thought. *I do.*

Father approached me. He looked dazed. "You should go with him," he said.

"I already asked if we both could. He said there's not enough air."

"Bullshit. I'll talk to him."

He mounted the ramp. Seeing him approach, Silas straightened; I could see his apprehension from where I stood.

Father stopped just below his level. "Remember me?" he said.

"I do. I apologize for being rough that night."

"You were more than rough. What you did ruined our lives."

"Come on, Mr. Crisp, let's not be dramatic."

"Everything that happened to us since has been a result of what you did. You owe us."

"Your daughter had a price and I paid it. Here. I believe this is yours."

He retrieved Mother's cylinder from inside his jacket and pressed it into my father's hand. It made me sick; I was supposed to give it to him. Not Silas. Another thing stolen from me, then. I turned my back to them, my face burning. I climbed into the back of the wagon, intending to help Joe carry the fuel.

"What is this?"

"I think it's a recording of your old lady. Your kid went to a lot of trouble to get it. Put a lot of people in harm's way, too. Brought death into my home."

I pressed my forehead against one of the fuel canisters, squeezing my eyes shut to stop the tears. I felt Sally's hand on the back of my head, gently smoothing down my hair. The shock of it stifled the urge to cry. I froze, allowing it to happen, afraid that if I moved or said anything, she would stop.

"Don't listen, kid," she said.

"All for this?" My father's voice sounded weak. "You ruined her life."

"No, you dumb bastard. I heard what you did to that miner. His buddy followed them out into the crater and tried to kill her, did you know that? *You* ruined her life."

Filth.

I remembered the word the War Engine spat, using poor Charlie's tongue.

Filth.

The Engines were right.

Joe's voice broke through. "Hey, excuse me. I need to get through, since I'm the only one actually working here."

I turned away from the wagon. Joe was holding a fuel canister in both arms, blocked from getting into the *Lamplighter* by Silas and my father.

My father looked broken. With that last sentence, Silas had finally done it. "I'm sorry," he said, and stepped to one side.

Joe made a huffing sound and dropped the canister onto the ramp. He took a step forward and pressed a hand to his back.

Blood seeped through his fingers. Then the *crack* of a rifle shot reached us.

Sally was the first to understand. "They're here! Get down!" She was moving as she said it, diving into the wagon bed with me, pulling me down alongside her, the rifle already in her hand.

It took me another moment. Yanked backward, I stared into a sky slowly breaking into evening. A single star burned. I wondered if it was Earth, if it was Mother looking down on me.

A voice carried over to us: "Put down your weapons!"

Sheriff Bakersfield. The law had arrived.

Joe had fallen off the ramp. He cried out: a low, pained moan. "Dad!"

"I'm here. I'm okay." His voice was coming from beside the wagon, sheltered from Bakersfield's sight. "Are you?"

"Yes," I said. I realized Sally and I were hunkered down with two remaining fuel canisters. One bullet could blow us all to mist.

"Everybody shut up!" Sally said. "I need to listen."

She got up on her elbows, peered carefully over the side.

I watched her eyes flick back and forth. "Can you see them?"

"I said shut up."

We waited. The only thing I could hear was Joe's labored breathing.

Silas said, "Sally, goddamn it! Say something!" He was peering from around the corner of the *Lamplighter*'s open hatch.

"I think all three are here. We're flanked."

"But how? I have Jack's cylinder," I said.

"You think the law don't have spares? You can bet they've changed the command word, too."

Joe's voice carried up to us. "This . . . hurts," gasping between the words.

Another shot rang out. It must have been fired into the air, because I didn't hear it hit anything. "I won't say it again!" Bakersfield called.

Sally yelled back, fury in her voice. "You son of a bitch! You shot Joe in the back!"

"I ain't taking no more chances with you, woman! You showed me what happens when we treat you with respect! The only reason we ain't rained fire on you is the kid!"

He let that sit for a minute. I felt a weird shame, despite the fact that it was the only thing keeping the others alive. I was still being treated like something less.

He continued, "You hear that, Sam? You and Anabelle come on out, and I guarantee you'll be safe! You really want her caught in the middle of what's about to happen?"

"He's right," Father said.

It was my turn to call out to the sheriff. "You still planning to hang him?"

He didn't answer right away. When he did, I heard the reluctance in his voice. "Justice still has to be served, Anabelle. I'm just hoping we can do it civilized, instead of like this."

Of course. This wasn't the kind of killing New Galveston favored. They liked the clean kind, where you pulled a tidy lever and listened to a quick snap. The kind where you got to talk about how sorry you were while you did it.

"Then I guess you're gonna have to do it the messy way, Sheriff."

"Belle," Father said, but I ignored him.

"Oh Christ," Joe said. I listened to his hitching breath. He was trying his best to keep quiet, but each exhalation came with a little keen of agony.

Sally's rifle exploded into life beside me. I risked a look over the top, to see what she was shooting at. Dig Town hunched like a great black beetle several hundred yards away, dark under a darkening sky; aside from that, the land looked like a barren series of small ridges and a few scattered rocks.

"I see him," she said. "Just keeping him honest. Once they realize you're really not coming out, they're going to fall in on us. It's about time we planned our exit. Joe, can you stand?"

"I don't know."

"Silas, I'm going to need you to get him up there."

"The hell with that," Silas said.

Bakersfield started talking again. "I see you got a ship there. I don't know where it came from or who it belongs to, but it might just change things with the governor. Might be we can work out a deal. Maybe this don't have to end hanging from a rope, or bleeding to death in the sand."

I looked at Sally, to see if this had any effect on her. I was startled to see tears in her eyes. She said, "He already passed sentence on Joe. You want to trust him, that's on you. I'm staying right here."

"I'll get Joe on the wagon," I said.

She didn't try to talk me out of it. She just watched me as I stood up and clambered over the side. I was gambling that they wouldn't shoot, that they'd believe I was conceding to reason.

I dropped down to where Joe lay prone, my back exposed to their rifles. My skin prickled and my muscles tensed, waiting for the bullets. I could see Silas in the ship, a few feet from the entrance. My father was to one side of me, crouched beside the wagon. Seeing me sitting in the open, his face blanched. "Belle! Jesus! Get over here!"

Blood continued to spread beneath Joe. His head was turned to one side, and his eyes, delirious with pain, focused on me for a moment.

"Hey . . . Belle . . ."

I was transfixed by the hole in Joe's back. It looked so small. He was shivering in the cold. Somehow it was worse, that he should be cold. I rolled him over and he cried out. The wound in front was bigger. His shirt and trousers were soaked in blood, and it left a puddle on the ground. I took my jacket off and pressed it into the wound, and he hissed through clenched teeth.

Sally called down. "How is he?"

". . . not good," I said quietly.

I heard the heavy tread of footsteps coming from inside the *Lamplighter*. Too heavy to be Silas. I looked up and saw Peabody standing in the open hatch. The failing sun was behind the ship, so it looked like he had stepped from an absolute darkness. The faceplate was aglow. Moths climbed along the outside of his suit, made a fluttering black halo around his head.

I heard my father say, "Oh. Jesus."

A sudden feeling of hatred crawled across my brain like a tarantula. This wasn't the scientist. This was the other, darker thing. This was Mars.

The psychic energy radiating from Peabody was a cousin to what I'd experienced while in the Throat, except more defined. This was a cold, killing contempt. A ravenous want. Joe shuddered with it, and I draped my body over his, trying to shield him, as if such a thing were possible.

I heard Mae Ackerman's voice. "Who is that? My God, who is that?"

Peabody began to speak, addressing us all in that weird, unknowable language, the sound of something dead and alien trying to express itself through a mechanism built for gentler sounds.

Joe grasped my forearm. His eyes were locked on to something unseeable behind me. "I'm scared, Belle," he said. And then he died.

I knew the moment it happened, as momentous and as trivial a thing as I have ever witnessed. The first stars of the coming night reflected from his staring eyes. Eyes that would soon frost over.

Joe Reilly's last experience in this world was the repulsive buckle of fear that this horror carried with it like a stench.

Gunshots erupted behind me. Three, four, six. And then a thundering fusillade, which had to be Jack. Bullets thumped and ricocheted off the *Lamplighter*'s hull. Jack's pounding ordnance hammered a series of deep dents into the metal. Only the horror Peabody exuded could have deranged them to the point at which they'd fire on a working spaceship.

Sally, still in the wagon bed by the two fuel canisters, returned fire at a steady, measured rate. It was hopeless, like one woman standing against a small army. She paused to reload, taking the opportunity to toss the revolver she'd liberated from Deputy Ackerman to the ground at my feet. "Help me!" she said, and resumed firing.

Peabody retreated inside.

The terrified mule started baying and strained to leave. Father, huddled with his hands over his head by the slowly turning wagon wheel, was about to be exposed. He looked at me in helpless terror. "Belle?"

All his life, he'd taken beatings. All the life he'd had, and all the life that remained to him, if these people had their way.

Behind me, the *Lamplighter*'s engines rumbled to life.

I picked up the gun. It had a terrible, exhilarating weight. I remembered the stink of blood from the massacre, the appalling sight of what bullets did to human flesh: Percy's flayed head, the gushing hole in Joe Reilly's gut. I recalled all of this not as a warning but as a promise, a certainty that I had corralled a godlike power.

The shooting ceased. Sheriff Bakersfield, made foolish by despair, stood up from behind the rock he'd been using for cover and stuck out an imploring hand toward the ship, as if he might pluck it from the ground like a toy. "Wait! No!"

Sally put a bullet through his chest. He fell backward like a plank of wood. She dropped the rifle and grabbed the mule's reins. Then she whipped her head around to me, her teeth bared like a feral dog's. "Go!"

The *Lamplighter*'s ramp began to retract. I grabbed my father's shirt collar and hauled him to his feet, screaming with determination. We raced up the ramp and dove into the hatchway before it closed.

BEING BACK INSIDE felt different than before: oppressive and heavy. I felt Peabody's presence everywhere, like an infection in the air. I nearly tripped over the suit's tether in my haste to get into the control room. Three empty fuel canisters crowded the corridor. I navigated clumsily over them, Father stumbling along behind me.

"She killed the sheriff," he said, dismayed. "There's no going back. Not for any of us. My God, Belle."

"Hush!" I didn't want him to panic; I was on the verge of it myself.

We paused at the entrance to the control room. The makeshift camp Joe had built for us was still mostly intact, our heavy packs—the ones we had to leave here without Watson to carry them—still lined up against the bookshelf. Joe's near-empty bottle poked from his rolled heat tent. Peabody sat in the pilot's chair, facing the viewport, which offered a beautiful, panoramic view of the night rising over the crater. Both moons shone coldly, a band of stars like a silver brushstroke behind them.

Silas stood beside him, breathing heavily, face flushed, sweat coating his brow. He was aiming his gun at us. His hands shook. How different from the confident image he'd projected in the diner, not even two weeks ago yet.

How quickly the world collapses.

The floor vibrated underneath us, the *Lamplighter*'s engines grumbling with power.

"Get off my ship," he said.

I raised the deputy's gun. My hand didn't shake.

This was the first my father saw of it. "Anabelle, no. Oh, no."

"Take us to safety first. Drop us outside New Galveston. That's all I ask."

Peabody turned in his chair to watch this display. The ugly presence that accompanied his dark aspect had retreated; we were dealing with the dead Southern man, at least for the moment.

Silas shook his head. "There's two fuel canisters still on that wagon. I don't even know if we have enough to get back to

Earth without them. So you can be damn sure I ain't taking any detours. Once we leave, we're going straight up. Now I'll tell you again: get off my ship." He pulled back the hammer of the gun. "I'm not playing, kid. You know that."

I did know. He'd let every last person in the cavern die, just so he'd have a ride home. I knew it wouldn't trouble his conscience one bit to kill us both.

Peabody spoke up. "Now, Silas, is this really necessary? Can't we do as they ask?"

"Yes, it's necessary." Silas struggled to maintain his composure. He was afraid of Peabody's dark aspect. "It's necessary, Mr. Peabody, because we didn't get all the fuel we wanted."

"We have enough, I think," Peabody said. "Let's be courteous to the lady."

"Yeah, Silas," I said, smiling sweetly. "Be courteous to the lady."

"Since when do we show hospitality to thieves, Mr. Peabody?"

"You call *us* thieves?"

He smiled. "She took one of your cylinders from the garden, Mr. Peabody. I watched her do it."

The atmosphere in the room curdled. Peabody arose from his chair, forcing Silas back a few steps. Silas lowered his gun, his face relaxing for the first time since the sheriff had arrived.

Father took my shoulder and forced me behind him. He stared into Peabody's face. "I don't know what he's talking about. My daughter's not a thief."

"He's the one who's got it," Silas said. "It's in the pocket of his jacket."

"Return it to me, sir." Peabody held out a gloved hand, some of the fingers long since rotted through, showing yellowed bone beneath.

It dawned on Father what Peabody was demanding. He pressed his hand against the pocket where he kept it. "No," he said. "No, that's . . . no."

"It belongs to me."

"It doesn't! That man took it from us. *He's* the thief." When Peabody showed no sign of relenting, Father's tone became imploring. "Please. It's my wife."

"No," Peabody said, and I could hear the change seeping into his voice. I could feel it fouling the air. "It is not yours. *Nothing here is yours.*" By the time the sentence was finished, the dark aspect had resumed control. The moths fluttered behind the faceplate, agitated.

From behind him, I reached into the pocket of my father's jacket. I placed my hand over his and took the cylinder. He released it to me. His shoulders slumped. I showed it to Peabody, bringing his attention back to me.

"I know what this is. I know it's part of you in here and you want it back. But part of us is in here, too. I want to play it once, so we can hear it. And then you can have it."

Peabody said nothing. I didn't expect him to. The dark aspect filled the *Lamplighter* itself; it didn't use the suit. I couldn't shake the comparison Silas had made between it and a god. It felt that way in here: omnipresent, radiant, terrible. Peabody's suit stood in the middle of the floor like a pagan statue, a holy fetish.

I scanned the technology on the walls, looking for the bank of crude cylinders that had initially powered the *Lamplighter*. It was easy enough to find: six illuminated circles, a simple flip-lock over each. These were designed before the *Lamplighter* ever reached Mars, of course, before the Strange was mined here and refined on Earth, allowing us to add the illusion of personality to our Engines. So I didn't know if it would play her recording at all. But if it was my last chance to hear Mother's voice, I would take it.

I popped open one of the locks and ejected the cylinder inside. It was cracked and corroded, like an old battery.

"Don't do that," Silas said.

I pushed in Mother's cylinder.

LATE ONE NIGHT, years ago, I listened to my parents talking when they thought I was asleep. Watson was stationed at the foot of my bed, as always. Hearing me wake, his head swiveled to watch me, the soft orange glow of his eyes bathing me in an eerie light. I felt a sense of unreality, of being suspended between two worlds. My parents were in the adjoining room. My mother had just awoken from a dream, and she was crying. A parent crying is one of the most despairing sounds a child can know, and I lay in my bed terrified and transfixed.

"Shhh, honey, it was just a dream." My father's voice was foggy with sleep.

"I know. I'm okay."

"A bad one, huh?"

She sniffled, waited a moment before answering. "No. It was a nice dream."

"What was it?"

"We were back home. We were hiking in the Blue Ridge Mountains. Remember when we did that?"

"I do. That was a great day."

"Yeah. And Anabelle was with us, even though she hadn't been born yet."

"That would have made it even better."

Her voice broke as she said, "I know."

I stared at the ceiling, waiting for more. The wind was blowing hard outside; I could hear the faint *tik*s of sand peppering the hab's walls.

"We were going up the trail, and Anabelle was talking about what she did in school that day—I know it doesn't make sense, we wouldn't be doing a day hike after school. . . ."

"Shh, it's okay. It's dream logic. Keep going."

"And we got to that field. That big blueberry patch in the valley, the mountains all around us. You remember that?"

"Sure I do. It was hot. The whole field buzzing with insects. Birds. Filled with life."

"Green mountains all around us. It felt like a church."

"That sounds like a good dream, Alice."

"What if Anabelle never gets to see it?"

There was silence. My heart hammered. I was the reason she was crying.

"She will. We'll take a trip back one of these days."

"But what if she doesn't? What if we can never afford to go back, or what if something happens to us here? What is something happens to her? What if all she ever knows is this barren, godforsaken place?"

"Honey . . . it was your idea to come here—"

"I know!"

There was a beat of silence. Watson watched me, his orange light seeming to grow brighter, hotter.

"She was so happy in the dream. She carried blueberries in her dress."

26

H ello, my loves."

It was her voice, but it sounded wrong: slowed down, deepened, as though it were being stretched like taffy.

"I'm going to miss you both so much and I . . ."

Her voice was coming from Peabody. The suit rippled with the sudden furious activity of the moths, tapping against the faceplate, flitting through the tears in the fabric, crawling over the tipped skull inside. He was painted gold by the light from the lamps.

Father took a tentative step closer to him. His body shuddered with emotion.

". . . wish I could take you both with me . . ."

"Alice?"

The voice dipped into another register. "Who are you?"

Father looked dismayed. "Alice, it's me. It's Sam."

I remembered that the cylinder had been split, exposed to the Strange in the cavern. Silas had warned me: whatever had been contained there before would be changed. I glanced at him now, still standing away from everyone else, holding the gun at his side. He watched us with an expression I couldn't read.

"... I want to understand ..."

Her voice was full of confusion, of loneliness. It broke my heart to hear it. I knew something else was in there, too, some splinter of Mars, but it was still my mother's voice. It was her, talking to me. I needed it. I'd been pushing so hard. I'd lost so much.

"... I'm sorry you can't come, Anabelle. You have to stay here ..."

The suit extended its arm to me.

"... but I'll be back very soon ... I must go back ..."

Her fingers beckoned. I stepped closer, and she embraced me. My muscles felt loose. Exhaustion overtook me. I curled into her.

"... I know this will be hard for you, Sam ... we've never been apart ... this long ..." She extended her arm to Father, and her message changed. It was no longer the recording we heard, but new thoughts. "Come with me ..."

The pitch of the engines increased, and the *Lamplighter* jostled gently into the air. I looked up into my mother's face. She stared back at me. Mushrooms crowded one of her eye sockets.

A chorus of sound filled the air, a strange undercurrent to the engines: whispers; weeping; splintering rock, like the language of stone. The garden of ghosts, packed neatly in their crates, awakened by something—the *Lamplighter*, perhaps, but most likely by the swelling presence of the dark aspect, the thing that was Mars, so heavy in the air that it slicked the back of my throat. It was like a holy visitation.

Silas stepped forward, putting his hand on her shoulder. "No. No! We can't take them! There's not enough fuel! Not enough air!"

She looked at him. This intruder into our reunion. This crawling mite on her body. An invader. *"Filth,"* she said. *"Get away from me."*

"What?" Desperately, he put his hands on Mother's arm, tried to force her around to face him. "No. You said you'd take me. This isn't even you, it's that goddamn cylinder she put in—"

"Never touch me," she said, turning on him. *"Never look at me."*

Turning away from him, she faced my father instead. My father stepped into her embrace.

Silas's expression went flat. To be rebuked by God. To be rejected by the very ground you stood on. I watched something dim in Silas's green eyes, some essential energy exit his body. He stepped away from us. Through the viewport behind him I could see the landscape of Mars scrolling slowly by, at little more than a walking pace. He honored her wish: he did not look at her again. Instead he looked at me.

"I told you," he said. "We're a disease."

He put the gun to his temple and fired.

". . . I'M AFRAID . . ." she said. ". . . I'm afraid . . ."

I didn't know how much of that was Mother, how much was Mars. I guessed mostly the latter. Silas's death snapped me out of my dream. We sat on the floor, arms around each other. Father was lost to me. He stared in wondering adoration at the thing that held him, that held me, too. I knew it wasn't her, but it felt good to pretend, even for a few minutes.

I knew, too, that Silas had not been lying. There was only enough air for one person to make the trip. And somebody had to. Somebody had to speak into the Silence.

But I could pretend for a little while longer. At least until we drifted over Dig Town.

Silas's blood streamed around us. I took my father's hand, felt it clasp onto my own. I leaned into Mother one more time. I looked into her face: the bare skull, the moths streaming in and out of the cracked faceplate, a black, shivering halo against the light. I told them both that I loved them, and that I was sorry to see them go.

I JUMPED OUT at Dig Town. The *Lamplighter* was moving low enough, and slowly enough, that it wasn't any risk at all. Mother's presence, what there was of it, was already receding into the dark aspect, which cared about no one at all. Father—the man I knew, anyway—was gone. What remained of him was in the only place he wanted to be: with the woman he loved, the one who gave him the strength he never had himself. Neither made any effort to stop me. There was no place for me there anymore.

The cold was ferocious. I had to get to shelter quickly or it would kill me. The Shanks' place was close by. I didn't know what had happened to Sally, and I thought—without much hope—that maybe she'd gone there afterward.

But first, I wanted to watch the *Lamplighter*. I hadn't understood why it had traveled to Dig Town—I didn't think my mother's cylinder had that much influence on the intelligence that controlled it—but once here, it became clear. It roamed slowly toward the center of town. To the Throat.

Sound began to flow from those great depths. It rose in volume, slowly at first, and then with gathering speed. Screams, wails, long sonorous notes, the glad noise of a woken devil . . . I know of no way to accurately describe it. It was the sound of a desolate world, the bodies it had claimed and broken, the voice it had taken for itself. The Strange geysered from the Throat in tiny green particles, little ice chips rising into the night sky and falling around it in a gentle snow.

I let it cover me.

The *Lamplighter* hovered briefly over the mine shaft. The Strange floated over and around it, sliding from its sides in glittering trails. Was the entity in the Throat different in any way from the one inhabiting that ship? Was it the same mind peering at itself? Or had Mars fractured, as Silas had believed, melding with explorers, soldiers, Engines of war? And with lost mothers, too?

What monster was going back to Earth, to sow its ghosts in an alien soil, my father curled at its feet?

The *Lamplighter* radiated light like a chandelier, throwing heat below, stirring the cloud of green dust into eddies and whirlwinds. I looked for the window, hoping to catch a last glimpse of my father. But it was too high, the window too dark. It continued to rise until its light was little more than a candle flame, then a pinprick, and then it was gone, swallowed by the darkness between the moons.

27

That's most of it, save a few minor details.

Sally wasn't at home. All of Dig Town was empty, all gone down to the gardens. I stayed in the old shack anyway. I knew I could never go back to New Galveston, not after what they'd done to me and what I'd done to them. We were through with each other, and that was fine. I was able to forage food from the abandoned homes in Dig Town; I knew it wouldn't last forever, but it would last a little while at least, until I figured something out. I found books there, too. I missed my little home library, and even though I found reading difficult in the immediate aftermath of what happened, their mere presence was a comfort. One in particular—the collected essays of Montaigne—would prove an anchor for me in the years to come.

I even got used to the voices from the Throat, which occasionally ebbed but never stopped.

Two weeks later, Sally showed up. She had a bullet wound in her leg that she'd taken care of herself, and she walked with a limp. We were surprised to see each other, and a little wary at first. We filled each other in on what had transpired. I might have left out some of the more personal details, but I gave her the gist of it.

She'd killed Bakersfield, she said, and escaped into the crater, though Deputy Ackerman had managed to land that bullet in her before she got out of range.

I felt bad for Sheriff Bakersfield, and I said so.

She shrugged. "He killed Joe," she said. "Shot him in the back. My only regret is I killed him straight out, didn't make him suffer like he made Joe suffer. I hope the crows are picking his flesh in hell."

"Do you miss him?" I asked. It was a stupid question, and I knew it. But I missed my family more than I could fully express, and I guess I needed to hear someone else confess to a similar feeling.

She was quiet a moment. "Yeah. I do."

"He hated me in the end," I said. It felt like an open wound.

"No, he didn't. Joe carried a lot of fear in him, that's all. The only person he hated was hisself."

I recalled their banter on our trip through the crater, the way she teased him and pushed him around, the way he said maybe he needed that. "Did you . . . well. Did you love him?"

The word made her uncomfortable. "Hell. He was my friend. That's all. And you're my friend, too, Anabelle Crisp."

I blushed.

"So what's your plan?" she said.

"Stay here, I guess. Keep foraging until things run out."

She considered that. "That noise out there don't drive you crazy?"

I shrugged. "You get used to it."

"Hell, kid. You might as well be moving into your own grave."

This struck me to my core. I felt the despair I'd been keeping at bay come tickling the edges of my gut.

"But I can't go back there," I said. "I can't. They all hate me there. And I hate them right back."

"They're city people. They can't help what they are. Any more than you or I can."

Something powerful moved inside me when she said that. Claiming me as one of her own.

"Well, look. You can't stay here. Nobody down in New Galveston wants to come nowhere near this place, especially since that devilish sound started up, but sooner or later Ackerman and that big Engine of hers are going to come up here looking for me. I'm amazed they ain't done it already. And if they find you, well. It won't be good for you."

"Then what do I do?"

She looked at me for a minute, like she was searching for something. "Here, reach me some of that moonshine, will you?"

I sighed and passed one of the big glass bottles over to her. There were still half a dozen left from whenever the Shank kids were last here.

"You know I'm a carter, right? You know what that is?"

"You take things from place to place. Sell and trade. My friend Brenda's dad is one, too."

"Yeah, Arthur, I know him. He's a good enough guy. He's official, though. He just goes to the sanctioned places. Here, New Galveston, Brawley's Crossing. Well, not here anymore, I guess. Anyhow, I go farther out. I go to the unofficial places." She paused. "It's a lot of work, and sometimes there's different kinds. Escorting a caravan from one place to another. Bodyguard work sometimes. It keeps me busy, and sometimes it gets a little dangerous. I could use someone to watch my back."

I stared at the floor, not sure I was hearing her right. "You want me to go with you?"

"Well, you know. I could use some help. I need somebody with some backbone. If there's one thing you got, it's that. Will you do it?"

I nodded. I felt the tears in my eyes again. I didn't bother to hide them.

"Let's load up then. I don't want to be in this shithole a minute longer than I have to."

IT WAS HARD, dangerous, dull, exhilarating work. I worked with Sally for years, until her fate came to claim her at last, as it does us all. Then I worked on my own for a little while, until I grew tired of it. I will tell you this: Mars is bigger than any of us knew back then, bigger than most know today.

I did go looking for Watson. On one of my journeys with Sally, we went back out to that cave. We found the War Engines, rusted and dried to a standstill, and we found bones. A lot of bones. We even found some of those ghosts, grown to vast proportions, exhorting their strange philosophies. But Watson was gone. I was sorry in the moment, but I knew that meant the cylinder had slid back into him, and that he'd finally been able to leave that mausoleum. With one notable exception, I had only known Mars when it had been channeled through vessels bent out of true by fear and rage. It pleased me to consider how it might express itself when channeled through a sweet, gentle soul like Watson.

And, of course, I did see him again.

As of this writing, the Silence endures. We're no closer to an answer than we ever were. For the most part, no one even thinks about it. Earth is just another light in the sky, one we sometimes tell stories about.

Mars, though. Mars is not silent. Everybody has the green eyes these days; everybody is part Martian now. Sometimes I think it's a good thing. But there are nights when I feel the old animosity, when I feel sure that some primal force is gathering its strength. Dig Town has fallen into ruin, but you hear stories of people still going there sometimes—suicides or fanatics or simply the curious, all being called down to the gardens, which sing to this very day. I stay away as much as I can. Whatever's coming, it'll come whether I'm there to see it firsthand or not.

I still keep to myself. I live in a tent in the high desert. I'm old now, and it's difficult to get around. I've rebuilt my little library. I still read Conan Doyle for comfort, though it's hard for me to imagine a rain-soaked London these days. In my mind, the sky there is butterscotch, and the avenues run with blowing sand.

I don't have much to do but remember, and to write my big adventure story. I tell it to Watson as I write. He's come back only recently, appearing as if by magic one night at the foot of my bed, his parts all clean and polished, telling me his own stories about the life he's lived on his own.

"I went deep underground," he says, "and I saw a field of floating green lights. Were these fireflies?"

"Yes," I tell him.

"They were like an ocean. They were beautiful."

His voice is strong and soothing. He's shed the British accent; he sounds like me now, and like my father. His stories carry me to a warm, comfortable sleep. They remind me of the feeling I had on the *Lamplighter*, that last embrace with my family.

I do wonder what happened to Father once he got home—if he got home at all. I wonder if he found Mother there, and if they went to the blueberry patch, thinking of me. I imagine them coming back to get me: descending from the sky in that big lantern of a ship, filled with the people I love, waiting to receive me once again into their company.

"Will you watch over me while I sleep?"

"Of course I will."

The walls of the tent flutter in a light breeze. Outside, Mars is vast, a place of mysteries. In here, I'm warm in the orange glow of his eyes.

"Good night, Watson."

"Good night, Miss Crisp. Dream well."

acknowledgments

I started writing *The Strange* more years ago than I like to think about. I wrote the opening scene, abandoned it, came back to it and wrote the next 20,000 words, abandoned it again. I was intimidated by the prospect of writing a novel. More than that, I was unsure of how to write *this* novel. I'd made what small reputation I had as a writer of contemporary horror stories focusing, for the most part, on working class men. What business did I have writing Anabelle's story?

Three people convinced me it was my business. The most constant voice of support is and has always been my friend Dale Bailey, who has endured countless hours of fretting, moping, whining, and Homeric monologues of self-doubt. This book exists in no small measure due to his unflagging friendship. Then there is Ann VanderMeer, who heard me read an early portion of this in the long-ago, and dropped me a line years later expressing hope that I would finish it. That tiny message was like the glimpse of a lighthouse on a stormy sea, and did much to bolster my flagging faith. Finally, and most importantly, there's my daughter, Mia. She was a young teenager—Anabelle's age— when I wrote the first words of this novel, and will be twenty-two when it sees print. She is Anabelle's backbone. Though they do not share temperament or personality—Mia is far more patient and generous of spirit than Anabelle, far less prickly and not at all pugilistic—she is every bit the inspiration for Anabelle's grit and endurance. She and others of her generation are growing up in a strange, turbulent world, in which everything we once took for granted has been thrown into doubt. I believe in her ability to endure.

Thank you, Dad, for reading the rough early chapters and pushing me along. I wish you could have seen it come to fruition.

Thanks are due to the writers of the Sycamore Hill workshop in NC who read and critiqued the early chapters of this novel, most especially to Karen Joy Fowler who used the line "*The Martian Chronicles* meets *True Grit*," which delighted my agent, Renée Zuckerbrot. ("I can sell that!" Renée said.)

Thanks to Maureen F. McHugh who, in the early days, told me about including dairy goats on Mars in her excellent novel *China Mountain Zhang*, and assured me I was worrying too much about realism.

Enormous gratitude to my agent, Renee, and her associate, Anne Horowitz, for their tireless work and rigorous attention to detail. What you see here would be unreadable without them.

Abundant thanks as well to Joe Monti and his team at Saga Press. When I turned in the first draft of the novel, Joe's response was, "Well, Nathan, I think you've got your work cut out for you here," and proceeded to hand over copious edits which pierced my heart at the time, but saved the book. I'm forever grateful.

Thank you to Davi Lancett and his team at Titan Books in the UK. I'm thrilled to be part of the family.

Thank you to Sean Daily for his enthusiasm, encouragement, and support.

Finally, I owe a debt of gratitude to the writers whose influence is all over these pages. *The Strange* is a love letter to Ray Bradbury, Isaac Asimov, and Frank Herbert. When I was a teenager, fantasy and science fiction provided life-saving doses of wonder and possibility as the world seemed to shrink and grow tight around me. When I returned to the genre as an adult, the work of Lucius Shepard, Maureen F. McHugh, and James P. Blaylock did the same thing, guiding me back to a place I thought I'd lost. This book is also a love letter to Westerns, a genre which has only become richer as it grapples with historical realities instead of indulging in mythology. Charles Portis is here, certainly, but so are Larry McMurtry, Molly Gloss, and Paulette Jiles.

And thank you, reader, for trusting me with your money and your time. I will never take that for granted.

about the author

NATHAN BALLINGRUD was born in Massachusetts in 1970, but spent most of his life in the South. His short story collection, *North American Lake Monsters*, won the Shirley Jackson award, and his collection *Wounds* was adapted by Netflix. His work has been nominated for the World Fantasy, British Fantasy, and Bram Stoker awards. Among other things, he has been a cook on oil rigs and barges, a waiter, and a bartender in New Orleans. He now lives in Asheville.

For more fantastic fiction, author events,
exclusive excerpts, competitions, limited editions and more

VISIT OUR WEBSITE
titanbooks.com

LIKE US ON FACEBOOK
facebook.com/titanbooks

FOLLOW US ON TWITTER AND INSTAGRAM
@TitanBooks

EMAIL US
readerfeedback@titanemail.com